I0527869

SOUL REAPER SERIES
BOOK I:
Masquerade

CRYMSYN HART

PURPLE SWORD PUBLICATIONS, LLC

SOUL REAPER SERIES BOOK I: MASQUERADE
Copyright © 2010 CRYMSYN HART. All rights reserved worldwide.
ISBN 978-1-936165-75-9
ISBN 10: 1-936165-75-9
Cover Art Designed by Anastasia Rabiyah
Edited by Brieanna Robertson and Traci Markou

Published by Purple Sword Publications, LLC
Tucson, Arizona, USA
www.PurpleSword.com

PART ONE
THE HERMIT

1

CHAPTER ONE

My name is Brenna.

The heaviness of the atmosphere rolled around my tongue, lingering in my nose like a fine vintage of wine. It was a hot, humid day. Clothes stuck to every inch of skin, and a sane person hungered for a shower after the slightest exertion. Traces of spices and sweat clung to the fragrance of the day as exotic food was prepared on every corner. Even a hint of magic wafted on the day's aroma. Spells had been cast to bar intruders and ignite passionate love affairs.

As these scents carried me into consciousness, a slight breeze blew through the Quarter, pulling the bouquets of the day with it. My nostrils flared at the odor on the back of the wind: the wet, dark, musty smell of death and an oncoming storm. Death was part of the culture here, always lingering like the ghosts in the city. Rain came often, but never lasted more than an hour or so, making this place more like a tropical paradise than a bustling city. Even the downpours couldn't keep the sightseers from exploring the small shops, as well as admiring the balconied apartments in the Quarter. Many were small oases, housing lush plants, which allowed the inhabitants to escape from the cameras and voyeurs. I inhabited one of these sought-after lodgings, but kept the windows shuttered so the sun couldn't creep in and disrupt my slumber.

I rose, yawning as the heaviness of sleep had not yet left me. Darkness caressed my naked form while the whirling fan cooled my bare skin. Stretching, I urged my body to rise and face the night. I opened the shutters to see the sun painting hues of purple and pink in the hazy air, signaling the fast approaching blue-greens of twilight. I smiled. This was the scene that had greeted me for years. I flicked on the light. I shielded my eyes from the sudden illumination until my pupils adjusted.

I admired my body in the bureau mirror. The overhead lamp gave my milky skin a jaundiced tint that contrasted against the pink of my nipples. My appearance attracted both sexes; it was something in the pheromones. The sex of my partners didn't matter. I only wanted the ones who could fulfill my desire.

The jasmine-touched breeze danced through my apartment as the coolness of full night blossomed like a moonflower inside my chest. I stretched, now entirely awake as the sluggishness of the day fell away like a misty shroud. The moon's silvery light already warmed my skin. Its blaze had replaced the sun in my memories and the power of it ignited my heart, night after glorious night.

Staring at my body a moment longer, I realized tonight was not the night for me to turn into Narcissus and be captured by my own beauty. I had eons for that. My gums ached, and hollowness filled my insides. Tonight I'd dress to kill, so to speak. I donned a black velvet dress, black thigh-high stockings, and black Doc Martens.

My gaze fell on the things I would need to complete my disguise. A contact case and scattered makeup: everything I needed to fit in better. From the lot, my tarot cards called to me. I smiled, wondering what Fate had in store for me tonight. Mentally, I checked my schedule and knew I had no clients to read. No one to tell a husband was cheating, or a sickness was devouring them, or a fortune would be lost in the stock market.

I smirked at the thought of how easily I peered into the minds of my clients, divining their futures and reading their emotions. After one session, they always came back. I had a good reputation, unlike the phony psychics who lined Jackson Square. Hotel managers and local occult shops referred tourists to me. I loved unearthing secrets from my unsuspecting clients.

I studied the cobalt backs, admiring the golden stars. I had owned them for years. My right hand passed over the line of cards, automatically settling on one in the middle and then another at the end. Energy sparked between the cards and my palm. I pulled those two cards to see how the evening would progress and to give me a glimpse into the more distant future. The first card I flipped was the Lovers. It signified I would meet someone to spend eternity within the next couple of nights.

Yeah, right! I giggled, wondering who my next conquest would be.

The card normally meant the beginning of a meaningful relationship, but this night I interpreted it as a lustful tryst card. I doubted anyone would spark my emotions. It had been years since I had known love. I didn't remember what it felt like to have warmth in my heart, to let someone have complete access to my innermost sanctum. My nature demanded solitude; I couldn't have a partner who might discover my secret, so I stayed away from the commitments and found other ways to pass my nights.

My mouth watered as I thought of all the willing partners I had been with. Sex made me remember what it was like to be alive. It gave me an excuse to feel, and I had as much as I wanted. Sometimes it overwhelmed me. Ah, but who was I kidding? One could never have too many good fucks.

Laughing, I turned my gaze to the other card.

It was the Ten of Swords, the true Death card of the deck.

Great, I thought. *Utter and total destruction.*

I doubted I'd literally be pinned with ten rapiers. My true demise would not be so horrible; it probably meant inner turmoil in the coming week or so.

Yes, that had to be it. I sighed inwardly, knowingly the suit of swords also meant mental stress. The card could mean I was near the end of my worries.

Customers weren't calling me to divine the stars for them. As a rule, business came in spurts as disasters struck the customers I entertained. Their money didn't matter to me. They just kept me busy and helped pass the long nights I lingered in. I glanced down at the cards once again before throwing them back in the deck. I wasn't too concerned. Even though the cards predicted my future, I forged my own path, not letting Fate govern my journey through life.

Moving the cards aside, I applied my makeup so I could blend with the goth crowd. The dark and misunderstood were a thriving part of New Orleans, drawn to the city's ancient heritage and otherworldly grittiness. Many of them applied white paint, molding acrylic fangs to their incisors; moving among them was easy for me. It seemed a crime to wear a suit and tie and lead a normal life. *But what was normal anyway?*

I put on a few lines of black kohl to accentuate my evergreen eyes. Contacts hid the real color. Next came the cranberry-red lipstick. Every time I wore it, men swooned over me, wanting—hoping—to fuck me. I only took a few up on the offers and wondered if tonight would be one of those nights. Many goth boys counted on pain to bring them to pleasure. I prided myself on knowing the right points to pinch and massage to get them to come. Some liked their asses beaten plum-ripened red. Only then, as they begged, did I give them their desire. Others preferred their dicks in my mouth, my tongue working the shaft while my teeth held the head in place.

These were only some of my many secrets. If I revealed them all, what interest would they have in me?

I sighed. I looked semi-normal, a cross between a bleached porcelain doll and the bride of Satan. I was perfect.

The energy of the tarot cards played against my arm, sending tingles across my skin. Tempted to pull another card, I paused. The night called.

I smiled one last time, checking my curved fangs to see if they were lipstick free. They were. Tonight was going to be fun. I could feel it.

2

CHAPTER TWO

My name is Veronica.

The setting sun warmed my back some as I made my way down Bourbon Street, marveling at the variety of shops, which offered every tool imaginable to fit into the city. Metallic Mardi Gras beads of green, purple, and gold filled the shops. Some were strings of beads; others alternated beads with doubloons or alligators. Masks lined the walls. Some sprouted elegant peacock feathers, while others were simple black and white bands to cover the eyes. No matter what disguise sightseers chose, it enabled them to lose their inhibitions, or hide behind the fancy feathers, drifting, undisturbed, among the throngs of people.

Numerous shot glasses stocked shelves, just the thing the inebriated tourist needed. My favorite tourist trapping was the T-shirt covered in the word "fuck." It was amusing, but something I'd never buy, even though I'm sure my ex would have.

Devon would fit in here better than I did. He'd easily get lost in a stupor and be cursed by some Voodoo High Priest. He knew how to piss off the right people.

This was my first visit to The Big Easy, and I wasn't entirely sure why I'd ended up here. I had hoped it would ease my restlessness, but I wasn't sure. Even if that didn't happen, I hoped I'd discover a way to put Devon out of my mind for good. He followed me everywhere I went. When I looked behind me to see if he was there, I'd realize my mind was playing tricks on me. Our last encounter winked through my mind, and I shivered at the memory.

I had grabbed a handful of money after he had broken my cheekbone. I was used to his fist. The pain was dull compared to the other humiliations I had suffered at his hand. I had told him I was getting something to eat. Finally finding my courage, I had flown from the house, never looking back. Now his memory haunted me as I tried to remember how to live, learning how to feel and regain what he had taken away from me.

I wasn't used to the heavy moisture in the air; I'd come here from the crystalline crispness of Boston, where the seasons changed and the streets were lined with people who didn't understand the meaning of hospitality. Here, people didn't assume I was going to mug them when I said hello.

I had always tried to blend in with the populace up north, but as much as I tried, they never accepted me. People seemed like aliens. I had always blended with the night, choosing black garments and other things that categorized me as goth. Corsets and clothes within the fetish world—vinyl, leather—anything to derive pain. That was how I knew I was still alive. Devon had trained me to believe that there was no more love in my heart. He lived to bring pain and fear. Sometimes I felt like some kind of monster, living the way I did. Several times I went against him and tried to live righteously, but every time I found some semblance of peace, he always pulled me back in.

Most of society called us nightkind freaks. I liked being outside of the norm in that sense and here I felt almost at home. I'd encountered other goths, stepping through the misty world, and I wondered if I could share my secrets with them. Only another true creature of darkness would understand the nightmare my life had turned into.

3

CHAPTER THREE

My name is Brenna.

Strolling down Bourbon Street, I listened to the music floating out of the clubs. I'd been walking indiscreetly up and down the Rue for almost two hours with my gums aching and the hollowness in my stomach growing.

I rested my tongue on one fang carefully. I grew bored of the drunken games many of the tourists played. Idiotic men barked at women, demanding to see their tits as if it were the biggest thrill. I groaned as one asked the same of me. I smiled weakly and then hissed, loving it as he fell on his ass, beer squirting out his nose as he spilled the rest on himself. More people ventured out into the hot, humid evening, looking for dinner or to shop in the tacky stores that lined the street. I wanted nothing to do with them.

I thought of the Lovers card I had pulled from my tarot deck earlier. It seemed Fate amused itself with me, as it always did. No matter how many times I thought I had discerned my own path, Fate threw me back on the course that it had plotted before I was born. There was no way to get away from it. It had thrown me on the path of working as a psychic when I never asked for it. Like tonight, it was leading me on a journey I couldn't see the end of—that was why I distrusted the whole system. I stopped, leaning against the front of one of the many strip clubs. From my vantage point, I could see up and down the street. A breeze kicked up, cooling me a little and taking thoughts of my hunger from me.

While watching the pedestrians, something caught my eye. A big, green hand grenade danced outside of a bar, enticing people to come in for the bar's signature drink. It was the strongest known to mankind.

My eyes wandered from the grenade and over the tourists, trying to pinpoint one who wouldn't be missed. Most traveled in groups and were not so easy to pick off. Suddenly the crowd parted, as if the gods had chosen for me, and a single male strolled my way. He had a drink in his hand. I licked my lips in anticipation. My stomach rumbled. I could already hear the rubbing of his jeans as he walked. His brown hair reminded me of chocolate, and his sculpted shoulders and lips were all to my liking.

I could see myself running a hand over his chiseled chest. His ass would be great to hold onto when he was driving into me. My hands wanted to explore every part of him. His lips would be full and would know what parts of me to explore as his hands played over my tits. I would laugh in his ear as he tickled my neck, thinking he could have his way with me. Then, as he moved his hard length deep inside of me, I would rise up and let him see what he had bedded. His eyes would open wide in fear, but he would be so caught up in his orgasm it wouldn't matter.

Then my fangs would pierce his throat as easily as his dick had slipped into me. Moans of unfulfilled pleasure would escape his lips, and I would drink my fill.

Yes, he would be very, very good.

My heart sped up some as I imagined what the oncoming night would be like. I stepped forward, centering my attention on him, when a woman collided with me.

Crazy bitch, I thought.

I growled low in my throat and looked up at the woman who had bumped into me. She kept going, not bothering to stop. She kept glancing behind her, into the hordes of people. I turned to see what she was searching for, but saw nothing. Focusing on my prey for the evening, I realized he had been swallowed up.

That did it. If I couldn't have him, she was mine.

I marched after her, darting in between the groups, closing the distance. I kept focused on her, but even though I followed closely, she never saw me as she kept checking over her shoulder. Something about her piqued my curiosity. I honed my mind and cast a line into her like hooking onto a fish. I brushed her thoughts and emotions, catching her name as well as the circumstances that had driven her to this city. Her name was Veronica, and she had run from an ex-boyfriend who had beaten her within inches of her life several times. She'd finally left, and underneath her fear of him, there was something else, a secret she tried desperately to keep walled away almost like a separate part of her personality.

I stayed attached only briefly. There were so many people on Bourbon Street; I didn't want to take the chance of their emotions settling in with mine. She was the only one I was concerned about. My rage from losing my prey died while waves of sympathy filled me. She may have been a loner and easy to pick off, but I had a soft spot for powerless victims.

She strode faster, weaving through the throngs of people because she assumed she might encounter her ex in New Orleans. Her fear was strong enough to drive her close to insanity, but beneath it laid happiness, struggling to survive. Each day she was away from her ex it grew stronger. It was this sense of feeling that had enabled her to break free from the abuse. I had to cultivate this seed within her.

I couldn't remember the last time I had actually loved someone. Each time I woke from my slumber, I had searched the night to ease my hunger for humanity. Even as I thought of this, I bit my lower lip, causing blood to seep into my mouth.

I swallowed the coppery fluid, letting it settle into my growling stomach. I licked my lips absently. Thoughts of my lost food vanished. I knew I'd sate my desires later.

Quickening my pace, I sensed someone watching me—which on Bourbon Street, of course, was everyone. However, this was different. Someone in particular watched me. My anger ignited at the invasion.

How dare anyone try to scan me, I thought. Then a tingling, an itching, started in the back of my brain, signaling my ignited psychic abilities, which normally warned me of impending doom. Scanning the street, I ignored the feeling, assuming it was a cautioning about Veronica and her ex-boyfriend. I smirked at the counsel, knowing nothing would happen to me.

I focused my attention on the entity observing me. It invaded my thoughts, forcing me to find it. I pushed against the presence, not used to having another in my brain. I followed it back to its source like a ball of yarn leading me out of a labyrinth and saw him directly across the street.

His hands were folded across his chest. One knee lifted, his foot resting against the brick wall behind him as if he knew I would find him with ease. An open black leather vest exposed his marble white chest. Skintight black leather pants clung to his form. His hair was black and spiked. He reveled in the fact that he held my attention so easily and grinned at me. The hint of fang gleamed in his smile.

I nodded in return. I had encountered several other nocturnal creatures in the city, but I normally ignored them. I didn't like to be crowded in my hunting grounds. Besides, there were plenty of victims in the city to go around. I wondered why he sought my attention. Maybe he wanted Veronica for himself. However, as our connection hummed, I doubted that.

An image of him kissing my neck played in my mind. The feel of phantom hands played over my arms as they traced the skin up to my neck and cupped my chin. The feel of his lips pressed against mine as he held my gaze. I smiled slyly as the creature across from me tried to show me what it would be like to be with him. I was not keen on the intrusion into my mind, but he was definitely making me think twice about what I had been planning with the mortal man I had lost earlier. His thoughts whispered that he could show me a night like no other. What could a mortal do that he would be able to do so much better? If I hadn't been so enamored with Veronica, I might have taken him up on his offer.

Veronica ducked into a restaurant just down the way. I sized up the man and felt no threat from him. His tether evaporated from my mind. I snuck a glance away from his piercing eyes. Through the restaurant window, I saw Veronica being seated by a waitress. When I looked back toward the man, he was gone.

A shiver ran down my back. The thought he had planted in my brain vanished, and I was able to concentrate on Veronica again. Still a part of me wondered what he wanted with me. Was it more than just sex? There were always ulterior motives behind our porcelain faces. What would it be like to be with another of my kind? I had never had that before. He left a part of me intrigued by the idea. I shook my head, realizing I had almost fallen under his spell as if I were a mortal. I had to be careful and remember I was something else, a creature of the shadows who answered to no one.

I slipped into the restaurant easily without the hostess noticing. It was fun playing with the minds of my prey. Choosing a table, I ordered a drink. My ears perked at the traditional sounds of jazz from the house band. The tune carried me away, taking me back to a time when my life had been much simpler, when I couldn't divine the future or peer into others' minds. To when I was younger and not so cut off from humanity. As a whisper of serenity came to my brain, my reverie was broken. My eyes snapped open. I gave the waitress a coy smile as she brought my drink and asked for my order. I brushed her away to look at Veronica.

Even after years of battering, her complexion remained perfect. Shoulder length black hair floated around her face, making her appear like a dark angel. Misty purple, her sad eyes peered out from under uneven bangs, and I found myself drawn to them. After so many years of searching, I didn't have to be lonely anymore. With Veronica here, feet from me, my heart leapt into my throat as I sipped my drink. There was a strength in her I could relate to. Whatever her dark secret, I was sure she would share it with me.

The hint of designer fangs peeked out from a white-painted face. I could see the grains of the make-up easily. I almost chuckled as I realized what she was doing. She hid behind a disguise, trying to be like me. Like many goths before her, she sought solace in the guise of my brethren. In this, we were sisters. Veronica's sadness hung about her like an ancient birthright. Her shoulders sagged under the weight of some unknown defeat. Every movement shouted her story. Try as she might to stay optimistic about life, to hold onto some kind of light in her life, her ex had taken her soul and left nothing save a stony abyss. Even with her weighty burdens, I knew I could make her forget the drama of her past.

Two women cackled for the band to go on as they finished their set. I smiled as their companions covered their eyes, pretending not to know them. No pity crossed my mind. It was their own fault the women had gotten drunk. Humans were so quick to indulge themselves. I licked my lips, thinking I was not so unlike them.

I focused on one of the drunken women, moving into her thoughts. It was actually quite easy since she was intoxicated. Almost like scanning a large-print book, the words and her thoughts stood out on the screen of her mind. They were not about bedding her husband. On the contrary, her eyes kept straying to Veronica. She was attracted to her for some reason her haze-filled brain didn't understand. She saw her lips on Veronica's. Her hands discovered the other woman's flesh beneath clothing. I bit my lip. This was unacceptable. Veronica was mine.

Narrowing my focus, I plunged a little deeper into the drunken bitch's mind. Tweaking her desire, I turned her attention to the bartender, whom she had eyed when she came in. He reminded her of an old high school crush. I made it so she wanted to leap over the bar and have the bartender fuck her on the counter in sight of everyone. The woman even began to take a few teetering steps toward the bar. I held back a smile.

Satisfied, I withdrew my tether from the inebriated tourist and focused again on Veronica. She had calmed a bit after her imagined pursuit and was content to listen to the band. Her ease washed over me as I drank in the emotions that helped to calm my aroused hunger. I took another sip of my drink. Signaling the waitress with a raised hand, I whispered that I wanted a drink delivered to Veronica. The server leaned in close, trying to catch my hushed voice over the tuning of a guitar. As my hand accidentally brushed the curve of her breast, I felt the nipple harden through her bra. Her pupils dilated from the sudden caress. Sadness and inflamed desire rose in her mind. Feeling playful, I pushed my mind into hers, using my emotions to promise her secret dreams.

I created pictures of her straining against me, my fingers buried inside her. She felt the softness of my lips on her, the wetness of my tongue encircling her areola, working the changing texture. She saw herself tickling my neck with her long fingers, but in the end it was she who gave up total control.

Her breath quickened as she became caught up in the vision. I pushed the images deep into her unconscious so she could return to reality and remember me in her own way. She blinked, coming out the daze, and left my table a little shaken to put in my order. Minutes later, she delivered the drink to Veronica. I caught the server's gaze sweeping over to me, and a hint of pink came to her cheeks, but she couldn't quite place what she was embarrassed about.

A look of puzzlement appeared on Veronica's face as the server pointed at me. Veronica's eyes followed her extended finger. I smiled carefully, keeping my teeth hidden.

Soon you'll be mine, I thought gleefully. I raised my glass, acknowledging her.

She nodded, testing the alcohol before taking a large sip. I smiled as Veronica tried not to look at me. Lightness encompassed my heart and blew away some of my own burdens. With her, I could explore all sides of reality. With her, the nights wouldn't seem so long or frosty, and I might actually find a renewed joy in the silvery starlight that dotted the fabric of the night sky.

4

CHAPTER FOUR

My name is Veronica.

"You're mine, always," I heard Devon whisper over the guitars.

I swung around, almost knocking over the chair next to me, but there was no one there. I took a few deep breaths, knowing my imagination had created Devon. He hadn't been following me on the streets at all. I cursed him for the fear he had instilled in me, but that was in the past. Now I was free, just a tourist in a strange city that captivated my imagination.

"This is for you," the waitress yelled above the din.

"I didn't order anything."

"It's from her, over there." She pointed at a woman several tables away.

Following her extended finger, I gazed at the woman. Her hair seemed to writhe like copper snakes. The cranberry redness of her lips stood out as she smiled. The shape of her face was more oval than round, but the way her hair hung gave her chin and cheeks a square look. The chalk-white smoothness of her skin gleamed like polished marble, but it was her eyes that drew me. They twinkled like stars in a crisp winter sky. I caught myself before I lost my balance.

She raised her glass to me as I lifted the drink to my lips and sipped, not taking my eyes off her. The taste of warm and cold hit my mouth as bitter tomato juice, horseradish, and vodka slid down my throat. The celery bumped into my nose, but I swallowed the awful concoction. She kept smiling as I forced myself to take a longer drink. I hated vodka in general, and I never could stand tomato juice. I made myself gulp the drink in two swallows because something in me didn't want to disappoint her. I didn't understand why I wanted to please this strange woman. Maybe because she was another goth or just because she bought me the drink. I felt drawn to her across the space. I yearned to discover what secrets she had hidden. Her eyes bored into mine, unearthing long buried emotions. One of them was hope. Hope that I could actually be someone again. As I stared at her, her will went into mine. I started to lose my breath and my heart sped up. By sheer force of will, I tore myself from those eyes.

Then the band started playing again, the same type of music, but heavier. The melody was so insistent it pulled my attention completely from her. It reached into my soul, tearing out everything I had buried. I glanced at the man playing the washboard as he dragged the spoon slowly.

Listening to the rasping of the spoon, I caught a glimpse of Devon's face as it had appeared the first time I met him. The sun played off his skin as he reclined against a tree, a slight breeze catching my dress and blowing up my skirt. He looked over at me with stencil shadows of leaves on his face.

His honey-brown eyes caught me first. They made me want to fall into them. When I regained my composure, he was by my side. His smile was a warm relief in the cold wind, and I wanted to have him forever. I would do anything for him. However, something more sinister lurked under the light exterior. I wouldn't find out how bad he was until I discovered the courage to leave him, but then it was too late.

When I drew my thoughts back to the present, I looked down at the table and discovered a folded napkin. Instantly, I knew the token was from her.

How did she get it here without me seeing her? I wondered, carefully unfolding the napkin.

The handwriting was old-fashioned and flowery, something from the eighteenth century when women learned penmanship, sewing, and nothing else. Now women were liberated—as they didn't need a lord and master telling them what to do. Then again, even in this day and age some women made the wrong choices.

Veronica,

I can awaken what you've kept hidden. I know you understand the shadows but yearn to rejoin the light. Meet me at St. Louis Cathedral in Jackson Square after sunset if you wish to consider my offer.

Brenna

I looked up from the note. Brenna had risen from her table. Her eyes were focused on me. I smiled and tried to hide my apprehension as she came a few steps closer. There was a look of anticipation on her face, but then it was marred by fear. I wondered what had happened and was about to say something, but Brenna was gone. My gaze shifted around the restaurant, searching the faces of the patrons, but nothing. I stood up, hunting for her outside. There was a hot dog vendor babysitting a Harley, but no signs of her. Blending with the other drunkards and wild college students, she had become just another body in the throngs of people.

5

CHAPTER FIVE

My name is Brenna.

The temperature had dropped since I had been inside. People crowded the streets, walking with drinks in their hands as the hour grew late. Here in the city of shadows, anything could happen. Ghosts walked along rooftops, unwary psychics predicted impending doom, and unsuspecting monsters lurked in the darkness. Because of my attire, some gave me a second glance, but I didn't care. They knew nothing of the world I aligned myself to. Their thoughts pressed against my mind, just like Veronica's had, and that had awakened my hunger. I knew my fascination would have to wait as my stomach rumbled and my gums ached even more than before. It was time to find something to eat.

Glancing around the streets, I noticed a boy in his early twenties. He looked all-American and something akin to the prey I had lost earlier that evening. I scanned his mind. He was alone and didn't have too much on his mind, save food and exploring the sights. I withdrew my tether and licked my lips. I followed behind him, knowing him to be the perfect catch of the night.

He entered a small diner, sat alone at the counter, and ordered a burger. Moving in beside him, I made sure the velvet of my sleeve rubbed against the bare flesh of his arm. He looked over at me, assessing my appearance. He didn't seem too pleased with my intrusion.

"Sorry," I said, giving him the biggest grin I could.

The look on his face was cold and set, but when I smiled, his harshness melted away.

"That's okay," he said, his voice thick with a northern accent.

"Where you from?" I asked.

"What do you want?" the waitress asked me.

I glared at her. She gave me a death look and left to wait on another patron. I patiently turned back to my prey, waiting for him to answer.

"What's her problem?"

I shrugged, trying to fawn over the man's big, blue eyes, playing the part of an interested human. After a moment, he picked up on the vibe. I ignored the waitress as she dropped his burger on counter.

"I'm from Boston," he said.

"Oh, really! I went to college there. How do you like it here?"

"It's great. I'm not used to this heat, though. Man, the sun can kill you."

I laughed. "I'm a night owl myself, but I understand. This place takes getting used to. Once you do, it's hard to leave."

"It's wonderful." He paused and took another bite of his burger. I noticed that it looked like it could still moo as he put it down. "I'm Cain." He stuck out his hand and I took it. The firmness of his grip surprised me, but it was his slender, delicate fingers that stunned me more.

"I'm Brenna."

"You want to get out of here?"

I nodded. This guy was a tourist and probably thought I was a whore. If he thought that, then I'd give him the night of his life.

"Good." He slapped some money down on the counter and got up. He fought his way through the incoming people and pushed out chairs.

Already I envisioned myself sinking my teeth into his warm, salty flesh. The taste of him lingered in my mind as the smell of his musk rose in my nostrils. The whispering of the rivers of blood called to me underneath his fair, freckled skin. I sighed inwardly, letting myself fantasize about what physical feats both of us would accomplish while I had my fill of him. Just the images got me wet. I smiled and licked my fangs.

Yes, he would be tasty.

CAIN WAS ASLEEP when I awoke. The sunlight splayed yellow bars across his chest, making his skin slightly red when I rose. I drifted out of bed quietly, wondering what it would be like to see this boy in the full light of day. Sadly, that was impossible. Being awake, I had to fight the dangers of the sun. Just the thought of its rays on my skin made me shiver. I'd have to be careful when I met Veronica, so I had to dress accordingly. Like any good goth girl, I was going to dress in style.

Choosing to wear a black miniskirt and peasant blouse, I threw my black leather corset over it all. When I finished lacing it up, the corset pushed up my tits. I looked through my closet, found long, satin opera gloves, and slipped on my floor length cloak, pulling its hood low over my face. Before I left, I needed one last moment with my midnight tryst. Leaning over, I nipped at his neck to feel the blood rushing underneath his perfect skin. The scent of him filled my nose: sweat, body odor, and the hint of aftershave from the day before. I lingered a moment at his jugular and took a deep breath, steadying myself as the beat of his heart drew me in. I knew better than to become entranced by the soft, slow sound. I licked his throat, sampling a small taste of myself on him, and then moved to his lips. Those I parted with my tongue, taking his bottom lip in my teeth. The curve of my fang caught the inside of his cheek, drawing blood. I savored the small amount of coppery sweetness as it clung to my canine and then mingled with my saliva.

As the sensors in his body sent pain to his brain, he jumped out of a sound sleep. Cain opened sky-blue eyes and cringed at the sudden brightness. He put his hand up to block it until I could close the shutters. I almost laughed, but held my tongue. My lover's lips were soft against mine, and he made my heart speed up, wanting to stay with him to pass the rest of the day. Difficult as it was, I pulled away as his hardness pressed against my thigh. He wanted to keep me, while I wanted to possess him.

"You have to get going," I whispered, surprised to feel the sadness of being separated. Normally, I just used those who crossed my path, but something about this Northerner was different. He made my brain foggy and tingly, as if my psychic abilities were kicking in. I shook off the thought. I wanted him to stay. There was something intoxicating about him that drove thoughts of Veronica from my mind. I didn't know if it was the subtle pinkness of his bare chest or the way his slender fingers traced the hem of my cloak. I stood silently, wishing to remain, but I had other business.

He stretched, pushing back the hood of my cloak so he could stare into the face of the woman he had gone to bed with. There were no signs of disappointment. The hood fell away, allowing some of my hair to tumble into my face. He brushed that away too. I caught his hand, my fingers encircling his wrist. I stared into his eyes and flicked my tongue over the soft lines of his inner wrist.

"If you want me to leave, you shouldn't do that," he said, his voice hoarse with impending passion.

I giggled, unsnaring myself from his hypnotic appeal and remembering my pressing business with Veronica. I licked his lips one last time, reluctantly moving off him. If I stayed any longer, I would miss Veronica. Pulling the hood back over my face, I stared at him from its darkened depths.

"Last night was fun," I whispered.

He got up, tugging on his socks and his boxers. I didn't remember where his pants were, but he found them under my bed. His shirt was nowhere in my room, but I was sure it was somewhere in the house, along with most of my clothes from the night before. Cain gazed at me, contemplating what to say. His emotions were easily read on his face and in his mind.

He wondered if this one-night fling had some kind of potential. The sex was better than any he'd had before, and he craved that. I saw the lust in him as he undressed me with his eyes.

"It was more than that," he finally whispered. "I think I'm in love. Don't you feel the attraction between us? You're something special. You could rule the world."

I laughed. "You're cute, and yes, you're intoxicating. You make me forget I have places to be. I wonder if you have some otherworldly power over me."

"You never know." He smiled devilishly as he kissed me again.

I had a hard time pulling myself away from him. I looked into his eyes and was almost caught. "I'm not busy tomorrow night if you want to get together again," I suggested.

"What time?"

I smiled, showing a hint of fang. "After sunset, of course."

"Of course!"

He stood by the door, scanning the bedroom while waiting for me to say something, but an awkward silence settled between us. I smiled and looked at the room myself, noticing how much I needed to dust. My eyes met his and I followed his gaze to my deck of tarot cards, which I had left out from the night before.

"You're psychic?" he asked.

"Yeah, since I was fifteen. You want me to pick a card for you?"

The corners of his eyes crunched up as he thought about my suggestion. I detected something stirring beneath his composure, but I took it as his indecision.

"Sure." He smiled. "But just one. You don't want to be late."

I got up and ran my hands over the backs of the cards. I concentrated on them, but the cards weren't alive beneath my palm. They had no energy, which was strange. I shook my head, took a breath, and closed my eyes, focusing again, but my intuition didn't kick in. There was nothing, only a hollowness where it should have been. It was as if the energy around my Northerner was dead, as if he weren't even in the room. Ignoring the deadness in my mind, I chose a card and pulled it out.

It was the Ace of Wands. My instincts told me nothing so I relied on the book definition of the card. It meant he had found a new passion in something and wanted more of it, wanted perhaps to possess the thing his mind was fixed on.

"Am I going to turn into a demon and ravage you? Or will I come to a horrible demise at your hands?" His arms came around my waist, and he pecked at my neck.

I smiled, settling back into him before I answered.

"Neither. It means you have a fiery heart and know how to re-root wherever you go."

"Hmm…sounds promising. I agree with the fiery part, but…you smell so good. I could keep you busy for the rest of the night if you wanted." His grip tightened on me.

"I wish," I purred. "But for now, take this." I wrote my number on a scrap of paper. "Call me if something comes up."

"Oh, I will." He kissed me one last time and walked into the other room, finding his shirt.

The apartment door clicked shut, and it was over until tomorrow night. A part of me missed him already, but that was only lust talking as I thought of the places he would ignite with his touch. I don't know what it was about him that had all but pushed Veronica from my mind. Now she was the most important thing, and I couldn't disappoint her.

6

CHAPTER SIX

My name is Veronica.

I barely slept that night, tossing and turning through the hours, anticipating the meeting. When I woke up, all I thought of were the different scenarios of what could happen. The woman would confess her love to me, or that she was some kind of long lost relative. Or maybe she was just a crackpot who wanted to worm her way into my life. In all the images, I found myself being unresponsive because I was afraid I'd break and not know how to pick up the pieces. At the last moment, I almost stayed in my hotel room. However, something made me face my fears and go to meet this woman named Brenna. Even the sound of her name seemed to hold power over me. It was only on my way to our designated meeting place I let myself utter it aloud.

The sun was high. I squinted against the brightness of it as I tried to stay in the shadows. I'd come out a bit early, eager for her encounter, and now the sun was starting to make me itch. I tried to ignore it as I stared at the passersby from behind a column of St. Louis Cathedral in front of Jackson Square, watching the crowd getting duped into having their fortunes told by vendors who sold the future as if it were cheap jewelry. I'd been told by some of the local shop owners that most of the readers were charlatans, preying on drunks and misguided souls by divining the mysteries of time and space. I believed only a select few possessed the gift to predict the future, and they didn't exploit their abilities to entrap others. These true psychics were like the gypsy woman who read my palm years ago.

Alone in Boston Common, I had been approached by an old woman dressed in a patched skirt and a black shirt that drooped on her shrinking frame. Her dark eyes were hidden by wrinkles. I imagined she had once been beautiful, but age and harsh living had worn her down. Silvery hair escaped from a kerchief and hung about her face.

She had appeared out of nowhere, but I was not afraid of her. Her aura was grandmotherly, so when she motioned for me to follow her, I did so without hesitation. I sat next to her in the grass while she studied the lines of my palm, tracing a few with her finger. After a moment, she clasped my hands in her own and stared into my eyes. When I returned her gaze, she didn't see me. She saw something in a distant time and place.

"Child," she said, her voice cracked with age, "you must not let him fool you. He'll be your death."

I stared, wide-eyed, not understanding why she told me this. "I don't know what you're talking about. Devon is wonderful. He loves me. He—"

"Already he drains the warmth and gentleness from your soul. There is still time, but I fear you'll think me crazy and not listen. Years from now when decades have passed, you'll remember the gypsy woman who told your fortune. Alas, it's too late. I already see his mark on you." She pointed at my neck.

I cringed and fumbled with the collar of my blouse, covering the bruise Devon had given me. He had gotten carried away and bit my neck during our last encounter. He apologized and told me he was just eager for us to be wed.

"Wait! What do you mean?" I asked. She shook her head, got up, and walked away, but I jumped up and ran after her.

"Child, the face you wear is sincere and pure, but soon, the light in you will extinguish. You'll crave the darkness, shunning the kindness of humanity and killing everything in you that is human. All for him." She paused and then patted my cheek. "In the end, you'll meet another who will deceive you, but will bring you back into the light." She let go of me and strolled away.

I started to go after her, but something held me in place. I thought it was my disbelief in what she'd said, and yet as she moved away, I realized it was something more. Part of me believed her, even though I told myself Devon would never hurt me. Who was the other she spoke about? She confused me, so I turned from her, dismissing her advice. I went back to my home, letting the sunshine lift my spirits and the thought of Devon's kisses drive her predictions from my mind.

If I'd listened to her and walked away from Devon then, I would be a different creature now. I was too lost in my own stupidity and happiness to see beyond. Now my heart was doomed to be cold and barren forever. I hadn't found the strength or courage to be close to another. Maybe Brenna could reach into my soul and bring me back to life. Maybe she was my salvation. Maybe she was the one the gypsy had spoken about, the one who could bring me back into the light.

I sighed, scanning the crowd, searching for someone who could change my life. Resting my head against a pillar of St. Louis Cathedral, I tried moving further into the shadows to escape the sun. It was no good. I was in its sights and if Brenna didn't come soon, I was going to give up. I would seek shelter indoors where it was cooler and the heaviness of the air didn't choke me. Each ragged breath I drew seemed to be filled with cotton. I coughed, tasting the humidity and wishing it would dissipate just long enough for me to take a normal breath. This deception forced me to face my own reality.

I grew weary of the masks I wore, tired of hiding behind a curse. And then this woman came.

She intrigued me, accomplishing something I never thought another human being could do. Brenna got into my soul, hypnotizing me. For years, the darkness had kept me safe, and now I wanted to break free.

Maybe she's like the gypsy from years ago and can read the future. That was something I had to discover after I found her in the crowd.

Most of the tourists didn't notice me. They were too busy looking at the sights in the square. As I watched them, none looked at ease. A few sat on benches sketching or snapping pictures of the cathedral, but none of them stood out. Even as I watched them, I wondered what it would be like to have a normal life: to think of children or friends or to take a relaxing vacation. That was why I came here. I thought it'd be a nice place to escape. The city was a mystery.

I never thought I'd meet a woman who'd turn me inside out. The more I thought of Brenna, the more attracted I was to the idea of her. There was nothing sexual about it, but I yearned to know if she was real. What did she eat? How did she brush her teeth? I wanted all the minute details. Then again, maybe the whole encounter had been something created by the darkness in my mind. It would want me to think the imaginary Brenna was a lifeline back to the outside world. Just like that small part of me that would always crave me being Devon's perfect slave. It would give anything to make him happy.

I shook my head. No. My mind did not create her. Brenna was extraordinary in a city filled with ordinary things. When I saw her she'd be breathtaking, something from a darkened fairytale, with the quiet calm of a princess and the beauty of a wicked queen.

And then, there she was.

Brenna traversed the square as if floating above the cobblestones. A black cloak billowed around her, but black gloved hands held the hood down over her face. Copper hair spilled from the folds of the material. No one seemed to notice her. She was only a mirage traipsing through the crowded streets. I knew she was there. I heard her footsteps crossing the square on the cobblestones.

What was I going to do? Run or stand my ground? Should I try to face her, forcing words out of my mouth? She'd look into my soul and see me for who I really was. Could I face the reality of someone getting close to me?

The last time it happened, I turned into an indescribable thing.

Maybe she had seen past the darkness and truly knew what was there.

She was within steps of me, but a stupid sightseer crossed in front of her—and when the tourist passed, she had vanished.

My heart skipped. Where had she gone?

The hairs on the back of my neck rose like bodies rising from the earth. A chill ran down my spine as I wondered where she had gone, and then, without a sound, a gloved hand clamped down on my shoulder. I couldn't help but jump. The hood covered most of her face, but the dying light snuck under it, catching her jade green eyes. She looked away, breaking contact, and put up a gloved hand to shield herself from the sun.

"Would you like to get out of the sun?" I asked hesitantly, knowing I needed to.

She nodded, drawing the hood further over her face. She stood in front of me and motioned for me to follow. I struggled to keep up with her hurried pace as she darted in between people. Each step took us deeper into the French Quarter. We entered a small café where she chose chairs in the back. I sat across from her, perched on the edge of the seat, waiting for her to make the next move.

Slowly, she slid the hood of her cloak off. Next, she meticulously worked on her gloves, pulling at one delicate finger at a time. I held my breath, drinking in her beauty. This was Brenna. This was the woman who could help me. When I had spied her before across the square, I had only gotten a hint of what she looked like, but now I knew she truly was some kind of creature out of a fairy tale.

Her skin glittered in the light from the café. I yearned to stroke it, to discover if it was as soft as it looked, to see it was a trick of the light or if it was makeup. A subtle hint of vanilla wafted from her, which made her even more intoxicating. My eyes followed her hair and neckline, settling on the rise and fall of her breasts, which were elevated by a corset. The garment conformed to her body perfectly. I knew how corsets worked and even owned two, but I only wore them while clubbing.

Her breasts rose and fell, each straining to fall out of the black, peasant blouse as she took long, even breaths. This strange woman was a phenomenon like I'd never encountered before. I craved to know all about her.

I smiled, the muscles in my face straining to remember the gesture. At first, I thought they might not respond to my mental command, but after a moment they moved mechanically.

She grinned, showing a hint of white, sharp teeth. It appeared she had fangs like mine. I didn't know what to do next. I hardly dared breathe. Some part of me feared if I blinked she'd evaporate and float away. So I sat, staring, as she relaxed into her seat and studied me. I saw nothing but her, ignoring the mule-drawn carriages that passed outside the window giving tours of the city. I drowned out the whirring of the cappuccino machines, the employees rattling dirty dishes, and the pigeon that flew into the café and settled contently under the table next to us.

"We can sit all night if you like, but I don't think it's going to get you anywhere," she finally said.

"Do you want to order something?" I asked, not ready to delve into conversation with this woman. So much had begun to change so fast, I thought that if I uttered a word everything would shatter.

She leaned over, putting her hand on my chin. The ends of her fingers brushed against my flesh, sending jolts of electricity through my face and causing the little hairs on my neck to salute. I shivered a moment, then a feeling of calmness descended over me, like someone had taken me out of a storm. I was serene and comfortable in my own skin.

"You have nothing to fear from me. All I want to do is talk with you." The concern in her voice was genuine.

"All right," I whispered as I tried to stop my voice from trembling.

I dared not look into her eyes again, and somehow I managed to swivel out of her grasp and stand up. I caught myself on a chair as I crossed the floor to the counter. I looked up at the menu board, but with so many coffee lattes, cappuccinos, and espressos to choose from, I didn't know where to begin. I glanced at her helplessly.

"Two chai lattes, for here," she said behind me.

I had no idea what she had ordered, but I trusted her. I stood as she pulled bills from between her breasts and gave them to the cashier, throwing a dollar bill into the tip cup. Brenna took the concoctions to the condiment counter and sprinkled cinnamon on top of the hot liquid before we walked back to our seats. There she settled down again and took a sip of the latte.

I picked up my drink, testing it with my tongue. The cinnamon gave it an earthy flavor, but when I took a larger swallow the liquid worked its way to my insides, warming me. As I sat sipping, the silence consumed me, making me angry. That was a feeling I related to. The darkness Devon had instilled in me reared its ugly head and slipped into my thoughts.

What am I doing here? She's just another goth chick pretending to be something she's not. This perfect stranger waltzes into my life and expects me to fall all over her? She doesn't know who she's dealing with.

My insides burned as the thoughts churned in my head. It was time to get down to business.

"What game are you playing with me?" I asked coldly.

She blew some of the steam from her piping drink, curling her nails on the hard, white enamel surface of the cup before answering.

"You caught my attention. You bumped into me on the street, and when you turned, I saw the years of pain in your eyes. It called out to me like a light in a storm. You try so hard not to remember your past. You've written yourself out of society, yet you find yourself here, in a city full of emotion. Just by walking down the street you cannot help but acknowledge this city has worked its magic on you. It calls to your soul. That's what got my attention."

I stared at her. Her answer was truthful. Every word of it. I vaguely remembered running into someone as I raced down Bourbon Street the day before. I'd thought Devon pursued me, but I had been wrong. The city had begun to work on me as soon as I stepped off the plane. The atmosphere was heavier, more mystical, shattering my finite exterior. How and why I didn't know, but this place had changed me in the two days I had been here. The city wanted me to stay here forever. It needed me to stop hiding from the darkness in my mind. I had to stop running from the memories of my past. One of them being Devon and what he had made me into: a monster with a pretty face. If I had only known about him I never would have let him in, but his power over me was absolute from the first moment he saw me. He wanted me, so I became his.

"And what can you do for me?" My voice was cold enough to chill my scorching drink.

She laughed. "I can give you back everything you lost and show you an eternity where you don't have to be afraid of the darkness inside your soul."

"Really? And how can you do that?"

Brenna smiled again, showing me a pair of designer fangs that could have passed for the real thing. Then her eyes ignited with green fire that brightened her entire face, making her even more eerily beautiful. She seemed to grow taller, expanding in the seat, commanding my attention, like a dragon might do when it opens its wings preparing to fly. My eyes widened. *Was this woman for real?* I didn't know what to say. Maybe I truly had found someone who could understand my nature.

"You're afraid of me?" A look of worry crossed her face and the hunger I'd seen in her eyes died as fast as it had appeared. She shrunk back in her chair, returning to normal. "Please, I didn't mean to frighten you. It's just… I wanted you to know who I am. I thought it was only fair to be open if you were going to let me help you."

At that moment it didn't matter what I'd seen or if she was real. She was sincere, no matter what she was. She truly wanted to help me, so when I stared into her eyes again, I still found myself falling into their depths. It was by no power of hers I'd been hypnotized. It was by my own will. I'd forgotten what it was like to be drawn to another so strongly.

"No, I'm just surprised. I never thought…well, it doesn't matter. You're right, I am scared. I'm frightened of myself. I haven't been able to see inside myself for so long I don't know if there's anything left to call human."

"That's okay. We can discover that together."

I laughed. For the first time in a long time, pure laughter rang out of me. The sound of it surprised me and silenced the room. I'd no longer run. I'd face the dark beast I'd locked away so I could be whole again, and this strange woman would help me do it.

7

CHAPTER SEVEN

My name is Brenna.

We talked together for most of the night, discussing ordinary things. Once I stated my intentions to Veronica, she relaxed. We became two people meeting for the first time, welcoming each other's company. We whispered nothing of our pasts, knowing the time would come later for sharing secrets. Instead, we spoke of our politics and other interests of the day. The hour grew late, and the noise of the crowded café dwindled to a mere din, until we were the only ones left. When the staff started putting up the chairs, we realized it was time to leave. I threw my cloak over my shoulders and escorted Veronica out of the café.

The night was quiet, and the temperature was as cool as a temperate pool. Birds twittered in the trees as we walked side by side on the outskirts of the Quarter, avoiding the garish lights and sounds of Bourbon Street. Considering her fragile state of mind, the people would be overwhelming, and I craved the quietness only the fringes of the Quarter provided; however, she stopped me after a few minutes of silence.

"What is it about this place that forces me to face what I am?"

I turned, staring into her eyes, knowing it was inevitable her mask would break. I couldn't tell her this, though. I sighed, gazing up at the sky, trying to find some guidance in the cloudless expanse. There was none, just the wisdom that came with age.

"This city is one of the oldest in the country. It has a history. It brings things to the surface for some, while allowing others to hide behind made-up faces. The one thing you have to figure out is: which one are you?" Pausing, I felt the moon graze across the sky and fill me with its cold light. "I know someone did terrible things to you, but can't you let that go and learn to love again?"

My voice dropped to a whisper as it drew her in. She was more under the spell of her own mind than of any thoughts of mine. Still, she didn't know what to make of me. Just by spending these past few hours with her, I desired her more. She was everything I wasn't, and she was so close to the breaking point. This one night of close company made her walls transparent and flimsy. The darkness in her was close, but she still held it at bay. It seemed that part of her personality was observing me to see what I would do next. My interaction with her overwhelmed her with feelings. They came off her in ripples. Each one confusing her, yet bringing her joy all at the same time. It was too much for her mind to digest. As her emotions moved from her, I let them sink into me and settle into my chilled heart. I found myself almost as intoxicated as she was.

She leaned into me, her eyes half closed. I noticed the slight rocking motion of her body. Resting my fingers on the underside of her chin, I steadied her, drawing her closer. I kept my eyes locked on hers. Her breath came in sweet pants as the last of the cinnamon from the tea clung to it. It made me want to devour all of her. Inches from pressing my lips to hers, something alien invaded my space.

Someone, something, was watching us from the shadows. I had never sensed it before. It was not an apparition pointed out on the frequent ghost tours, nor was it any type of human being. It was an alien energy. I heard a low growl. Ready to pounce, I turned to face whatever it was. I hissed. I saw movement in the shadows. It was quicker than me. My first and last thought was of trying to protect Veronica. Whatever attacked me hit me hard on the side of the head. Pain exploded and my vision darkened. I made out an outline in the dark, and I thought it was Cain. My would-be hero. Before I could call out to him, blackness overtook me.

PART TWO
THE TOWER

8

CHAPTER EIGHT

My name is Veronica.

While we were out enjoying the night, I slowly sank under her spell. We only talked about unimportant things, but even as we discussed them I knew she was the one who could rescue me. When I turned to look at her in the night, I saw how unchangeable she was, how her beauty would be picturesque forever. Brenna showed no fear of the night or the unknown, and was ready to help me, no matter the consequences.

For that, I was grateful.

Suddenly, she turned to investigate a noise, but when I heard the sound, I knew what it was. Who it was. I tried to warn her, but a large, meaty hand clubbed the side of her head, and she crumpled to the ground. The moment the wound opened, I knew what she wasn't.

It had all been an illusion.

The warm, sweet scent of her blood filled my nostrils, and I knew how human she was, how vulnerable, how easily hurt and killed.

At first, it shattered my image of her; my savior was nothing more than a mere mortal. It made me realize she was like the rest of my kind, tricksters whose every word was a lie. I should have recognized the signs, but I was blinded by my own stupidity. I only saw one of my own who actually cared about me and wasn't enthralled with tormenting prey. She had a life, and I desperately wanted her to show me how to be warm and somewhat sane. When I caught the perfume of her blood, all of my aspirations shattered.

Turning my attention from her, I gazed into the darkness, knowing immediately who the hand belonged to. My beloved. The one who gave me this cold, undying life.

"Devon, I can smell your putrid breath from here."

"It's wonderful to see you again, Ronnie," he cooed, his smirk branded into his features.

"Let go of me," I whispered.

He moved forward, stepping over the crumpled form of my companion.

"Not this time," he purred.

"What do you want?" I hissed. My gums tingled as my teeth ached to descend. I held myself in check, not knowing what to say or do—I only knew I didn't want to be around him.

Looking deep into my eyes, his mind snaked past my defenses, trying to find where I had been. His power called to my other half, the beast he had birthed, but I was not about to release her from the cage she occupied in my mind. His will demanded I come back and fall under his power once again. I was stronger than before, and he was not going to keep me. I clamped the shields around my mind when he tried moving deeper to get to her. He snarled at this and pushed me away.

I landed hard on the ground, the sidewalk scraping my ass. I was more dazed than hurt as I sat, staring up as he looked down at me with contempt in his eyes. He lowered himself to the ground, cradling Brenna to him as if she were a child.

If no one knew what had transpired between us, some would have thought he was her lover, or her husband, picking her up because she had fainted or had too much to drink—either of which were possible in this strange place. I crawled a few inches forward, reaching out so he would not harm her. He grinned, his teeth growing as he did. He pushed the hair from her neck, positioning it to the side so he would have an easy pathway to where he would bite. His triumphant sneer radiated on his face because he knew it was that easy for him to have her, using her to get to me.

"No—"

He looked up from her throat, just before biting. The hunger in his eyes begged me to follow suit and join him in the ravaging of the mortal at his feet. I bit down on my lip, holding my passions in check as the beast roared from its slumber in my mind. It sensed its master was close.

"You've grown soft these past few years. I never would have thought you would want to spare one of them. They're nothing but meat. You used to tear them apart, drinking them up from the inside out. What happened to you?"

"You made me do that. I never wanted to kill. It's only when she gets out that happens."

"Oh, yes. Your other half. The beast you keep locked away. You stalk hospitals drinking from those Death is about to take so you don't feel so guilty about killing them. You're a meat-lover, but your hunger is never sated unless you feel the thrill of the hunt rushing through you. Your beast is not something to shun. Embrace it."

"Why? So I can be like you?"

"Ronnie, we've had this conversation before." Devon sighed.

"Stop calling me that. My name's Veronica. That's her name."

"Yes, my true child is locked behind the walls of your mind. I know she wants to come out. She would do anything for me. The hunger is growing, Ronnie. Soon your control will slip and she'll come out, the vampire you hate so much. What will you do then? If that happens, you won't be able to save this one. You know how much we like to play with our food. The fear makes them taste so much better. Just like this one."

He brought Brenna to his lips again, and then flicked his tongue over the line of her neck, familiarizing himself with the terrain of her skin. A low growl, something akin to a cat's, echoed in the night. It was lower, more feral than the angriest panther scream. It took me a moment to realize it had erupted from my throat. Every muscle was taut; I wanted to spring at him. The sidewalk was hard beneath my hands, its coolness seeping into my skin, trying to chill my rising temper. My nails scraped the cement and my teeth rested on my bottom lip, long and sharp, ready to tear into flesh. Saliva dripped down the corners of my mouth like strings of torn meat. Absently, I wiped them away.

I moved my hand forward, balancing my weight so I could propel myself into the air.

"Move one more inch, and I'll tear her throat out," he warned, caressing Brenna's neck with his elongated claws.

Brenna's head flopped to the side like a child's doll. Her innocence hung in the air. If I destroyed it, I was no better than Devon and he had won.

The last vestiges of his control over me slipped away. I wouldn't let him provoke me until I let her out. It didn't matter that he was the one who brought me into a world where there was no light. I stared at Brenna's prostrate form, wanting to help her because she was willing to help me. Devon was right. The beast in me called out for her blood, but I ignored it and the hunger that raged in both of us. I wouldn't let Devon ravage her body.

I relaxed, letting my talons become blunt and squared off. My teeth retracted somewhat, but remained tiny pinpoints in case he decided to harm Brenna.

"Let her go!"

He smiled. "But she smells so good. Can't you pick up the coppery scent of her blood mingling with the vanilla of her skin? It makes my mouth water. Her blood still runs like a molten river, ready to warm us. I know you want her. Your hunger scents the air like human fear."

I closed my eyes, staying in control. He wasn't going to tempt me into letting my guard down and the beast take over. I would not give in. I would remain as I was while the beast ravaged my insides. I bit down on my lip, drawing blood, but I kept my focus. "No, damn you, Devon. No more games! What the hell do you want?"

He studied me before answering. "Isn't it obvious? I want you. Did you really think you'd get away from me so easily? You're mine. Always!" He glanced down at Brenna, running his hands over her face.

I watched the rise and fall of her chest. She rested as peacefully as an innocent babe, unaware of the danger around her. I couldn't wake and warn her of the impending doom. If I did, Devon would kill her.

"If you let her go, I'll—" I feared no matter what I said he would hunt her down and take her anyway.

"You'll what?"

I shook my head. Tears formed in my eyes. "M-m-aster. Please." I couldn't bring myself to say anymore. Devon knew how much I hated to call him that.

He chuckled. "Since you're being so cooperative, you can have your fun now with this human. Remember, I'll be watching. Night, night, Ronnie!" He laughed, and in a blink was out of my sight, though not out of my life.

I thought when I ran away it would be forever. But no, after two hundred years he still couldn't let me go. It wasn't good enough, not even after he had killed everything inside me that was human. He wanted to dominate the whole package. However, I was no longer in his possession. I'd grown strong over the last decade. He'd seen this when I shoved him out of my thoughts. I didn't know what he had in store for me. I could only imagine what went on in his sadistic mind after the horrible things he had done to me and to his victims, playing with them as if they were paper dolls, shredding and tearing their limbs with his razor-like claws. He admitted he'd followed me, and I knew he probably had ever since I'd run away.

Now I had to worry about Brenna. I could break contact with her, or show her what I really was. I could shatter the image she had of me and take the mask off. Maybe it was time I did, time I stopped denying my true nature. I'd been playing human for so long I'd forgotten what it was to be myself. Denying my nature was something I was used to, but I had let my guard down and Devon had found me. I shivered at the thought of what I had been when I was with him. I fought my hunger and stalked those close to death, but there were times I was lost in my own hunger. My beast, Ronnie, as he called it, was the only thing that pleased him. The things they did together now haunted my dreams. So I kept her caged as much as I could. He found fault in everything I did, beating me until the hunger consumed me and my control slipped. He would never draw me back in, not even with images of when he used to hold me and whisper that he loved me. How I cared for him then, but that was centuries ago, before I understood the true meaning of what my life had become.

I sighed, crossing the pavement between Brenna and me. Her weight was nothing to me as I picked her up gently. I tried so hard to fit in with the humans I let my powers run on reserve until I needed them. Well, now was a time I needed them, and my system was still in high gear from facing Devon. Carrying her back to my hotel on Bourbon Street, I shielded myself so no one could detect us. In my room, I laid her down on the bed, arranging her arms so they lay across her heart as if she were a corpse awaiting a funeral.

I smirked at the thought, and then turned to the window. I pulled the cord for the blinds and looked out into the normally warm and pleasant night. It had turned deadly and cold. This was not a sight for me to lounge in. It was a place for me to survive in. The city had just become an unfamiliar hunting ground, and I was the prey. I didn't know how long Devon had been here or how well he knew the city. I prayed that he was as new to the surrounding area as I was for my own sake and for Brenna's, but for now I kept watch on the city that never slept, waiting for my little one to waken.

9

CHAPTER NINE

My name is Brenna.

When I opened my eyes, almost everything was dark. I tried sitting up, but the pain in my head warped my balance. I felt a small lump on the side of my head. Forcing myself to sit up through the dizzying pain, I found I was in a strange bed in a hotel room. When I listened closely, I heard the hooting drunks and the noise of bands; Bourbon Street was close. I scanned the room and saw an entertainment center and an open suitcase on the floor.

Looking further over, I saw Veronica staring out of the open blinds, the glow from the city lights casting long shadows on her upright form. I waited for her to speak, but when she didn't, I reached out a psychic tether and tried to move into her mind. I sensed nothing warming within her psyche. She was frigid and held some part of herself in check. It was the thing she kept hidden behind the walls of her mind. It was near the surface. Its emotions were raw. Hungry. It wanted out, but she held it at bay.

There was nothing left of the frightened girl I had met. There was only the coldness of a steel trap, waiting to be sprung. I tried steering deeper to see what else she was feeling, but with the ache in my head and with her walls in place, I couldn't. Silently, I cursed myself for not being able to focus.

When my weight shifted, she heard the springs on the bed and turned around. The look on her face was alien. The original fullness had been shaved away to reveal descending cheekbones, almost elfin in their angles. Through the purple, her eyes burned red, and her hair floated around her face as if it had a mind of its own. Her skin seemed paler than mine and almost transparent, reflecting the light like polished moonstone. This was her true self.

My gaze slid down her body, settling on her chest. I watched her for two or three minutes before she took in a breath and even that was forced. Something was off about her, like the air parted around her as if she were an intrusion in the space.

This strangeness made me desire her even more. I assumed she wanted to terrify me. It wasn't working.

Veronica was as she always was: an interesting creature in need of help. The more I examined her, the more I saw beneath her façade, discovering the vulnerable girl under the porcelain face.

"At first I thought you were like me," she whispered. "It would explain so many things, answer so many questions I had about you. You deceived me. You're not like me at all, and I still don't understand why you intrigue me so."

I silenced her with my hand. First I had to know what had attacked me before I could answer whatever questions she had. "What happened?" I asked, crossing the room to meet her. I ached to touch her face to see if it was as smooth as it looked.

"Do you really want to know? Because if I tell you the truth, all masks come off and there is no going back for either of us."

I nodded, needing to comprehend the great mystery in which she shrouded herself. I traced the outline of her cheekbone with my fingers. Her body temperature had dropped dramatically since earlier that night when she was sun-warmed like a stone. Now she was colder than a dead furnace. It made me want to thaw her. She allowed me to outline her lips with my fingers. I picked up every indentation with the tip of my thumb. She stood patiently as I did this, and when I stopped, she stared into my eyes and raised her hand along my cheek, mirroring my gesture.

"So warm," she whispered. "I'd almost forgotten what it's like."

I smiled when her thumb brushed my lips and then moved down my neck.

"Then let me help you remember." I pressed my lips against hers, darting my tongue between them.

She moaned, and her hands wrapped around my waist and ran over the tightness of my corset, trying to get to the body underneath. I placed my hands on her hips, moving one to caress the curve of her ass. Her mouth left mine, kissing and nipping my throat. Her tongue circled my pulse point, and then the hardness of her designer fangs pressed against my skin. I breathed in a sigh, but she looked up and backed away from me.

"What's the matter?" I whispered.

She cocked her head quizzically, studying me. "You still don't get it, do you?"

"What's there to understand? You're a goth chick who's been fucked up by an ex-boyfriend. You hide behind the vampire image to express yourself better. Just like I've done for years."

She laughed, a dark laughter layered with meaning. I didn't think I had said anything funny.

"Look and see what I hide." Her mouth formed into a snarl, and I saw her perfectly white teeth. Then the impossible happened. Her canines grew longer than the rest of her teeth, and her eyes changed from purple to complete blackness as if a squid had released ink into them and covered the white. I backed up a few steps and sat hard on the bed.

Impossible. It can't be! She can't be! But she's real. My dream, my desire is standing in front of me. My wish for eternity has appeared out of nowhere. She's real!

I looked up with tears in my eyes. "It's not possible."

"It's more than possible. And you…" She smiled, running the back of her hand along my cheek.

I tried not to flinch beneath her touch, but I couldn't help it. The primal instinct of flight ran through me as she revealed her true nature. I saw the hurt in her face as sadness touched her eyes.

"I thought you'd be my savior, letting me reveal the story of my past to you. It doesn't matter now because everything I touch turns to shit. You're just a human who has no idea what a true vampire is. You cling to an image that has been created by a crazy Irishman. You can't help me. Just go." She turned her back on me and seemed to forget I was ever there.

"I'm not leaving! I don't care what you are. I still want to help you." I was stubborn. I had always been that way and never listened to anyone. Not even my own instincts that told me to run and hide from the predator. My body was yelling for me to do that, but my mind was whispering something else. I was drawn to her, not because she was a vampire, but because she was in need.

I saw her fists clench, and suddenly my head was yanked to the side and her hand was wrapped in my hair. Her fangs grazed my throat. One of her canines sunk into my neck, sending pain shivering through my skin. My mind tried to latch onto hers, but there was nothing of the woman who was there minutes ago. There was just hunger and pure enjoyment. Whatever she had been hiding was now in control.

"Wait!" I screamed and pushed with my mind. The thing faltered. She withdrew and looked up at me. Hunger burned in her eyes and something of the woman I knew reappeared. It seemed I had the attention of both her personalities, but only for a second or two before the beast took over again, this time completely.

"What?" she breathed.

I placed my fingers under her chin, forcing her face to my level. I studied the shadows playing off her flesh and saw nothing I was frightened of. This was still the woman I was drawn to, still the Veronica I desired to bring back into the light. Brushing away a hair that had fallen into her face, I traced the outline of her cheek again. Closing my eyes, I kissed her, working my lips to hers. The sudden gesture intrigued the beast. My mind lingered on the outside of her thoughts and it seemed her other half was not used to being accepted. It shied away and let Veronica back into the mix, which seemed to surprise her.

At first she did nothing, her lips still drawn back in a fearsome snarl, but then, after my tongue grazed her fangs, she responded. My tongue caught the tip of one, drawing a drop of my blood. She sucked it and my tongue into her mouth, locking me to her. With that she locked down her other half and forced it back into the recess of her mind. I thought I heard it howling as I left her thoughts as well.

"I'm not afraid of you. I meant everything I said. No matter what you are or what lies inside your mind. I still want to help you. I guess I'm not the only one masquerading." I wanted so much to protect her from her own demons.

Veronica smiled at this. "No. I think we both were craving to become beings we couldn't. We each thought the other didn't exist, and because of that, you've gotten mixed up in my mess." She reached up, touching the lump on my head.

I winced at the pain, but it didn't matter. "Will you tell me what happened? Will you tell me all of it?"

"I'll tell you only if you want to listen. It might take all night."

I brushed a stray hair from her face, finally able to experience the silky texture of her skin. "It doesn't matter. I'm a night owl." I laughed.

She smiled at the remark, her eyes returning to their violet hue, but her expression turned distant and cold again as she stepped away from me and back into her own memories.

10

CHAPTER TEN

My name is Veronica.

How could I tell her of my fall from humanity? Could I confess I used to be happy living in a world where the night was a scary place, where women were expected to marry and have children? A world in which I had a future as a teacher, as a mother. Was Brenna going to retreat, leaving me on my own after I bared my soul, tearing down what was left of my crumbling walls? I glanced at her as she sat on the bed, her heartbeat keeping rhythm with the ticking clock in the next room, counting down the minutes until her life stopped forever.

No, she would not desert me. I knew this deep within my heart. Brenna truly cared, no matter what kind of thing I was. She had seen the beast and hadn't turned away in fear, but rather had accepted me uncon-ditionally. She saw into my soul and past the monster who had ravaged children, torn apart women, disem-boweled men. I'd done so much horror in my life. I didn't think anyone would want to be close to me. Devon turned me into a vampire and birthed a beast who thought that people were raised for pleasure: to fuck and feed from. I, meanwhile, hated the life he had given me. I despised myself for the blood I needed to keep myself going. As Devon had said, I hunted hospi-tals and took the lives of those close to death. I tried not to kill them, to just sip a little from each one. Even then, I ended up taking their lives. At least they went peace-fully, unlike the victims of my alter ego. She craved fear, obedience, and like other vampires, she wanted to be used and abused by her Master.

I didn't understand how my kind could do such things. How could we prey on the things we used to be? Mortals reminded me of ants, living out their lives unaware of the dangers in society. For years, I craved what was stolen from me, a chance at a mortal life, and all the joys and problems that went with it. It had been ten years since my facade had broken and I'd had to face my true nature again. Of course, it was when Devon showed up. The beast always knew when its master was close.

I sighed as my train of thought turned to Brenna, who waited expectantly for me to begin.

"Why are you so sad all of a sudden?" Brenna broke the silence.

The look on her face allowed me to see how much she shared my pain. She might not have known what I was thinking, but she knew how I felt. I walked over to her, touching her hand, feeling her energy. Then a warmth came over me, like being covered with a big quilt. It settled first in my heart, then moved to my arms, legs, and finally into my head. A sense of reassurance and peace lingered in my cold soul. I didn't take my eyes off of her. My legs wobbled as I fell into her eyes, as I had when I hadn't known she was human. I sank down on the bed beside her, her hand still in mine. As her pupils expanded, I was pulled farther into her grasp. All I wanted to do was let myself go wherever she wanted. She was my whole world.

I blinked, clearing my head. The warmth in my limbs slowly dissipated. Some of my pain had been removed. Not even an echo remained. Something in me panicked when the contact with Brenna ended. I wanted to be with her again—a junkie needing a fix. She had done something to me, akin to what I did to my victims, giving them pleasure to ease the pain. However, when I left my prey, I never took their pain away, just their blood. When I killed, I ravaged those I had chosen. When I fed, I'd keep them alive, but the feeding was always hollow as I never lingered too long in their minds to learn their true emotions for fear it would rouse my own beast. I instilled in them feelings of pleasure from the feeding, but when I left, they always seemed empty and unfulfilled, despite the pleasure I could make them feel. So I moved on to another.

"What did you do?" I inquired.

She pulled her head up, looking at me through tear-rimmed eyes. The pain she took in swirled inside her head like a whirlpool, being absorbed.

"So much pain. I didn't know." She sniffled.

I sighed. I knew it. Somehow she had picked up on all of the horrible things I had done over the years. She hated me now, despised me for what I had done, but I couldn't let her go, not with Devon lingering in the city with his eyes on her. I had to keep her with me because if I didn't, she would be consumed.

"It's how I lived, how I was taught. It was natural. I kill or I die." I sat back on my heels and looked up at the small bits of dust hanging on the plaster ceiling. If I squinted, the particles seemed like the small dots of an Impressionist painting, creating their own design.

"No, it's not that. All this time you've spent alone, locked up in the cage of your own mind, putting yourself through hell. All to try and be human. Thinking you could never find a friend. It's so sad. You have so much pain. I mean, I knew you did before, but I didn't know to what extent. I thought I could help. I wanted to help. But there's so much darkness..." She trailed off into more tears.

I stared at her in disbelief. I hadn't uttered a word, yet she knew all of this by touching me. Maybe I'd been right to think this mortal had put me under some kind of spell and hypnotized me. Before me was a human who had a touch of the powers bestowed upon my kind. I didn't know what to do or say.

"How do you know all of this? You can't have read my mind. I would have known if—"

Brenna shook her head, wiping her eyes. "Not your thoughts, your emotions. I read what you felt. I'm an empath. I feel the pain of others, as well as their sadness or joy. I was able to get inside your head because of all the cracks in your shields. You didn't feel me because you were distracted by the image I projected."

"I understand you feel others' pain, but you took some of mine away. How did you do that? And how is it you can hypnotize me? No human has ever done that to me before." I was intrigued as much as I was mortified. This girl had been able to get inside my head.

Brenna laughed. "I manipulate energy, just like any good psychic. It's how I do my readings. I can read people's energy fields like others can read a book. The aura catalogs everything a person experiences. It's a matter of knowing what to look for. I've been doing it since I was a teenager."

I laughed when I realized what she was. "You're a psychic. Like those I saw in Jackson Square. That's great."

"No, not like those in the Square. I'm the real thing," Brenna spat. "I've been feeling things since I don't know when, but I learned how to use my abilities. How the hell do you think I make a living down here?"

"I'm sorry. I don't believe people are able to divine the future. Well, not many, anyway."

"How can you say that when you exist? When your kind is supposed to be a fairy tale? Wait a minute...you're lying. You do believe in what I do. Someone told you that you were going to become a vampire." Brenna looked at me expectantly.

Glee sparkled in her eyes because she knew she had caught me in a lie.

"A gypsy told me to beware of Devon, that he would make my life a living hell. She said I'd curse myself for not taking her advice. I guess she was right. But how did you figure all this out? How did you hypnotize me? When did this start for you?" I asked her these questions not to deflect the subject away from myself, but because this new tidbit increased my fascination.

Brenna smiled. "I thought you were going to tell me about yourself."

"Your life is more interesting at the moment."

"You really want to know?"

I nodded.

Brenna didn't say anything, but took in a deep breath, closing her eyes. She willed her heart to slow and her breathing to lessen. I watched intently, wondering what she was going to do next. When she opened her eyes, the pupils expanded. Her presence dominated the room, surrounding me as if I were in its way. The waves of energy radiating off her were invisible to the human eye, but I saw them in bright blues and purples, with a light shade of yellow surrounding the edges of her body. This was her aura.

My kind perceives the energy field around humans when we're in hunting mode, our senses sharpened. But I saw the colors with my own eyes, felt them moving off her, each one having a different vibration. The yellow was high strung, reminding me of the buzz of a bee's wing. The blue, the subtle hum of the streetlights, calming and yet annoying at the same time. The purple was heavier, pushing me to sleep. If I listened, the sound was the lapping of water breaking on the shore. Then I turned my attention away from the colors and the feelings when something moved inside my mind.

At first I panicked, dropping the walls surrounding my thoughts so nothing could penetrate my stronghold, but then I felt Brenna's tether. Her presence reminded me of a subtle itch in my brain. If I hadn't focused on it, I wouldn't have known she was there.

As she moved in my mind, I watched her face. The muscles by her cheekbones slackened, but her eyes gazed past me, looking at something I couldn't see, or didn't want to see. The intensity of the stare was overwhelming. She literally looked inside my mind, reading what was there, absorbing what she needed, but within a second she was gone, her presence no longer lingering inside my head. The emptiness she left behind consumed me. I wanted to cry out.

"Did you feel me in your mind?" she asked.

I nodded. "It was strange. What do you use the colors of your aura for?"

"The purple hypnotizes. The frequency of the energy calms people, capturing them in the beat. Most of the time, I don't intend to use it. I just do readings and people are tranquil afterward. When I dress up though, I project an air of mystery and use my aura like a cloak to hush my energy, or unfurl it so it grabs people's attention. My aura is an extension of myself. I work it without a thought. It's like you reaching inside someone's mind, taking control of their bodies. You just do it without thinking."

What Brenna said made sense, and it was relevant to how my powers worked. Vampires performed most things on instinct. I'd met some of my kind who could hardly hypnotize a dog, but they had great physical strength. None of the vampires I knew were weaker than humans, but like mortals, all had certain things that came naturally. This was what Brenna said. She knew how to manipulate energy just as I knew how to control people. It was part of her physical make up.

"How did you discover you had these abilities?" I asked, fascinated at the thought of what else Brenna could do.

Brenna sighed and went over to the window, taking the spot I once occupied. I brushed my thoughts against her lightly, like a butterfly touching her arm. She fought with something internally, wondering whether or not she could tell her story to the supernatural creature who had spun her life upside down. She looked at me when she realized I was in her innermost sanctum, monitoring what she thought. Smiling, she gazed back out into the night, letting it carry her away.

"When I was four, I saw a ghost. I woke up and looked over at the stairs. A head was staring at me through the slats of the banister, grinning at me. I knew it wasn't my grandfather. He was asleep. So I got scared and shut off my abilities. Then when I was twelve, something followed me around at night. I stayed up late watching movies and it would come with me into the kitchen. The manifestation was scary, like it wanted to harm me, so I'd run into the light and it would go away because the light meant protection. That continued until I was fifteen. Then one day, I sensed things, saw images of the future.

"I figured most of it was because I was close to a nervous breakdown. Things in my house were not good. I'd come home from school and go straight to my room, avoiding my mother's boyfriend. When Mom got home they always fought. The stress of it got to me, so I started sewing to keep myself sane. Then one day my friend gave me her earrings to hold. I saw pictures of her dead aunt in my head, and when I told her what I saw, she freaked and never talked to me again. After that, I picked up emotions and images about people. I didn't think much of it until it started to get out of hand. I was eighteen by then and sought help online to control my abilities. I found a man who offered to help. I went in for an interview and he hired me on the spot to do readings. I started two days after graduating from high school and continued there until the September after I finished college. I worked at a restaurant until I had saved enough money to come here. And here I am."

"This man must have been a wonderful teacher," I said, envious of her story. Where my education had been demeaning, hers had been nurturing.

Tears came to her eyes again, but this time my pain had not caused them. "He's a wonderful person, and he treated me like his little sister. I miss him very much. Edmund is the best. We had our problems, but they never interfered with our relationship. He was my boss, and at one time my roommate."

She wiped tears from her eyes and turned to me. "Now it's your turn. What's it like to be a vampire? You keep part of yourself caged. Why?"

"It's complicated."

"Try me."

I sighed. "You were inside my mind when I attacked you. You felt the hunger of the beast. It was born in my soul when Devon gave me blood. When it awoke, its first instinct was to sate the hunger. Every vampire is like that. Normally the demon personality and the human personality merge together and co-exist. There are varying degrees among vampires, but you get the idea. The demon always wants to ravage and treat humans as meat.

"That didn't happen with me. When my hunger was sated, I looked Ronnie in the face and saw the destruction we both had caused. Guilt overwhelmed me, and I separated from her. I realized I had become a monster. I hated myself and Devon. I swore I would fight Ronnie and keep her locked away. She wanted out to torture more humans, but I told myself I wouldn't kill. I would treat humans fairly. However, the hunger proved to be too much and even though I preyed upon the sick and dying, I always ended up killing them. Ronnie gets out when my control slips like it did earlier."

"I didn't realize how it was. Books and movies paint a different picture. Even my pretend life was different."

"Now you know and understand how dangerous I can be. What else do you want to know?"

"Tell me about your transformation."

I smiled half-heartedly. This was going to be a long night.

11

CHAPTER ELEVEN

My name is Veronica.

"It was drearily cold the night he came for me. Frost stuck to the windows no matter how much the maids stoked the fires. It wasn't snowing, but the draft in the house cut through the bricks like a guillotine severing heads. I lived in one of the brownstones on Beacon Street; my family wasn't prestigious enough to live on Beacon Hill. My sister and I shared a room on the second floor. I slept close to the window. The third floor was for the servants.

"I had just gotten to bed when I noticed the light rapping of fingernails on thin glass, more like a tree brushing against the panes. I should have been scared, but I wasn't. I got up, wrapping a shawl around my shoulders as I went to the window, filled mostly with curiosity. There, hanging from the latticework, was Devon. I blushed. I looked deep into his eyes, knowing he meant me no harm. I opened the window, letting the coldness of death into the room, into my arms.

"I shut the glass, and then I heard my sister moan in her sleep, but she didn't wake.

"'Devon, what are you doing here?' I asked.

"The grin on his face spread further than ever as he looked at my shape through my nightdress. I was cold, and my nipples showed through the fabric. His look made me hot, despite the temperature of the room. Lust stirred in me for the first time, and shame, because I wanted him to see me. But this feeling only lasted until I regained my senses, and turned to grab my robe, which hung on a chair near the fireplace.

"'What are you doing here?' I asked him again.

"He said nothing. He just took a long step and I was in his arms, his mouth locked to mine. Stunned at his outburst, I went frigid. Never before had he shown such forcefulness. After the shock wore off, I melted into him like warm snow, pressing myself against him as his hand traced the outline of my thigh and ass. His hands were as big as any man's, but his fingers were long and slender as a woman's. That was an odd thing about him because it was the only thing delicate about him.

"He kissed me, moving down my neck, nipping at the skin, mixing pain with ecstasy, drawing me to the brink, all with his teeth and hands. He massaged my breasts, my nipples hard against his palms. Then he stopped, backing away. There was a fire in his eyes that was almost demonic. Or maybe it was the light reflecting off them from the fire, but in my naiveté I assumed it was his lust."

I paused, peeking over at Brenna. She listened intently, reminding me of how I once was, a human child ready to take on the world.

"Devon composed himself and sat next to the fire-place. He leaned against the chair. He glanced up at me and motioned for me to sit with him. He wrapped his arms around my chest, so I was locked to him. My heart sped up, and I could barely breathe. His breath chilled the skin of my throat. We stayed like that for a while. Time slowed and seemed to stop. The warmth of the dwindling flames was enough to keep us warm while we listened to my sister's easy breathing. It was good, and peaceful.

"'Do you want to be with me? For all time?'

"'Of course,' I whispered.

"Why wouldn't I want to be with him? He had awakened so much in me, how could I ever let him go? No one else was coming to ask for my hand, no matter how much my father had in the bank.

CRYMSYN HART

"'The day I met you in the Garden I knew you were the one for me. You were so quiet, caught up in your books. It seemed I'd never get to see inside your thoughts, but the longer I was around you, the more I saw that fire. But I didn't know if you'd survive the change. There's always a chance it'll drive you insane. There is nothing to worry about, once you get over your first kill. Oh, I remember mine. It was the most glorious thing I'd ever done. Yes, you should be fine. I can feel how strong you are, so strong...' He trailed off as he began kissing my neck.

"I listened to him, thinking he was drunk. That was the logical thought because the things he talked about were impossible. How could one live forever? And the nonsense about killing? I was flattered he thought me strong, but what did I know?

"He worked his lips harder into my neck, using his teeth to tug on my flesh. His intentions became feral. I tried turning in his embrace, but his hands locked around my tits, pulling me into him. I screamed, but no sound came out. Fear spread in my veins as I kicked my legs, trying to get away. My attempt was futile.

"Devon's lips and teeth tore at my skin. Somehow, I got loose from him, but it did nothing more than allow him to tear huge gashes into my throat. This spurred him on. I panicked, but it just gave Devon the time to grab hold of me and lock himself to my wound. I heard a horrible sucking. I struggled again and he dropped me, satisfied for the moment. Weakened from the blood loss, I tried crawling away, but I only got a few feet. Tears streamed down my face as I tried to hold in my sobs. All that escaped was a hiccup, since I still couldn't scream. Devon's laughter echoed softly in my room and seemed to be in the confines of my mind as well. I tried moving away, but something tugged at me, and I was forced to look at Devon. My eyes widened at the sight of the man I was going to marry.

"His fingers were bloodstained. His mouth smeared with my blood, his lips curled back in a grin so I could see his two stained teeth still dripping blood. His face was more angular, almost pointed. His ears elongated, coming to a point at both ends so they resembled bat ears. His nose had flattened, looking like it been the victim of an errant frying pan. But his eyes scared me the most: they were completely black with pinpoints of red in the center. There was no white at all.

"As I looked into them, I stared into the face of a demon. I couldn't even scream. He'd stolen my ability to call for help. Just as he had willed my sister into a deep slumber. What was I to do except let silent tears stream down my face?

"Devon smiled, reaching a curved finger to wipe a tear away. His nail, hard like bone, touched my face. He brought the tear to his tongue, tasting it, savoring the saltiness. I wanted to whimper for him to kill me.

Extending my torment was a nightmare, but that was what he wanted.

"He traced my body with his eyes. The hem of my nightdress exposed my bare knees. His hands gently caught my foot as he kept his claws from contacting my skin. His touch was frigid on my warm flesh as he outlined the arch of my foot, moving slowly to my ankle, and then to the bend of my knee. All the while his strokes elicited both disgust and pleasure. Whatever he was doing to me was beyond my emotional comprehension. I wanted it to continue—and God, how I hated myself!

"His hand slid slowly up underneath my gown, caressing my thigh. I arched my back at the coldness. His hand covered my pussy. Devon felt how warm and wet I was. He rubbed his thumb over my clit, watching my reaction. At first I didn't know what he was doing, but soon I could barely contain myself. I writhed and whimpered underneath his touch. I couldn't get enough of him. Everything was building inside of me, but he stopped.

"Using one of his taloned fingers, he slid into me. His entrance was smooth, but so cold it felt like a knife had impaled me. I cried out this time as a gush of wetness retreated with his finger. He smiled, licking his stained claw clean like a cat grooming itself. The worst of it was that I wanted him more than ever. He embraced my rising pleasure, tasting it on the air.

"But he wasn't done toying with me. He bent down, but this time, instead of using his hand, he worked his way up my legs with his tongue, stopping every once in a while to nip at a vein. These bites I didn't feel. I was still lost somewhere inside my mind, screaming for help and absolution for being fucked by a demon. Then he made his way to my clit again where he took me delicately in his teeth and worked me with his tongue lapping at the blood that seeped from my wounded vagina. Every time an orgasm threatened, he kept me at the brink, only letting me taste what was on the other side, but never lingering there.

"This kind of torture went on for hours, until finally my clothes were in shreds, and his had all been neatly piled on the chair. In all of this he had given me a taste of his blood. That small sip kept my soul locked in my dead body when he stole the last bit of my life. I didn't know it then. Only now, after seeing him do it to some of his victims to torture them, did I understand.

"Finally, when he knew I couldn't take any more, he moved his dick into me, slowly, letting me feel how it was to expand around him, taking all of his enormous length in. It was painful because I was raw from all his intrusions, but I gritted my teeth and let him plunge into me. By this time his appearance returned to normal, except for the fangs and his eyes. During the night, his skin had grown warm as I grew colder.

"I bucked under him when he entered me. Pleasure mixed with the pain and I was lost to the sensations. His arms wrapped around my back as he moved in and out, holding me up. My body was numb, but I felt his every movement. He must have kept my endorphins going or tweaked the pleasure center of my brain as he fucked me. But something else was happening. I was dying. He was fucking the life out of me as the passion built. At the brink, his fangs buried themselves in my neck as he drained the rest of my spirit.

"I remember the last push of my near-dead heart as Devon took the final draught of my blood. The familiar pounding in my ears stopped. No breath passed over my lips, but I could still think. The process was slow, like there was mud in my brain. Oxygen stuck in my throat as it closed in on itself. It dawned on me through the haze that I was dead, but there were no trumpeting angels waiting for me. Nothing. I wasn't filled with endless joy at joining heaven. I was frigid and stuck in cold, dead flesh. I was neither vampire nor human. I wondered if hell awaited me, but I saw no flames or devils. The only true devil was Devon. Fear didn't even touch me. I was extraordinarily calm as true death was denied me. It seemed a unique adventure, and little did I know the hell it would become. There were only the dying coals in the fireplace.

"Tiny particles of dust floated in the air above me. Drifting freely, some came to rest on the floor, while others settled on my staring eyes. Their heaviness blurred my vision. I tried moving my eyes, but nothing happened. It was then I knew heaven had been, and always would be, denied me.

"Devon took himself out of me and dressed. I only saw the outline of his legs. When he appeared again in my full vision, he'd thrown his jacket and vest on, but left them open. Picking me up, he cradled me, supporting my head. He positioned my face so it rested against his neck. Even though I was dead, I smelled the blood though his skin. It reminded me of freshly dug earth. The scent made me want to rip him open, to have the substance underneath. That was when I felt the first stirrings of hunger in my system.

"'It's time to be mine,' Devon whispered to me.

"With that, he opened a gash in his throat, letting blood the color of kerosene spill out. At first, the thought disgusted me as drops moved onto my lips. Warmth seeped onto my tongue, sliding down my throat. Where each drop touched my skin, something inside me came back to life. It went into my stomach, igniting my body. Strength returned to my mouth so I could suck in the life-giving liquid. I lapped up his blood; it tasted like crystallized honey, but was thick like molasses as it went down my throat. Pins and needles worked in my toes and fingers as I came back to life.

"With more blood working into my bloodstream, my heart skipped to life and the cobwebs in my brain blew away. I pulled on the wound in Devon's neck until he pushed me away. I landed hard on the floor, knocking my head on the flagstones of the hearth, but the impact didn't hurt like it should have. My skull should have broken, but there was only a tingling as the skin knitted back together.

"I took a moment before getting up, and I peered around the room. Everything looked so crisp. Glancing at the windows, I saw the intricate patterns within the frost as though it were a lace doily spread on the glass. I looked at Devon and saw a red and black light surrounding him. It was his aura, I learned later. It reminded me of foxfire, the ghostly light seen in marshes. It flickered intensely, and then disappeared when pain exploded in my body. I felt like someone had put my insides through a meat grinder. Devon grabbed my shoulders, forcing me to focus.

"'Look at her, on the bed. She can make the pain go away. Do you want that?'

"'Yes,' I breathed.

"'Then take her.'

"The creaking floorboards screamed with each step I took. I wondered why my sister didn't awaken. I watched the rise and fall of her breasts, entranced by their subtle movement. Then I heard it. The drumming. A steady beat, keeping time with the rhythm of life. My hand settled over my sister's chest, absorbing some of the warmth her body gave off. But it did no good. I was still cold, frozen like the frost on the window. This warmth made me mad. It was then my canines extended into fangs, but I didn't think anything of them. I needed her blood. My hand dove into her chest, tearing apart her ribcage. Blood splattered everywhere: the ceiling, the bed, the rug, and me. Bits of bone, muscle, and discarded flesh plopped onto the floor. I separated her chest bone with a smash of my fist and took her heart in my palms. It was slippery, emerging with a loud sucking sound. I held the organ above my face. I inhaled the scent of life, and it smelled like spring after a winter thaw, like cool mountain water. My tongue darted over the muscle and took in the crimson liquid. It slid down my throat, warm and salty, igniting my own system, allowing my newly transforming body to come into its own. The first taste was so sweet, I needed more. In my frenzy, I gnawed at the heart until it was pulp. It was only then, after sucking the blood from every last bit of meat, did I notice how much blood I had wasted. I desired more. I listened a moment and caught two more heartbeats down the hall. Licking my lips, I glanced at Devon for his approval. He nodded, knowing what I wanted.

"I rushed down the hall toward the sounds. This time, I savored the kill. First, I tackled my father. After a couple of bites I got the technique right and sliced open his jugular. Blood squirted from his artery like a fountain. It hit me in the face and went up my nose, but I didn't care. I opened my mouth, covering the wound, while blood ran down my face and dried in my hair. I pulled hard, drawing in the substance my newborn body craved. The more I took, the more I wanted. Each drop warmed my body, burning my insides. All I remembered was being frozen, and that something inside me knew that by taking more I would be alive again and the chill of death could no longer touch me.

"After draining him, I moved on to my mother.

"Lodging my fangs into her jugular, I drank until I was full and warm. When I looked up, Devon stood at the foot of the bed. Blood covered his body. I listened and heard no more heartbeats. Devon had massacred the servants.

"Entranced by his slick, red body, I circled him, sniffing him like a dog. I smelled myself on him and that was good enough. I walked around him a few more times, never taking my eyes from the red liquid coating his body. I wrapped my hands around his torso, crushing my breasts against his back. One hand moved along his chest, feeling the marble smoothness of it, while the other embraced his shaft. He hardened under my touch as I slid my hand up and down his dick. All the muscles of his back clenched when he was ready to come. It was then that I sunk my fangs into his throat. He released, moaning and writhing against me at the same time. It's funny, but that was the only time he let me be in control. And it was only for a split second.

"The acrid smell of cum split the air and settled with the blood-scent. I took his blood only for a few moments, still feeling how hard he was in my hand. I worked him again, but this time he squirmed out of my grasp and tackled me. Both of us landed hard, rattling the room. Bits of plaster fell from the ceiling, turning into red paste from the blood on our bodies. He dug his nails and teeth into me, licking and biting until I didn't know where he began and I ended. It continued like that until dawn, when, finally the lethargy of sleep sucked me down as the orb rose in the sky.

"When I woke up the next night, I truly understood the nature of what I had become: I was a monster; a demon, pure and simple.

"My kind can't see the beauty in the humanity they originated from. Once my kin open their eyes to vampirism, they cast off their humanity like an old skin and become what the blood makes them into. There are only a few of us who betrayed our origins, realizing humans were more than things to fuck with. Many vampires consider this way of thinking weak, hunting those like me because we are the black sheep of the species. Devon hated that he had created one of these. That was one reason he loved to torture me. However, my other half was satisfied with killing, especially my family, and wanted more. That night I swore I would never be what Devon wanted. That's when my beast and I started warring."

I turned from Brenna, my tale told. I had just divulged my history, something I never thought I could do. Now it was up to her to stay or leave. If she left I'd protect her from Devon, watching out for her until she died, even if she never knew it.

Silence descended on the room like the eye of a storm. She thought about all I had told her. I dared not peek into her mind in case I let out a maelstrom of emotion. So I stood, motionless, listening to the echoing footsteps of people passing in the night, of other guests dozing in their rooms, they're breathing slowing. Dozens of heartbeats filled my head, each one a different song, adding to the chorus. They all tantalized me, igniting my hunger. I swallowed it down. Soon I would have to feed, or I would lose control. Brenna's presence was a horrible distraction. It made me remember everything I was. I salivated just having her so close; my other half wanted out again to taste and ravage her, but I pushed her away. Brenna's arms crisscrossed over my breasts as she rested her chin on my shoulder. She took in a few breaths, tickling my ear, thinking about what to say. Then, to my surprise, she kissed my neck, tracing the delicate line of my throat with her soft lips. My gums tingled as my teeth ached to descend.

"You do a dangerous thing." My voice was shaky, as was my control.

"I trust you."

"I'm glad someone does."

"So what happens now?"

I shrugged, unsure of how to answer. It seemed fate had thrown a wrench in my path. I didn't understand how this human could be my salvation.

"I don't know. I just don't know."

12

CHAPTER TWELVE

My name is Brenna.

My reflection showed the tiny lines around my eyes, little tick marks showing my age. They were almost invisible, but I knew they were there.

Tears sprang to my eyes when I thought of Veronica—alive for over two hundred years, an ancient woman wearing the guise of a twenty-five-year old. All because she fell in love with the wrong man. As she told her story, I sensed how much she yearned to be with humanity. I could bring her back to life and show her the light once again. I laughed while scrubbing off my makeup, thinking of what I had said about unmasking.

My true likeness stared back at me. My skin was now a subtle shade of pink from rubbing off so many layers of cover up and eye shadow. Underneath it all it was a pale white complexion. I strove to keep out of the sun. The sun didn't bother me; I just didn't like it. Its garish light hurt my eyes and browned my milk-white skin. I'd always been drawn to the night. To me, the midnight blue sky was endless and kept my secrets when no one else could.

I wrapped my tongue around my fangs, wiggling them loose before I pulled my lips back in a sneer to see their sharp points suspended among my other teeth, and then I plucked them off, throwing them into an empty contact case. Then I took out my evergreen contacts. Underneath the imitation eyes, my irises were a dark dull brown that saw the world with a human blurriness. Without my props I was a mere mortal, as Veronica would say. It's funny how humans have a way of deluding themselves.

Veronica wanted to know why I understood her so well. It was because I snuck inside people's minds, into places that had been shut up for a long time. Little did I know that while I was living my life, I was also living my dream. When I saw her for what she was—an immortal, a living vampire—everything I pretended to be crashed around me. I could no longer go on seducing men into believing I was one of the undead than Veronica could continue to try and blend in with humanity. We each failed miserably at being something we were not.

It astonished me how each of us had forgotten what we had once been. When I popped my fangs in, I became a creature that couldn't be touched or understood by mortal minds. I was a vampire. Now my mask had been torn off. My reflection began to show my true age, and with age would come great changes. That was one reason I clung to the idea of the vampire. The thought of an eternity spent in the cool night, being a marbled beauty for all time, just understanding the mysteries of life and death. The vampire knew what it was like to be human, seeing the world from two spotlights, two different points of view.

Being psychic, I tapped into a small part of the vampire's powers and read others' emotions. I lured in those I wanted to fuck. I used this ability to my advantage because it heightened the sexual experience. I never used it on my clients though. I even chose a new name—Raven. The name defined who I was. I was a prophecy giver, one of the associations with the name. It also meant being a harbinger of death, and vampires certainly were that. I got so caught up in the vampire lifestyle I had fangs fitted, as well as contacts to make my eyes look deeper, more alluring. The tricks worked, almost too well.

Men at clubs pulled me aside and wanted me to drink from them. I always turned them down, but the more I played out the fantasy, something happened. Not only did others believe I was a vampire, but I believed it, and that belief had changed my aura.

At first I didn't understand how easy it was to fool people and then one night while dancing at a goth club called the Black Rose, I expanded my senses, mingling with the emotions of the other dancers. From my work as a psychic, I'd learned that the aura could be used to tell and do many things. Each color revealed something about the dancers' personalities. The subtle shades and how the colors were arranged relayed the emotional state and physical state of a person; auras could also be used as shields or walls around the mind to keep other psychics out, or just keep thoughts in. I knew how to do all of this, and as I danced, I caught the sight and feel of my own aura.

My normal colors of yellow and blue were there, but there was a purple, a deep violet I had never seen. I paid attention to it and felt the slow, steady beat. As I focused on it, it grew deeper and I noticed the eyes of the other dancers, which was rare in the self-absorbed world of goth clubs. Feelings of lust and the thrill of the other world radiated from them as the purple began to blanket the dance floor. I pulled it back. My aura withdrew from the minds of the people, whipping itself back in place to just the normal yellow and blue.

When I first settled in New Orleans, I received strange looks from goths, but that didn't bother me. Then I became a fixture, like the many ghost tales and the never-changing humidity and sudden rainstorms. I never minded though. I was what I wanted to be: my fantasy.

Now that had disappeared. Everything shattered because the one thing I pretended to be had appeared out of nowhere.

Unlacing my corset, I got up from my vanity and glanced at the blinking number on my answering machine. Six messages waited for me. Most of them were clients, seeking my guidance to steer them on the right path. I sighed, thinking how nice it would be to bow out of the business and watch people fend for themselves, like rats in a maze as they sniffed at the walls trying to decipher where the end was.

Corset off, I punched the play button. The whining voices of five clients reeled out, all wanting to see me by Saturday, three days away. I doubted I'd meet their demands, but I made a mental note to call them back. It was the sixth message I was more surprised and pleased over. It was from Cain. His accent reminded me of the crisp cold Boston winters I'd forced myself through.

"Hey Brenna, was wondering if you wanted to get together early tomorrow night, say like around seven thirty. We could do one of those ghost tours or something. You probably know all about them, but it would be nice to get together. If you're interested, meet me at the Moonwalk—at least I think that's what it's called. If not, I'll see you at my hotel around ten."

The message clicked off, ending with a loud beep.

I smiled, realizing how much I'd taken a liking to this new boy. It was strange I had latched onto him so swiftly. When he was here the other night, I had almost forgotten about meeting Veronica. It was as though he had some hold over me. It was sad to think he would not be in the city for very long. The thought of him on a plane, returning to a place thousands of miles away depressed me. Even after he left, I would still have Veronica. She wasn't going anywhere any time soon. I didn't question her reasons, but was happy that such an unearthly creature would keep company with an ordinary girl like me, who hoped to be something else.

I WOKE UP around six and spent the last hour pondering the events that had taken place in the past twenty-four hours. I still couldn't believe them. I'd been attacked, met a vampire, spilled my life story, and become entranced by the fact that a creature of myth and legend was real. I wondered what other kinds of monsters she had associated with or seen. Maybe there were werewolves roaming around in the Bayou, or even in the city, pretending to be human while munching on a few mortals at the same time. I would believe it because fantasy had now become reality in my book. Vampires were real, but underneath the fangs and glowing eyes was a sad, intriguing woman who held me captivated.

I yearned to feel her hands on my body, her fangs buried in my flesh. I wanted those soft lips kissing and caressing every part of me. I'd slept with women before, but Veronica intoxicated me. She commented on my ability to hypnotize her—well, she had me mesmerized to the end of my toes. She made me feel strong, like nothing could get in my way. Veronica made me desire a life I'd never have, a life I pretended to live. She had removed my mask, and now I was just me. I didn't know if I could put on my fangs or contacts again, pretending to be one of her kind. It was all I knew. How could I give it up? And if I did, would that mean Cain would consider me an ordinary plaything, to have, to hold, to fuck? I sighed. I didn't know the answer, but I didn't want to give up the chance of seeing my new lover tonight.

The thought of his warm, wet mouth on mine made me tingle inside. He had a power over me Veronica didn't possess. Perhaps it was pure lust because the sex was amazing. He reached an animalistic part of my psyche, enabling me to give myself over to sheer abandon. He made me aware of every part of my body. Besides, he was only a ten-minute walk from my apartment, hoping I would be scared by the tales of the city so I would need his protection.

Yes. I giggled. I'd go to him, and I would have the best time of my life.

I jumped up, throwing on a simple skirt and white shirt. I dressed lightly, knowing that the summer, even though it was coming to an end, was still hot and heavy. If it rained, the shower would pass, and I didn't care if I got soaked.

Racing out of my apartment, I made my way over to the Moonwalk, arriving just as the clock on St. Louis Cathedral struck seven thirty. I crossed the street, glancing around the steps, searching for Cain. He talked to a tour guide who was dressed in a pink crushed velvet shirt. I went up behind my date, waiting for him to notice me. When he did, a huge smile appeared on his face.

"You made it!"

"Of course! I wouldn't miss it. Besides, we might actually see some ghosts," I said as I pushed a piece of hair out of his eyes. As I met his gaze a sudden sense of calm came over me. Nothing in the world could break the moment.

"Is this your other half?" the tour guide asked, his voice thick with an English accent.

"Yup. She's all mine."

MASQUERADE

"Mine's up there." He pointed to the front of the tour group. "We were married about twenty minutes ago."

"Congratulations," I said.

"Thanks," he said before walking off to address the rest of the group.

Cain and I listened as the guide explained the tour. The rising excitement of the crowd washed over me, filling me with anticipation. I didn't bother to erect the shields around my mind to keep out the emotions. Tonight I wanted nothing more than to be content and warm on the arm of my date. I just wanted to be his.

As we ambled along I took Cain's hand, just as lightning illuminated the sky. I jumped and huddled into the curve of Cain's arm. The warmth and smell of him made me feel safe, but even as the tour continued on, I knew we would get very wet. We ventured through a residential area while the guide showed us a few places where movies had been filmed. As he talked I pressed myself closer to Cain, catching the scent of musk and earth.

A few drops of rain fell as we arrived at our next destination. The guide told the story of a man who dared his lover to prove her devotion. In order to do so, she had to stand on the roof naked until dawn. Her lover didn't think she'd fulfill the challenge, but as the night ebbed, she didn't come down. He checked on the woman and found her huddled against the chimney, her lips blue with death. It was said people saw the woman on top of the roof gazing down at them, keeping her vigil until dawn so she could prove her loyalty. It was a sad and interesting story.

I glanced up at the chimney just as a roll of thunder exploded above us. I saw nothing, but Cain stood, transfixed, as if he waited for the ghost to appear. His gaze was fixed intently on the chimney. A gust of wind came up, blowing my hair in my face, obscuring my view. In that instant, a shrill scream split the air, and Cain's hand crushed mine.

"Look, there she is. Did you see her?" a woman's fear-filled voice exclaimed.

By the time I cleared the hair out of my eyes, there was nothing but an empty roof, and wild rain dropped like bombs from the sky. I glanced over at the woman and then back at my date. His face seemed pointier, but I thought it a trick of the light. I put a hand on his shoulder, sensing the muscles ready to spring underneath his T-shirt.

"Did you see anything?" I asked.

It took Cain a moment before he looked at me, and when he did, his eyes were unfocused, almost hungry. When he saw me, they returned to normal, the tension draining from his body.

"No. It was probably just a trick of the light. People see what they want to see. Right?" He smiled.

I nodded, not sure what to make of his answer. "Come on, we'll get left behind." I grabbed his hand, dragging him after the retreating group, which had taken refuge in a local tavern.

"Well, wasn't that interesting?" the guide said to Cain. "Nothing this exciting has happened since the time a woman thought a cockroach was a flying rat."

I laughed, knowing how big the roaches got in the city, but my date didn't get it. The tour guide walked away and my boy looked disgruntled. I wrapped my arm around him and rested my chin on his shoulder, trying to cheer him up, but it wasn't working. He grew quiet and withdrawn, lost in his own thoughts. I kissed the side of his neck, flicking it with my tongue, hoping to get his attention. After a few more nibbles, some of the tension emptied from his tight muscles as he took me in his arms.

He looked into my eyes, and I lost myself in the depths of his sky-blue ones, but the sensation only lasted a second. I glanced around and we were the only ones left in the tavern. Cain caught my chin, gently turning me to him. He leaned over and caressed my lips with his, making me forget about the tour.

"We should get a move on if we want to catch up with the others," he said after letting go of me.

I nodded and followed him, not concerned about the ghostly sighting from before. Outside, the rain had stopped as suddenly as it had started. It took a moment to find the group, but we did, and kept with it as the tour guide led us through the French Quarter, recounting sadistic murders and gruesome hauntings. The English guide knew New Orleans was a place where anything could happen. I had already found that out as the city helped reshape my life once again. The thought of losing Cain to an airplane and obligations in Boston was excruciating. I didn't want to let him go any more than I wanted to let Veronica go. I had both, and I was content.

The rest of the tour passed uneventfully. The woman who'd spotted the ghost had sworn she wasn't drunk. No one discounted her, but the crowd's disbelief of her tale sunk into my psyche. I smirked, wondering if she, along with Cain, had seen anything. He declined to answer when the crowd turned to him. The tour guide looked at Cain and shrugged, letting him know it was his prerogative to say what had happened or not.

The tour ended where it had begun in front of St. Louis Cathedral in Jackson Square. The tour guide hawked a book that had been written about the hauntings of New Orleans. I chuckled. Everyone in the city was out for a buck, but I had to give him credit because he made a living doing something he liked. The crowd dissipated, going off to an endless night of drinking and partying. I craved something to cool my insides, but nothing alcoholic. I wanted to spend the night keeping myself busy with my boy. Yes, I wanted him, right on the street if that were possible. Just his presence made me hot and wet. My body hardened, readying itself for him, just from gazing into his bottomless eyes. If anyone tried challenging my authority over him, I'd rip out their throats because he was mine and mine alone.

"Are you all right?" he asked me.

"Yes." I couldn't believe I'd thought of tearing someone open. To be jealous was one thing, but to kill? I didn't think so.

"You want to get going?"

I nodded. We moved away from the last of the lingering tour group. I scanned them, wondering what their lives were like back home. If they had families, or thought of their futures, something normal. With Cain beside me, I had a chance of that dream, but then I spotted Veronica. She leaned against an iron fence, one hand on the top of the main spike that formed the gate. I waved to her, but the look on her face stopped my hand in mid-motion. Pure malice and hatred adorned her expression. I'd never seen a being so full of anger. My voice caught in my throat as she stepped across the Square, but before I blinked she had disappeared, reappearing in front of both of us.

"Veronica, what're you doing here?" I asked, trying to even my voice, but it wobbled in and out because of the seething anger radiating off of her. It filled my head like molten lava, red and runny. It encompassed her aura in a crimson glow and seeped into mine. My insides churned as they boiled. Sweat beaded on my forehead. I tried backing away, hoping the distance would help diminish the intensity of her energy.

"What are you doing?" she hissed.

I looked at her in shock. "We're on a date," I stated.

Veronica kept her eyes locked with Cain's. He seemed amused with her as she challenged him. I understood she was jealous, but my being with him didn't mean I was neglecting her.

"Veronica, it would be better if you left. We'll discuss this later; I'm busy at the moment."

Again she ignored me.

"I think you should do as the lady says. After all, we are on a date and she's asked you to leave," Cain spoke up, keeping his voice calm, though I caught the hint of amusement.

I wondered what he thought was so funny about the standoff.

"Damn it, I told you to stay away. You have no right," Veronica chided.

I glanced down at her fists and noticed how clenched they were. I spotted the blood clinging to them, running down her tightened fingers. I became fascinated with it. I heard blood as it dripped down the palms of her hands, splashing on the cobblestones. As Veronica's anger mingled with my aura, my own frustration rose to match hers, pushing out thoughts of blood.

"Look, Veronica, it's not my problem you're jealous. What I do is my business. Now leave us alone."

"Yeah, Ronnie, why don't you butt out? Can't you see me and Brenna are having a wonderful time?" Cain cooed, enflaming her even more.

"Don't provoke her, okay? You have no idea what she can do," I said to my date. *How does she know him? This can't be happening.*

"Oh, I'm sure she wouldn't hurt little old me. Besides, I'd like to see her try." Veronica didn't answer. Both of them stared at each other, having a silent confrontation. Cain loved every minute of it. I stood watching, unable to do anything. Her rage built in me along with my own, and if I didn't find a way to release it, I feared I might just burst into flames.

"Fine," I yelled. "You two want to play? Have fun!"

I turned, walking away, not believing the woman I'd been so close to just a few hours ago would turn on me, or the boy I found myself so enamored with could abandon me to play such childish games. If both of them were like that, then they were made for each other.

I realized Veronica only projected the things I saw in her. She was truly a beast that toyed with people's lives, and I was her new plaything. She allowed me to fall in love with her, screwing up my perfect life. She made me think she was human and convinced me I had to help her.

It wasn't over as I walked back to my apartment. I'd see her again. My vampire would apologize and say it was all a mistake. By then, it'd be too late. I'd have shut myself off from her and turned back to what I knew. I'd go back to being the mysterious vampire, gluing my mask and persona back together, reinstating myself back into the lifestyle I thought I had left behind.

I strolled into the night and stopped after a few blocks and extended my senses, trying to let the darkness cool my temper. Taking a deep breath, I tried pushing the confrontation between the vampire and my date out of my mind, but even as I did, faint shadowy figures of ghosts pressed against my consciousness. Their presence was nothing more than background noise, but if I focused on them, their voices would float into my mind as wispy echoes, reminding me of windblown screeches. I didn't need to hear them or even want to see their transparent forms hovering on the streets. Nor did I want their cold fingers pressing on my body to get my attention. No, I wanted her. It was in these times my abilities were nothing more than a burden, when I wanted to throw them away and somehow be normal.

Maybe then I'd never have met Veronica, never known about the other side of reality I was keyed into.

As much as I wanted to dismiss my powers, I'd be lost without them. I'd never be able to glimpse the emotions of others or get the exciting thrill of knowing there was a cold, terrifying watcher following me in the darkened night.

Something powerful slammed into my psychic mind, dampening the whining voices of the spirits. Its power drew me to it as ghosts were drawn to me, like bugs to a flame. Following my mind, I decided to discover what threw me off balance. Veronica.

I yearned for her. I would dream of her hands on my body, of her fangs buried inside my throat, but that could never be because I knew what I saw was true. She was a demon preying on those she saw fit, and I was the one her eye had fallen on.

13

CHAPTER THIRTEEN

My name is Veronica.

I didn't hear what Brenna said, but she stormed into the night and left the two of us alone. Devon changed then, becoming the lovable vampire I knew him to be.

His eyes darkened, the pupils growing like thunderclouds to cover the whites in his eyes. His shoulder blades cracked, rearranging themselves, stretching to make room for his wings. Nails grew long on slender fingers, and his hands stretched to accommodate the weight of his dagger-like claws. His face elongated slightly. I watched the bones in his chin rearranging until they settled into a small knob.

"That hurt, bitch."

I stepped forward, strengthening my shields. I wanted to be ready for a psychic attack if it came to that. Both of us had disappeared from human view; we had become invisible.

"Good. It makes up for some of the years you fucked with me," I growled.

He laughed, more a hiss, as a black, forked tongue darted out between his lips.

"You have no idea what I'm going to do to you when I get you back. First I'm going to start with the sweet thing that just left—and my, is she tasty, like sugar and cinnamon. Her blood melted on my tongue. I had her the first time I fucked her, but you wouldn't know what she's like. All you care about is baring your soul, trying to be like them. Now she hates you, and she's all mine. All mine!"

I felt myself turning, my beast taking over. My arms lengthened as my shoulder blades rearranged. My shirt split as leathery wings unfolded from my skin, thick with mucus and runny from the change. Fingers and nails hardened into bone, my face elongated. My nose flattened, and my knees buckled to support the weight of my wings. My ears grew hair on the tips, as well as becoming four inches long and pointed. Toe talons ripped through my shoes as I lost the rest of my clothing. All this happened in a movement of the second hand. Devon didn't expect I'd give in to my urges. He assumed I'd whimper before him as I used to. No more.

I swiped at him, running deep furrows over his eye, down his cheek, and into his jugular vein. Foul-smelling blood exploded from the wound. His hand came up to catch his dislodged eye, which hung from the socket by the nerve endings. He snarled at me, holding his injured face, all the teeth in his mouth pointed. I had wounded him, caught him off guard, and he didn't have the strength to fight back. Devon growled, his tongue visible through the hole in his face. He turned from me and ran into the crowd. He would be back. It would take him a few days to heal, but when he returned, he would be out for blood. I had what I needed — time — and I had to use it.

I lingered in the square, wondering what to do next. I had to get Brenna, but the scent of Devon's blood and my recent transformation called to my lust. I had to feed. I looked at Devon's life drying on the ground, remembering a time I begged to suckle at his neck, to drink in his wonderful nectar. I shook my head, trying to rid myself of the thoughts of my other half. The walls I had erected suddenly fell away and my beast smiled. I tried to lock it down, but it surged forward, drawing on the strength of the hunger coursing through our body. I was a fool. I tried to remain in control, but it took over, driven by its lust for blood.

Please. You can't, I pleaded with it.

Oh, but I can. I'm hungry. And there's nothing you can do about it. So many people. Let's see...where do I start? The beast laughed. Then with a quick shove, it moved me into the prison where it normally stayed.

14

CHAPTER FOURTEEN

My name is Ronnie.

I stood in the shadows completely naked, still invisible to the human eye. The temperature had dropped after the sudden rainstorm, making the Quarter muggy, and the moisture clinging to my skin, chilling me. Every so often, I shivered as a slight gust tickled my exposed body. I didn't mind the weather, but with the hunger stirring in my veins, the combination of the cold breeze and the flames inside me made for an interesting mix. It had been so long since I had been the dominant personality in this body; I wanted to enjoy it. Poor Veronica, she was so pathetic. If she had only accepted her destiny when I had been born then we would never have to fight. It wasn't my fault she couldn't see humanity as the meat they were.

From the square, I worked my way back to Bourbon Street, walking among the tourists, who started drinking earlier than usual. I darted in and out of the human cattle that were getting drunk, narrowly avoiding colliding with a girl with a daiquiri in her hand. She brushed up against me, looking confused, wondering what she'd bumped into when there was nothing to be seen, at least no physical object she could perceive. If she remembered the encounter, she'd write it off as something from a drunken haze. I didn't care.

I wanted to get away from the hordes of people. I had to find a place where I could settle down and gather my thoughts. It had been a decade since I had mingled within the sea of humanity. The sweat of the humans enticed me. I tasted the alcohol from so many bars on the wind. The noise from the bands came in spurts, overwhelming my heightened senses. Mortals' thoughts pressed against my head like a vise. I had to get off the main drag before I lost it and let them see the beast I really was. If that happened, everyone would have a tale to tell their grandchildren about the time they encountered a demon in New Orleans.

Glancing around, I knew I couldn't go into one of the restaurants or shops. I needed a human who was not going to be missed, and the tourists in these places were all visible. No, I required a darkened room or an alley, away from everything. Then I noticed the strip clubs.

I smiled.

Pulling my shields in as tight as I could, I strolled past the bouncer. I walked into multicolored flashing strobe lights and blaring new wave music. The place looked like something from a bad seventies porno. The scent of cum and sweat overpowered my nostrils, but I pushed it away immediately, focusing on the heartbeats in the room. The place wasn't packed yet, but what was in here would suit my needs.

I scanned the minds of the men lingering at the bar as they watched the girls dancing on the tables, all in various stages of undress. Each man at the bar was married, or had a girlfriend. They would be missed. As I patrolled the place, one of the girls caught my attention.

Silver pasties in the shape of stars covered her nipples. Around her waist were a thong and a gun belt. She gyrated against a pole, bucking her hips into it, moving her hands over her tits, and then down to her pussy, a finger lingering over her clit, before moving again into the beat of the dance. I realized her attentions were on a weak looking man. I scanned him and found nothing interesting, except the fact that he was alone; he was my kind of target, but when the girl's gaze locked to mine, I knew what she was.

She was young, not more than forty years old, but she was a vampire and saw through my shields, or at least knew I was there. Her warning in the back of my brain pushed me away. The man she fawned over was hers. I nodded, acknowledging she could have him. With that her vampire persona retreated and she melted back into her dance as the song ended. Still I watched the way she moved.

Her body was taut, every muscle defined. I stared into her eyes, detecting the darkness about them. Her hunger stayed on the surface. As she danced, her shoulder blades kept rearranging themselves like a liquid puzzle. She was insane, struggling to pass in a human world. Her insanity made her strong. Even though I wandered into her territory, something in her sensed my age; she wouldn't challenge me. However, if I had not been in such a need for blood, I would have taken it upon myself to put her out of her misery. She was an abomination to our kind. Now was not the time for me to deal with her. My gaze shifted from her, and I noticed a man sitting in the corner nursing a beer with two empty ones already on the table. He sat sprawled in a booth, looking on the show with a passive expression. He hadn't had sex in a while and nothing in the club really interested him.

I put on a big smile and worked my way to his table, snaking my thoughts into his mind, allowing him to see me standing before him, naked. When I appeared out of nowhere he gasped, spitting out his beer, covering the table in saliva and warm alcohol.

I smiled and slid into the booth. The leather cooled my bare skin as the wool of his shirt tickled my nipples. They hardened against his suit jacket. I pressed myself into him, running my hand over his thigh before caressing his crotch. Rubbing my hand over him, I breathed heavily into his ear, feeling him harden underneath me. My hand worked over his dick as my tongue flicked over his jugular. His breathing became labored. He was getting ready to come. His hips started to buck forward, but I grabbed hold of his mind and stopped him in mid-thrust. Veronica stirred in her mental cage, begging for me to stop torturing him. I ignored her.

My prey moaned under my touch as I still massaged his cock through his pants. He wanted more, yearning for release. I held him there, licking at his neck, tasting the alcohol through his pores. The more I nipped, the more the fear rose in his brain, but he had no way to express it. He wanted to expel the tension growing in his body, but I wouldn't let him. I liked indulging my whims.

"Speak if you wish," I whispered heavily into his ear.

"What are you?" he whimpered.

"Everything you ever wanted," I purred.

The terror in his mind had me drunk as I played with him. This was what it was all about, what my kind did with the meat. Still I couldn't take him in this place. There were too many people, too many prying eyes. I sighed and eased his erection down, but I kept the pleasure centers in his brain titillated so he experienced nothing of the fear he had before, just intrigue and longing. I slithered out of the booth. The leather made a sucking sound as my bare ass slipped from the seat. I walked a few paces and didn't feel him behind me. I tugged on his mental leash as I would a dog and had him amble behind me.

We moved out of the club, and I was still invisible to all but him. To others walking by, he looked as if he were moving in a drunken stupor, which made it easier for me. I walked a few blocks, traveling further away from the crowded main streets into a more quiet area where tourists only straggled by. I surveyed my surroundings and noticed the New Orleans Historic Voodoo Museum.

I smiled. This was a good place to play.

The door was locked, but that didn't matter. I shoved it with my shoulder and it opened quickly. I went inside, waiting for my new toy to follow. I shut the glass door behind me and caught a glimpse of various types of voodoo dolls and tarot cards for sale. I smirked at the thought of the dolls. Whoever heard of such nonsense, putting pins in a doll to hurt people? I certainly didn't believe the technique worked. But who knew? If one believed hard enough, maybe it did.

I moved to my right through a curtain and found myself in a cramped hallway filled with pictures of past Voodoo High Priestesses. As I passed along the hallway, I noticed all the different implements used in rituals. I had no idea what most of them were for, but some of them looked interesting. Thoughts of using them on my prey flickered through my mind. The torture I could inflict...but I was not in the mood to play that much. We walked into the backroom where I noticed a huge, glass tank. Peering in, I was surprised by a big albino python that hissed at me. I jumped back a little, and then giggled at being scared by a snake. My fangs grew and I hissed back at her. She stared at me, realizing I was something not to mess with, and then she went on with the rest of her night. In the back of the room there was a door, which gave instructions to follow red arrows through a courtyard and into another part of the museum.

I stood, beckoning my prey. My fangs gleamed from the soft light of the snake terrarium. He came shuffling toward me, fighting the hold I had on his mind, but it was no use. I was the strong one. This fact angered him because he was used to being the dominant one. I caught glimpses of him slapping around a few of his girlfriends. He would be the perfect victim for me.

We followed the arrows outside into a small court-yard covered with flagstones. There was a small white table with chairs in the left-hand corner, and a few potted plants that secluded the table from the rest, creating a mini-paradise in the middle of the bustling city. The night had grown cooler as the hours pro-gressed. The stars sang something only night creatures could hear. I was happy, my belly rumbling with hun-ger from the thought of fresh blood exploding onto my tongue.

"Come here," I whispered. The sound bounced off the brick walls of the courtyard.

He came to me without hesitation as I reeled him in, all the while making him believe he wanted to come to me. I implanted images of me slapping his face. Of me straddling him, riding him until he begged me to stop like so many had done with him. I made him want to feel the pain of my fists colliding with his nose, the blood dribbling down his chin, him crying for me to stop when really he wanted more. The thought that he wanted to be dominated baffled him. I licked my lips in anticipation. His blood sang underneath his skin.

Stripping off his jacket, he surrendered himself to my waiting arms.

I smirked. He could wonder what made him want to be conquered like he had done to others before, but I wasn't going to linger and let him figure out he hadn't willingly given up his power. I ran my hands over his chest, feeling the hardness of his muscles underneath the shirt. My nails grazed over it, tearing furrows in the skin beneath. When the first explosion of blood hit my nose, I could no longer hold back. My plans to fuck him to death, to drink him in as he came, flew out of my mind. I wanted the elixir that would give strength back to my body.

Again Veronica rattled her cage. I gave her a quick mental slap that sent her reeling. I didn't need her guilt infecting me. My mouth became a maw of sharpened teeth as I smiled. It was then that I pulled all of my power from his mind and he saw me for what I truly was. Fear exploded in him. I licked my lips. His eyes grew wide and he backed away. He only got a few steps.

My smile widened as he tripped and landed on his ass. Even when he crawled away from me, I caught him. Like I had shown him, I straddled him. I had no intentions of riding him all night. He looked into my burning eyes and knew what I was. He tried to scuttle away, but my legs held him in place. He whimpered as I ran a hand over his neck and down to his exposed chest. I stopped at the wound on his chest, dabbing my pinkie into the blood. I tasted a drop. It was as sweet as ever. My realigning shoulder blades signaled the coming of my wings. They burst out of my back, dripping wet. The liquid crystallized, making them ready for flight. He screamed then, but I was beyond caring. My fingers stroked his jugular vein, feeling the heart beating underneath. I brought my teeth down, savagely tearing out a hunk of flesh. I swallowed it without thinking, becoming lost to the warm ecstatic sensations coursing through my body.

I sucked in everything he was. In that beautiful moment, I wondered how Veronica saw humans as things of beauty. I'd never been like them. I was a unique creature born into this world from blood. As I drank, the fount I sucked on grew weaker. To get more, I pressed against my victim's chest, but the flesh gave way and my talons encompassed the warm organ. I yanked it out and brought the blood-rich muscle to my lips. Yes, this was the way I was supposed to be. I was all-powerful. I could do whatever I wanted. I was immortal.

I drained the heart, smashing it against the points of my teeth, just like juicing an orange. When there was nothing left but a dry husk, I threw it aside. It landed somewhere in one of the potted plants. I laughed at the thought of one of the employees finding it tomorrow and wondering what it could be.

I extended my wings, missing the glory of moving through the night air. I could move with the birds and rise above them. God be damned, I was a fallen angel, and I would not be denied my wings. I spread them, enjoying the slight creaking sounds they made after their long confinement. My muscles tensed, ready to take off, when I heard something. It was faint, the screeching of an already opened door. I smiled as I caught the hint of another human coming to investigate the break-in. I moved into the shadows, my toe talons scraping along the flagstones. I hid in the corner behind the potted plants next to the door. This was a good night. I'd get a two for one special.

The door in front of me squeaked open, sounding like a screeching mouse. A head with long hair peered through the door, and then the body followed. After a few steps the human was in the courtyard. I smelled a hint of vanilla on her skin. I licked my lips, allowing my teeth to return to normal, except my canines. This one I was going to savor.

No, no more. Let her go. You played with your last victim. We don't need this one, Veronica whimpered. She banged on the confines of her cage, and I realized she might break out if I wasn't careful.

I moved out from behind the plants, cloaked by the night. When the mortal heard the noise, she looked in my direction and took a step forward. That was when her foot found the remnants of my last meal. A scream welled up in her, but before she released it, I wrapped my hand around her throat and put my face close to her ear.

"Scream and you die. Understand?"

She nodded. My hand automatically stroked her jugular. The fear ran hot in her blood, along with stoked passion. I brought my nose close to her skin, drinking in the vanilla.

"What are you?" she asked.

"I'm your death, little one. You've come into my waiting hands. How sad for you!"

"Please," she whimpered. She was pathetic like my meat-loving counterpart.

Saliva dripped from my fangs as I thought of the sweet liquid moving in her veins. I let the drool elongate and dribble down my chin. "Please what?"

"Don't kill me."

"It's a little too late for that, but since you are being such a good human, I'll make it painless."

I projected my thoughts into my victim's mind, wrapping around her brain as if I were a ball of yarn entangling myself. I didn't bother to look at her thoughts. I didn't need them to savor her blood. Something about her felt familiar. I dismissed the feeling and licked her throat.

She was sweet, tasting like cinnamon, a flavor I enjoyed.

Oh, she would be good.

I opened my mouth and sunk my teeth into her waiting throat, closing my eyes in the ecstasy of her. I swallowed a mouthful. At that moment, Veronica screamed. Her personality surged forward, pushing me back into my cage.

15

CHAPTER FIFTEEN

My name is Veronica.

Oh, God! Brenna!

Dislodging my fangs, I backed away into the darkness. My rationality returned as I forced myself into human form. Ronnie, the part of me that had been nurtured by Devon, cried out for her blood, but she was locked away again. However, just because my alter ego had been in control didn't mean I wasn't aware of what she had done. The man she devoured would haunt my dreams for centuries.

I spit out the last of Brenna's blood, wiping the back of my hand across my mouth, cleaning away the remains of her.

She mustn't see me. How could I ever confront her again? What would she do if she saw me totally un-masked?

My thoughts still encompassed hers. She was con-scious, wondering what had happened. I couldn't go to her now, even to soothe her. No, I needed time to think.

Forgive me.

I lashed out, shutting her mind off like a switch, pushing her deep into unconsciousness.

Then I went to her crumpled form and picked her up. She was so frail. The wounds I'd inflicted were still bleeding. They would heal. Her heartbeat thundered in my ears; she was nowhere near death. I brushed away a piece of hair that had fallen in her face, admir-ing Brenna's innocence in sleep. A tear spilled from my eyes as I cajoled myself for damaging her.

"My, my. I guess you haven't totally forgotten what you are after all."

I glanced over at the voice and saw Devon reclin-ing at the wrought iron table, his legs crossed and his arms over his chest. The wounds on his face had begun to heal, but slowly. A film resided over the hole. Blue veins brought blood to his scarred face. The membrane was transparent, and I saw his tongue through the healing cheek. His eye was cataract white as it also regenerated. I hugged Brenna close.

"I haven't forgotten what I am."

"She's good, isn't she? I knew you'd like her," he whispered in my ear. He moved across the courtyard, showing off as he always did, thinking he was better than me.

His arms wrapped around my chest as he crushed me to him. Devon was hard through his jeans, but no passion ignited in me. He took one of his lengthened fingernails and moved it along the side of Brenna's cheek, causing a line of blood to well up. The smell hit me, hard, and I almost moaned. Ronnie roared inside my mind. The tip of his finger traced my mouth. Blood settled on the ridges of my lips. I dared not move. The beast howled inside my mind for release as everything in me craved to lick his finger clean. The muscles danced in my back, and I felt my eyes changing color, bleeding black. I shuddered in my skin. It took all my strength to hold the beast back, but I did.

"Damn you, Devon," I whispered.

He laughed. "You say that a lot, but it's not me who's damned. I accept what I am. It's you who wallow in this misery while denying what you are. It's a sin. You shouldn't try so hard to be like them. Accept what you are and come back to me. Then it'll be all better. You'll think that this was all a daymare. And if you come back now, then I'll not punish you too harshly. Of course, you'll have to sacrifice your pet. What do you say?"

The beast in me called to its Master, yearning to feel Devon pat its head. It didn't care about using Brenna as a meal to show obedience. I was more than my monster, and Devon was no longer my master.

"Go to hell." I jabbed my elbow into his stomach, dislodging his hold on me. I allowed my wings to grow so I could get away from him. Away from the city.

"For now." He coughed, catching his breath. "But remember, I'll find you no matter where you go. I'm the one who made you. You're mine."

I didn't acknowledge him. What he said was true. He'd hunt me until I was his consort again. When he ensnared me, he wouldn't kill me. His torture would be endless and worse than having maggots in my face. There were no ends to the things he would do to me. I'd seen him keep victims alive for days, bleeding them slowly, savoring their fear. I'd witnessed him pouring boiling oil over prey just to watch the flesh melt away. I didn't want to think what he would do to Brenna if I went back to him. I wouldn't let that happen.

No. I shook my head. I grabbed Brenna as my wings propelled me out of New Orleans.

I didn't know where I was going. I was just flying to safety into the sunrise, praying I could make it. I wasn't impervious to its rays, but that didn't matter.

Brenna was my priority. So I flew off, letting my instincts carry me cloaked through the night.

PART THREE
JUDGMENT

16

CHAPTER SIXTEEN

My name is Brenna.

The first thing I saw when I opened my eyes was a crumbling plaster ceiling, yellowed and flaking with age. The odor of rot and must had tattooed itself to everything. I blinked, knowing it wasn't my apartment. I didn't know where I was, but I was alive. That was the most important thing.

I ran my hands through my hair. My fingers grazed my cheek and sent pain screaming to my brain. The long ridge of a scab traced the base of my jaw. I assumed I'd gotten it in my fall. To make sure I hadn't dreamed the whole event, I felt for the two wounds the monster had inflicted in my neck, and I found them, two small holes, puncture wounds. It dawned on me what had attacked me. A vampire.

Fuck!

All I needed was to have another vampire in my life. It was bad enough I had one who was jealous of others I associated with. Vampires. I'd had enough of them. Whatever mask I'd worn before to trick those around me, I couldn't reattach. Too many things had happened. It was time for me to be a plain old human. Funny how a brush with death makes one think rationally.

I shook my head as I swung my legs over the bed.

The springs creaked, sending an explosion of dust in my face. I coughed as it settled around me. Scanning the room, I noticed a sheet over a chair next to a fireplace. Dust blanketed the hardwood floor like snow. The walls, like the ceiling, were stained yellow from age and water damage. The drapes were moth-eaten. Pinpoints of light showed through the holes and allowed me enough light to see by. The faint beeping of horns and jackhammers echoed through the glass. I wandered over to the window and pushed back the drapes, wincing at the sunlight that streamed onto my face. I looked down and saw people walking along the street. Some looked to be students rushing to class. Gazing across the way, I saw similar houses, each in various stages of disrepair. Some had small, gated gardens, while others sported steps leading right to the sidewalk. I smiled. This was a familiar neighborhood, one I'd spent four years running through to get to my classes. Somehow I'd gotten back to Boston.

Cain crossed my mind. He was from Boston. I didn't know from which part, but maybe he had brought me back? I hugged myself, remembering the feel of him inside me. Yes, I could stay with him forever, as long as he desired me. I could make him happy. We could enjoy nights together, and I would do anything he wanted. I'd never thought of anyone that way, and I was grateful for that.

My mood darkened when I remembered Veronica. She was a problem. She could be cold. What would she do to Cain if we decided to build a life together? I shivered at the thought of seeing her in the full transformation she had hinted at. She might have been pissed, but she would never take me as a meal. I meant something to her. I was the creature to break down her walls and get to the being inside. No, she would not hurt me, but I feared for Cain. Their confrontation the other night hadn't been pleasant. Her anger directed her actions as she tried containing everything she was. I wondered if she had failed, and if she had, what had she done to Cain?

I didn't know the answer. I would have to wait and see. When I saw her again, she'd tell me the truth. If not, I'd force her to. I had some power over her. Of course, my psychic abilities were nothing compared to hers, but I could manipulate her.

I moved further into the light, watching as the people walked by, unaware of the creatures that moved among them in society. I'd always know vampires now, the unnatural look in the eyes, and the throbbing hunger just beneath the surface of their masked faces. Only some of them were like Veronica. Most ravaged anything they got their hands on, like the one that attacked me. When I felt its breath against my neck, I knew it was the end. Then it had stopped, throwing me aside. Why?

A moan interrupted my train of thought. Pushing the curtains farther open, I noticed a bed hidden on the far side of the room where the light didn't penetrate. I moved cautiously and saw Veronica's naked, sleeping form. I went to her, careful not to make any noise in case I woke her. The closer I got, the more I caught the smell of burnt meat. Most of her back was seared black around the edges. I wondered when she had gotten burned so badly. Pieces of skin littered the bed as it flaked off. The skin that wasn't damaged was lobster pink and scarred. I reached my hand to feel the texture of the flesh. Parts of it peeled off, showing alabaster white perfection underneath. Tentatively, I touched my finger to the new skin. It was warm, almost as though she had been in a hot shower. The burned skin was cold and clammy. That was unusual. I assumed all of her flesh should still be radiating heat, and sensitive to the touch. When I got scorched it hurt well after I iced it down. The burn marks on her back were frigid, dead marks. The more I observed, the quicker they healed, the skin falling off even in the places I had touched.

I caught a glimpse of her face and saw the rawness of it. It didn't seem her front was as bad as her back had been. The burn resembled a strange tattoo, creating a design in her already healing flesh. I wondered what had happened to her. Had she gotten this damaged trying to protect me? Had she gotten it when she fought with Cain? I didn't know. Watching her heal reassured me somewhat.

She didn't breathe, didn't even move. She was perfectly stiff, like a corpse in its coffin. I placed my hand over her mouth to feel for any moisture. There was nothing. I checked along her neck to find a pulse, but yet again, nothing. Her body was lifeless as it healed, as she slept somewhere lost in a dreamland I didn't understand.

I sighed and got up. Part of me wanted to explore the house, to revisit some of my old haunts. I wondered how the Tearoom faired, considering I wasn't slotted to return until Halloween. I volunteered my services for Edmund's annual séance. Why I had, I didn't know, but it was an obligation and part of me wanted to see my old friends again. It was a bonus I was back early and could figure out my arrangements with Edmund, considering I expected him to pay me.

I wanted to confide in Edmund everything that had happened. Maybe he could help answer some of my questions. Of course, if I asked him for advice, he would answer he couldn't give it to me because he knew me too well. That was bullshit. I knew he could read me; he just wouldn't want to. As much as I wanted to run to him for some sort of normalcy, I couldn't desert Veronica. She was too vulnerable to be left alone, at least until she healed. From the looks of things, there was no one in the house. Though my feelings about her were undefined, I didn't want to take a chance that a homeless person might discover her resting place.

I rose from the bed and worked my way around the room. Two doors stood opposite me. One of them was a closet. I opened that and went inside. To my surprise I found a pull cord for the light and yanked it. The closet wasn't very big, but it held a few dresses, each in their own dry cleaning bags, reminding me of body bags. Picking one up, I examined it through the plastic. It was a white dress. Lace ruffled the collar and the hem. The dress was in remarkable condition, except it was yellowed and had holes in a few places that I saw. Extensive beadwork had been sewn around the sleeves, and on inspection I noticed they were pearls. This dress was not a costume as I originally thought, but a wedding dress.

I replaced the dress and leafed through a few of the others in back, but there was nothing of interest. Glancing up at the top shelf, I saw a black, modern suitcase and a wooden box next to it. I stood on tiptoe and grabbed both. I opened the suitcase first and found nothing more than a few pairs of clothes. Mostly black jeans, T-shirts, and a few bras. I guessed this was for emergencies. I examined the box next. It was a simple, wooden jewelry box, something to keep mementos in.

I opened it slowly, in case any spiders crawled out. I hated them and didn't want any arachnids jumping out at me. They couldn't hurt me, but it didn't help my state of mind. A hint of cedar wafted from the box as I opened it. On top was a small gold circlet. A ring. I inspected it, and for the hell of it, I let it slide onto my finger. The coolness shocked me, but the ring was slightly too big. I took it off and held it up to a beam of light streaming through the holey curtains. I tried to make out the inscription, but it was so worn away I couldn't make it out.

I put the ring down and unwrapped a bundle tied with a green ribbon. I peeled back the fabric and found an intricately woven necklace. Tiny braids of human hair made up the chain. I'd only heard of such objects being made for the wealthy and usually given to a loved one. I gingerly picked up the heirloom, wondering who had made it.

"It was from my sister. Her gift to me when I was going to be married. The ring was from Devon."

I nearly dropped the piece of human jewelry when I heard the voice. I caught myself and placed it in the box before I turned to look at Veronica. Her face retained a slight pink color, but nothing else. I wondered what her back was like. Before I could say anything, she got out of bed, stretching like a cat. She walked over to the suitcase and pulled out a shirt and a pair of jeans.

With her back to me, I was able to examine her wounds. Most of it had returned to normal, except for a few splotches of red here and there. Other than that, she was perfect.

She ran her hands though her hair, testing the length of it. In legend, vampires' nails and hair grew every time they slept. Then again, they weren't supposed to walk about in the daylight and I had seen her do that. I watched as her nails lengthened and sharpened and she cut off the ponytail so she was left with hair down to her shoulders. Veronica picked up the hair, along with a trail of dust, and threw it into the fireplace.

I gazed at the place where her hair had fallen. The wood was darker than the rest. I thought at first it was the stain or age of the wood, but something about the color caught my eye. It was too dark, too reddish-brown. There was a huge spot by the fireplace and another by the window. Something about it was just wrong. I placed my hands on the spot, ignoring Veronica. Closing my eyes I opened my mind. Memories of pain and anguish swamped me as they once filled the room so many years ago.

The pictures that flooded my mind were hazy, like looking though a clouded window. My body went rigid as I began reliving the events of the past. I witnessed a woman go to a window to let in a man. He looked familiar to me somehow, but I couldn't place him. The girl was happy to see her lover. He had sneaked in before they were supposed to be together. Then the vision changed. There was no longer love and surprise associated with the woman. A demon stood over the cowering girl, its grin burned into her mind. It took her innocence in unbridled ecstasy, damning her soul while a part of her wanted him to fuck her to death.

My body bucked in response to the orgasms the demon inflicted upon her. The sensations were still embedded in the wood after so many years. And then everything went still.

The body I was in had no feeling, but I saw and heard everything around me. I was dead, or at least the woman I had picked up on had expired. She hadn't totally crossed over to the other side because her consciousness lingered in the flesh. I tried breathing, but couldn't. My hand flew to my throat. I sensed Veronica held me in some capacity, but I couldn't see her.

All I perceived was the warmth coming into my body. The immobility I experienced was passing away, everything coming alive. The coals threw off warmth in the hearth, and then I saw the body on the bed. It was warm and could sate the devouring pain in me.

In my vision, I pounded my fist into the body's chest. I drank and drank, not thinking of anything else. When the ghost of the past finished with the prey, the hunger no longer burned in me. Something was wrong. When I looked down at my hands I saw the blood. The blood of my sister, Veronica's sister. On my hands, on her hands.

I screamed; we screamed.

The visions and emotions overloaded my mind. They meshed and pushed against my thoughts. The psychic impressions tried to suck my awareness back to the past, melding my thoughts to the past Veronica. I tried wrenching my hand away from the floor, but it seemed the liquid was wet again after two centuries, and it didn't want to let me go.

The image of a blood-covered Veronica grabbed my hand, her fangs glinting in the moonlight. I tried to pull away, but I couldn't. I screamed louder.

"Brenna, what is it? What did you see?" Veronica's voice was inside my mind.

I shook uncontrollably as her mind pried me away from the apparitions I'd experienced. She found the psychic center of my brain and shut it down. One moment I was stuck in the past seeing her all covered in blood and the next I saw her as she was, dressed in a black turtleneck and jeans. The faint beeping of horns and voices filtered into the house. There was frost on the windows.

I huddled into her waiting arms, trying to erase the pictures from my mind. Veronica had told me her story, but I never imagined it to be so horrible. So much abandon in what she had to fight against. I knew the true reason she forced her other half behind so many walls.

I took a moment, feeling her strong hands around me, holding me like I was a small bird. It wasn't jealously the other night; it was protection. She guarded me, trying to make up for her sister. She wasn't envious of my relationship with Cain. She wanted to protect me.

"Are you all right?" she asked once I calmed down.

I nodded, wiping my dripping nose with the back of my hand.

"I'm sorry. It's just I never really understood what you went through. I know you told me about how you became what you are. How the vampire personality is. But I just experienced it, and the pain you felt after you realized what you'd done. I'm so sorry. What he did to you. And you loved him, invited him into your life. You were so entranced. You never knew what he was."

Veronica looked at me quizzically, trying to process what I said. "You saw all of that by touching the floor?"

I nodded again. "The emotions, the events of that night remained embedded in the dried blood. When I first woke up I didn't know this was your old home. How did we get here anyway?"

Veronica sat back on her heels. "I brought you here. I flew well into the day to get here. I had to bring you here to keep you from—"

"I knew it. You rescued me from that creature that attacked me."

Veronica started shaking her head. "No, you don't understand. I was the thing that harmed you. Ronnie got out. I finally got her under control again. I brought you here so Devon wouldn't find us. At least not for a while. Eventually, he'll catch up. I just hope we have enough time."

She had been the thing that assaulted me! Veronica had been the beast that held me captive. Was I a piece of meat? I backed away from her until my ass hit the wall.

"How could you?"

"I tried to stop her." She moved toward me, tears trailing down her cheeks. She pressed her fingers to my lips. I felt her heartbeat through her fingertips. It was beating faster than mine. "I never meant to hurt you. I was locked away. She didn't recognize your scent or your voice. It'd been so long since she was free. Seeing you with Devon made my control slip. Everything just boiled over. I'm so sorry. Once I tasted you, felt your blood in my mouth, I broke free and forced Ronnie back into her cage. I spit everything out I had taken.

"I threw you across the courtyard and shut your mind down, not believing what I had done. I took you in my arms, and Devon appeared. He was the one who attacked you the first time, taunting me with your blood. I resisted him." Veronica paused, running her fingers over the wounds on my neck.

I winced a little, but I saw true pain and regret in her lavender eyes.

"He said he'd already tasted you. The first night you met him."

"I don't know who you're talking about," I whispered. A growing sense of dread welled up in my brain. She said she saw me with Devon. I had been on a date with Cain. No, she couldn't be right. I knew what she was going to say, but I couldn't hear it.

"To you, he's Cain. To me, he's Devon. You don't believe me, I can see that. But some part of you does. So listen to me and heed my advice instead of pushing it aside as I did the gypsy's warning. You know who he is. You've fucked him. He wormed his way into your life just as he worked his way into mine. This time you won't have to suffer the same fate as me. But he'll come for us, and use you to get to me."

"I don't believe you."

"Yes, you do. You already know it's the truth."

I lowered my eyes, knowing she was right. Even when I didn't want to acknowledge it, I knew Cain was Devon, her master. How could such a monster come into my life without me knowing it? Without my intuition giving me a warning? I knew that answer too. I believed my mask for so long I didn't sense real danger when it kicked me in the ass. Now I knew better. I wouldn't let the monster into my mind again. The more I thought of him, the more I wanted his hands fluttering over my body, his mouth pressing against mine. Veronica was right. He was a demon, and he'd used both of us.

"So what do we do now?" I asked.

Veronica sighed, pushing back the drapes, wincing at the streaming sunlight filling the room. "Now we wait."

CHAPTER SEVENTEEN

My name is Veronica.

We walked along the darkened streets of Boston, smelling a hint of the oncoming fall in the air. I'd forgotten what it was like to be in this part of the country. To be in a place that altered seasons as a person changed clothes. I'd traveled, running for so long. I hadn't stopped to enjoy nature's wonders. Even with Brenna at my side, happiness was fleeting. Devon would soon intrude upon our serenity. The uncertainty inside of her overwhelmed her senses as she mulled the events of the past few nights. Deep down she didn't want to believe Devon was the man she'd fallen in love with. I knew Devon could manipulate things. I felt the same way whenever I thought of him and the past.

I wondered what it would be like to be a naïve young girl again, walking through Boston Common. If a wind had not come up that day, I might not have seen Devon, or he might not have seen me. I'd have been buried in the cool earth, next to my family and perhaps a husband. Wouldn't that be something? Dying of old age, instead of living as the creature I was today. Devon assumed that by destroying my family, I'd severed all of my ties with humanity and become like him, but he was wrong. Brenna experienced that when she zoomed in on the emotions left in the blood on the floor. How she achieved it I wasn't sure. The screams of the past echoed in her psyche as they did mine; the pain was horrible and deafening if I listened to it. She only suffered it second hand, like watching a bad horror movie. If only Brenna knew the true torment I endured day in and day out from my actions.

Through her, I remembered what it was like to see my sister's desecrated body laying on the bed in the aftermath of my transformation. I tried to shake the memory from my mind, but it was too strong. It took over my mind and once again I had to relive my past transgressions.

I WOKE AS the sun sank below the horizon, the events of the previous night sticky in my mind. Something had happened, but I didn't know what. I shielded my eyes from the receding daylight and struggled to get up. My muscles creaking as I stood. I looked down at my rust stained naked form, knowing I'd been the cause of the unlikely paint on my body. Tears threatened, but another voice inside my mind comforted me, telling me not to weep for the things I'd lost. They didn't matter because I had been reborn into something better.

My senses were still highly tuned. The wind hurt my overdeveloped senses. I searched for Devon but couldn't find him. I clamped my hands to my ears, shutting out the noises of the scurrying rats in the basement and the rumblings of the humans next door. As I thought about the noise lowering, it suddenly did. I took my hands off my ears and the sounds had lessened. I smiled and wandered out of the room, thinking I should wash up or I'd get a chill. In my room, I lit one of the lamps on the bureau. I watched a moment as black smoke billowed up from the cloth wick. The acrid stench of kerosene hit me. I crinkled my nose at it, not remembering a time when it smelled so bad. As the smoke came up it settled into my eyes, making them tear up. I sneezed and backed away, rubbing my eyes with the back of my hand.

A thin film of pink tinged ice had settled over the washbasin. I pushed my hand through it. The water temperature chilled the muscles of my hand, but instead of seizing up they bent easily. Gathering a handful of water, I threw some over my face. I scanned the bureau for a cloth and found nothing, but there were a few rags on the floor. I recognized them as my tattered nightgown. Using them, I scrubbed my body, the water turning redder and redder with each wringing.

My eyes closed each time the rag touched my skin, the cool water dribbling between my breasts. Even though the water was freezing, my body filled with warmth as I remembered Devon's hands on me the night before, his dick inside me. The pleasure of the memory enveloped me as my thumb found my clit. The rag fluttered from my hand, my eyes half closed in satisfaction. I half expected Devon to come into the room and take me right there. Just the thought of my Master, who brought me into the world with his blood, helped to free me of the world I had come from. I remembered the feel of his blood when I opened my eyes. It felt like warm silk caressing my insides. I knew my Master would only let me suckle him when I had been good.

The other blood was almost as good, and as I remembered the thought of the blood my body tingled. I let the sensations overcome me and I came. Languidness overcame me from my manipulations. I wanted my Master to take me in his arms so I could please him. He would know what to do with me. He was nowhere to be found, and when I opened my eyes all thoughts of Master vanished as I saw what was left of my sister.

The thing that craved Devon's touch receded as rapidly as it had come. I screamed. The windows and the mirror strained against the pitch and then shattered, sending glass into the street and into the room. I staggered over, looking down at the display. Mary's lungs hung half in and half out of her shattered ribcage. Pieces of intestines peeked out from the bottom of the wound. Her flesh matched the hue of Devon's eyes. I shook, not believing what I saw. My finger traced the fragmented lines of her chest. I tried to pull it back, but my body wouldn't respond to the command. Unconsciously, I licked my lips as I remembered the taste of her bringing me back to life.

Part of me wanted to hug the body and weep, mourning the loss of my life. The slice Devon birthed desired to take the corpse in a lover's embrace and dance, whirling faster and faster, laughing over the thought that I had escaped death. A strange duality raged in my mind. My sister's face held serenity in death. She never felt a thing when I ripped out her throat and then her heart. Mary had been my devoted sister, giving her life so I could complete my change.

I traced the line of her jaw. A little voice told me I had nothing to worry about. I should trust my instincts, giving myself over to unbridled pleasure. I saw the beast as it sat behind my eyelids, waiting to be freed.

Its maw of sharp teeth was slick with saliva. I felt its purr vibrate in my throat.

Let me out, it whispered in my mind. *We'll leave the corpse and find our Master. The human bitch is dead. We have been reborn. Let me out, and you'll never have to blanch at the thought of humanity again.*

I closed my eyes and found my body swaying, wanting to give in to the words and feeling of serenity I would have if the beast took hold. It begged to surge forth. I felt myself changing. My teeth were lengthening, my nails hardening to bone. Then the desecrated image of my sister flashed in my mind. It raced to the forefront of my thoughts and pushed the beast into the dark. It howled as I forced it back and sunk to my knees and cried over the body of my sister. Devon found me naked and weeping.

I looked up when I heard the weight of the boards creaking.

"Ronnie, why are you crying?" he cooed in my ear while hugging me to him.

The warmth of his flesh surprised me. I shivered as his wool shirt scraped against my skin, clinging to the little hairs on my arms. He brushed away a stray hair from my neck and kissed my throat. As his lips grazed the wounds he had inflicted last night, I moaned. The pressure of his lips on the puncture wound tore all thoughts of my sister from me. For a moment, the beast rose. My body temperature spiked with its emergence, but I fought it and my body cooled as the monster retreated. Devon felt the fire crawl over my skin and he responded, digging his fangs into my throat. I cried out in pain and pleasure as he sucked and then withdrew.

"Tell me your troubles?" he purred.

"How could you make me do this? She was my sister." I gestured to the bed.

Devon glanced over at the corpse. A sneer crossed his face. "I don't see anything but dead meat. You can't mourn for what you have lost. You have me now. Isn't that what you wanted? You had no complaints last night when you gorged on her blood. The blood of your parents. What's wrong now?"

A gust of wind blew a bit of snow into the room. It chilled me to the core as I pushed away from Devon. His hand closed around my arm and he squeezed. The bones creaked and cracked in my upper arm. I began to scream as the pain overwhelmed me, but Devon placed his finger on my lips, silencing me. His lips pressed against my ear as he spoke.

"They are meat, Ronnie. Nothing more. And don't think you are going away from me. You are mine. Just remember, it's my blood that flows in your veins. Nothing you can do will ever change that fact. If you ever think of leaving me, I'll do things to you you can only imagine. I'm sure that will never happen. This is just a phase until you mature, and then you'll crave my domination over you. Every second of your life, you'll do anything to please me. It's in our nature to want pain and dominion. I know part of you longs for it even now. I smell it in your veins. Now what are you going to do?"

He withdrew his finger and the pain began to diminish in my broken arm as it healed. Everything was true. He was my Master, but that didn't mean I had to kill. The beast desired to embrace him, to have him fuck and beat it into submission for its blatant disobedience. Part of me wanted to whimper at his feet, but no. I would never let that happen.

"Go to hell!" I whispered.

He slapped me. His claws scraped furrows in my check to the bone. I was thrown back against the wall into the mirror. Pieces of glass sliced my ass. Blood streamed down my face. Devon stood over me as I looked up at him. His eyes burned red in their already black orbs.

"Never speak to me that way again. Never show me defiance, Ronnie. I can be lovable or cruel. It's your choice. If you leave me, you'll die. You don't know how to survive on your own. Be a good girl and come to me."

He knelt down and licked my bleeding cheek. Underneath his black, forked tongue the skin tingled as it healed. I was getting lightheaded from the blood loss.

Devon stared at me and stroked the flesh between my breasts. "Come on."

I stared into Devon's eyes and felt my resolve melting away. He could be my safety. *No*, my rationality screamed. Anger overwhelmed me, initiating my transformation. My nails hardened and swiped the soft flesh of Devon's neck. It was only a superficial wound. His talons slipped into my chest, piercing my ribcage. The hardness of his nails caressed my beating heart. Devon began to pull, ever so slightly. Breath caught in my throat.

"Please," I whimpered. I didn't want to die.

"Please what?" Devon asked, his voice laced with frost.

"Don't kill me."

"Don't kill you. Why not? You have been such a bad child. Maybe if you ask me nicely, I won't," Devon hissed.

He squeezed harder on my heart. I convulsed underneath him. Stars appeared on the edge of my vision. I tried to breathe, but my lungs wouldn't work. I didn't want it to end like this and Devon knew that.

"Please don't kill me, Master."

Devon smiled. "Very good, Ronnie. For now you have been punished enough." He gave my heart one more gentle squeeze for good measure, making sure I understood how cruel he could really be if I ever stepped out of line again. I convulsed again and the stars totally took over my vision. I descended with them into blackness.

| STILL BORE the scars he'd inflicted upon me that night. Five small star-shaped puckers where his talons entered my chest. They were yet another reminder of his mastery over me, and each time he fucked me, sucked me, beat me to a bloody pulp, I told myself it was my punishment. It was always his way of showing me he owned me. He made me believe I deserved the treatment. He always hoped I would come to my senses and beg him to fuck me or beat me, letting the beast out, but it never happened unless he forced his way into my mind and pulled the monster out. As the years grew, his control on me waned as he began to lose his interest, and he let me have some freedom. I could go into the night and feed the way I wanted. I snuck into hospitals and fed on the dying. Then one night when he was preoccupied with two whores, my courage came up.

I grabbed money and told Devon I was going to feed. He waved me off, lost in the blood-haze, and let me go, not bothering to monitor my thoughts. I flew until the sun forced me to seek shelter. Even though part of me yearned for its rays to eat away at me, I was not ready to give up. I had a new chance at life and would embrace it.

I wasn't ready to curl up and die. I wanted to live. Even as I winged away that first day I didn't know how to care, how to reinstate myself into society. Devon had taught me humans were food. I'd been alienated and knew only pain and the warped love Devon had shown me. Always apologizing after he beat me. Touching me gently. Sucking at my old wounds on my chest. Those were times I forgave him and forgot his brutality. It was the voice of my mortality that gave me the nerve to run from Devon. When Brenna reopened my heart once again, I couldn't handle it. I lost myself to my nature, and in one sip destroyed the very relationship I cherished, using it to sate my beast.

"Veronica, did you hear me?" asked Brenna.

I looked at her blankly, shaking my head. I scanned the area we were around and found we had walked all through Boston Garden and the Common and were about to cross Tremont Street. I glanced up at the clock on the Park Street Church, noticing it was almost seven. The traffic was still as hectic as it had been in my time, but now the roar of engines replaced the clopping of horse drawn carriages. I missed the sounds the hooves made on the cobblestones, so crisp and clear.

The Boston I'd left had changed, but it was still very much the same. Except there were more shadows than I remembered. As I breathed, the stench of my kind lingered on the air. They were here, imbedded into the city just as the cobblestones had once been on the streets. Now was not the time to dwell on other vampires.

"I'm sorry, Brenna, what did you say?"

"I said we're here. I was wondering if you wanted to come up. It's where I used to work."

"Sure." I forced a smile. "That'd be great."

She nodded as we crossed the street. We walked into a building on Winter Street and entered through a set of glass doors into a building housing a Chinese restaurant the size of a closet, a lottery store, and a pizza joint. Brenna pushed a well-worn button for the elevator. A lavender sign hung on the wall next to the elevator indicating the Boston Tearoom was upstairs. Bats fluttered in my stomach at the thought of entering the establishment, but to please Brenna, I boarded the elevator.

The scent of stale cigarettes, cloves, and the whiff of old garbage penetrated the enclosed space. I tried not to gag. With each floor the bats in my stomach grew more frantic. Dread weighed me down as the elevator came to a crashing stop, landing on the third floor, with three loud thuds before allowing us to leave. As soon as the door released, the hackles rose underneath my skin, and the muscles in my back danced as my wings pushed against the inside of my flesh, wanting to burst out so I could escape. Danger lingered in this place. It wasn't the kind of threat I was used to, it

was unknown, the place that loomed before me possessed an energy that I could see. Its brilliance was
brighter than the sun. I turned my head from it, desir-
ing nothing more than to crawl back into the safety of
the elevator and run outside. Before I could back away
from Brenna, she walked off the elevator and into the
light. There was no choice but to follow. As I traversed
the few feet between the safety of the lift and the door
to the Tearoom, the tips of my wings stretched the skin
and poked the fabric of my shirt up. I took a deep breath.

This place can't be that bad, I thought as I settled my
wings back into their rightful resting place and walked
into the unknown.

The light allowed me to enter as I crossed the
threshold. The energy inside the Tearoom suffocated
me like I was breathing liquid air. The heaviness made
me dizzy, and I wondered if this was how humans felt
when they came in here as well. I didn't think the
energy just affected me. It would affect anyone who
walked in, but more so if the human was intuitive.

Brenna smiled as though she'd returned home
after a long vacation. This place was familiar to her.

A mural of a winged horse and griffin fighting
reared in front of me on the wall. Each creature battled
for something–good and evil probably? Then an odd
sensation came over me, as if someone were watching
me. A presence on my left pushed against my thoughts.
It wasn't unpleasant, just intrusive. I turned to find a

painting of a woman in white surrounded by pillars of stone. A sense of serenity descended over me when I gazed into her face. She smiled and winked at me, but when I stepped forward, touching the cool surface of the wall, the image was gone and she was just a robed figure looking down at me from a misty glade.

"Can I help you?"

A tall, thin black man with unruly hair and a mustache stood in front of us. He looked to be in his forties, but the only indications of his true age were the small shots of gray in his hair. In his hands he held a broken pair of glasses. Waves of knowledge and understanding flowed from him and hit me like ripples. There was no lie about him. He was a kind and willing guide.

"Gee Peter, has it been so long that you don't recognize me?" Brenna asked him.

His expression changed from business to pure excitement. A light appeared in his eyes, and he wrapped Brenna in a big hug. He looked almost formal in the gesture, but I realized it was just how he was.

"Raven! How are you?"

I looked at her quizzically. "Raven?"

She blushed. "It's the name I read under. It helps with privacy." She turned back to Peter. "Is Edmund here?"

"Did someone call me?" I heard a voice behind me as the elevator door opened.

I turned and stared into the eyes of a man who was truly all seeing. He saw through whatever shields I had, slicing my past and identity from me, taking them all in with just a movement of his power. His mind slammed mine so hard I dared not fight him. Even though I could do some serious mental damage to him, he could fuck with my psyche, and I didn't need that. This man had the same brightness I encountered before entering the Tearoom. This was the force that protected the place. I deduced he owned the Tearoom and was a truly gifted psychic. To him I was as easy to read as a street sign.

"You might want to leave," he said to me curtly.

Brenna looked at us and was about to say something, but he opened his mouth first.

"Raven, oh my God! How the hell have you been?" he breezed past me and took Brenna into a bear hug.

As he strolled by me, I got a whiff. There was an odor of decay about his body. A sickness lingered inside of him, and it had been eating away at him for years. It was not cancer, but something in his blood, a plague that medicine kept at bay. I wondered how long he had been infected. He turned to me while in his bear hug and his gaze bored into mine. He knew I'd scanned him in some sense. He didn't like it, but didn't dare lash out at me again. Edmund had made it clear I was not welcome. I nodded slightly and made for the door, trying to sneak out before Brenna spotted me.

"Where are you going?" she asked. "I hoped you'd get a reading."

"I don't think I need to know my future. I think we both already know it."

"Nonsense. Besides, I'm sure Edmund would be happy to give you a reading. He owes me one."

Both he and I turned to Brenna.

"It's not a good idea. I'll meet you outside."

"No. Edmund, you don't mind, do you?"

He didn't say anything, but he shot daggers of energy at her. If Brenna felt anything, she ignored it.

"Fine." He smiled. It took him a moment, but then he gestured for me to have a seat at his table.

I sat down, not knowing what to expect. The last thing I wanted was to find out my future, but as it was, I couldn't disappoint Brenna. As I shuffled the cards Edmund placed in my hands, a ray of hope blossomed in me for the first time in centuries.

18

CHAPTER EIGHTEEN

My name is Veronica.

The tarot cards I mixed had been used many times before. The lamination had worn thin in places, but I continued to move them, back and forth until I had the urge to stop. I placed them on the table in front of Edmund, looking at him attentively, wondering what he would come up with. He stared at me, his mind boring into mine like a hot poker. My instincts were to enclose myself in barriers to keep him out, but it would do no good. He would get through.

He gathered the cards and held them with his eyes closed, focusing on my energy. Edmund inhaled as if evaluating my present situation and gazed down at the cards in his hands. His fingers were long, and slender, but unlike Devon's, Edmund's were daintier, the hands of one who should have played as a concert pianist, but this was not Edmund's calling. He was one to protect the Tearoom and see it kept moving into further centuries. I envied him this because he had a purpose, where I had nothing, save a hunger that drove me to kill everything I'd ever loved. The reading made me hopeful because it might actually change my future. I wanted to believe that, but deep down, I knew I was doomed to be Devon's pawn for the rest of my years.

Edmund held the cards a little longer and then turned them over, causing them to click softly as he placed them on his small table. I scanned his table wondering if all of the things he'd collected were relics to help him focus or just personal items. A picture of his mother stood next to a pile of papers. Two chalices, one black, one white, adorned opposite sides of his table. The scent of old coins clung to their glazed surfaces. I assumed he used the goblets as representations of balance. In the middle of the table was a large crystal the size of Edmund's fist, standing on its base. Energy resounded off of it like a tuning fork.

The first card Edmund turned over was the Devil. I smirked as I examined the picture. The man in it resembled Devon with his cruel smirk. The next card was Judgment. The image on the card was an angel blowing a trumpet, its wings covering the sun and sky as the humans below cowered in fear. The next card, The Hermit, was the representation of a lone man inside a cave huddled near a rock. He had long white hair, a wizened expression, and a single light to guide him. The next was a skeleton holding a scythe. I chuckled as Edmund placed it on the table. Of course I'd get the Death card.

Edmund looked at me as I laughed. The chill cut from his eyes into me and I stopped chuckling, realizing how serious he took the reading. The next and last card was The Tower.

"You think that because a demon made you into what you are, beating you into submission, that you are enslaved to him. You punish yourself for killing your sister. Just because you stayed with a man doesn't mean you have to damn yourself for an eternity." He paused and took a drag of his clove cigarette and then hacked up a ball of phlegm.

I caught the whiff of old pot in his clothes and in his mucus.

"Judgment is something you give yourself every day. You feel because of what you are, you cannot communicate with anything around you, even your own kind. Again you blame yourself for staying with a man that rammed his fist into you. It was your duty to accept his proposal because you thought you'd never have another man ask you to marry. Your parents indulged you, but your sister hated you for taking so long. She wanted—"

"I know." I cut Edmund off. "I was stupid. Mary hated me so. I think she haunts my house. I mean, I eviscerated her to death. And—" I stopped, my mind catching up to my words. How had he known so much about me? It was unsettling. The information cut right to the heart of my soul. He was right. I hated myself for letting Devon control me so.

"Hush! Even though your sister was killed in the house, I don't think she lingers there, but I'm not sure. I don't think that's what you're here about. You want to know the future. Well, what I can tell you is this. The Hermit says you have been alone for a long time, searching the world, trying to regain what you once lost. You walk a path behind a mask that doesn't fit. If you had looked at the matters of faith in your heart, you'd have found the answers to your questions, but you were destined to meet Brenna.

"The next card is Death. This is present time. You're about to enter into a new stage of life. You've come out of the cave after so many years and now you have a companion."

I glanced at Brenna, who smiled at me as she talked with Peter. I didn't like what Edmund said. His train of thought was leading toward Devon.

No. I shook the thought away. Devon wouldn't have her. I'd kill him before he would get Brenna. I shuddered at what Edmund had said. He was good. Power radiated off him like a furnace. He truly was the real thing, but I didn't know if I wanted to heed his advice.

"The outcome of everything is The Tower. It shows your world crashing down around you. This card is the future, but it's already coming upon you as an old foe returns. He's already in the city, waiting for the right time to make himself known. He knows where to find you, how to get into your resting place. He comes to claim what is his. He won't stop until he has both of you, and in the end you'll have to choose between the better of two evils. It's all up to you. You do have help, but not in the way you think. Sadly, this is all I can tell you. The rest is up to you to figure out."

Edmund leaned back in his chair and took another drag of his cigarette. So many questions loomed in the back of my mind, but I couldn't ask him. How did he get the information? What was Devon going to do? Choosing between two evils didn't sound too good. Edmund had a key into the future that I'd never understand. Even though I had mental abilities, I didn't understand the sort of power he and Brenna possessed.

"Tell me one thing: how will Brenna fare in this whole event?" I had to ensure her safety. Maybe I'd face Devon alone and leave her in Edmund's care. Devon would never know where she disappeared. If I died, he'd leave her alone, thinking his conquest of her would no longer be relevant because I expired. If I won, then I would never have to expose Brenna to him again.

Edmund finished his clove cigarette and snuffed it out in a marble ashtray, forcing it down harder until it splintered and cracked.

"Brenna will get all she has ever wanted. Maybe even more than she bargained for in the arms of Death. Don't worry about that. Now, if you'll excuse me, I have to go back upstairs. You're welcome to stay and look around and, if need be, come again." Edmund wheeled his chair back and got out of the seat.

The chair hit the wall, causing small chips of green paint to come flaking off and pictures to rattle. I was afraid one might fall, but it seemed the nails were securely in the wall and were used to Edmund's rough treatment. I sighed as I stared at the cards on the table. This had been my first real reading. I understood why humans were fascinated by the prospect of having someone tell them their future. It gave them some reassurance and a hint as to what path to follow if they lost their way. I took one last look at the cards, wondering what to do next. As much as he had given me answers, he had left me with so many questions. What did he mean when he said that Brenna would get what she always wanted? It must have been something between them. I got up, noticing for the first time the mural on the ceiling. It was the universe with Saturn as the centerpiece. The artist had to be very talented to create it because drainpipe covers had been turned into different planets, others, asteroids. Shooting stars traveled through the painted universe like cars on a predetermined course. Stars twinkled around Saturn, and the sun dulled in comparison to the awesome planet.

"Cool, isn't it?" Brenna said.

I nodded. I didn't want to show her any of the doubt or fear I had when I'd gotten the reading.

"How was the reading? Did you learn who your next Romeo would be?"

"Hardly," I laughed, smiling at the thought. If only that were the case. "It was very informative," I said at last. By the look on her face she wanted to know all of the details, but before I could tell her, Edmund called her over.

Brenna glanced at me and shrugged her shoulders. She looked at the man she truly respected and cared for. He had been a generous person and given her much she had to be thankful for. I wondered what it would have been like to have someone like him, but no. My fate was to wander through the world alone.

19

CHAPTER NINETEEN

My name is Brenna.

Veronica was not happy with Edmund's reading. Her mouth tensed, causing wrinkles to appear around her eyes, marring her marble smooth complexion. I wanted to speak with her, but my old boss called me up to his apartment. I left her to absorb what he'd said. Besides, I needed to talk with him after so much had happened. I wasn't sure where the lines blended with Veronica and me anymore.

She had attacked me, but then saved me from herself. The conflict loomed in her whenever I looked at her. It was as if her brain danced in duality between what she was and what her scattered humanity dictated. She couldn't admit that part of her was a thing without the ability to feel pain, something without a conscience. She crossed that threshold over two centuries ago. I hoped Edmund could sort out some of my many questions.

As we stood together in the elevator, the back of my mind began to itch. I shook my head, trying to ignore the tingling.

"What's the matter?" he asked as we stepped off the elevator and into the lobby.

I closed Edmund's door behind me and followed him into the living room. I plopped down on his black leather couch while he went into the kitchen and got a drink. After a moment, the door opened again and the clicking of claws sounded on the hardwood floors as the dogs came running. Justin, a miniature golden retriever, pounced on me, licking me as if he were still a puppy. Next came Isis, a half Chihuahua-Jack Russell terrier mix. When she saw me, she yipped and barked. I pushed Justin off and put Isis on my lap, and she sat there as if she were on a throne. I smiled, remembering all the times she'd sat on my foot waiting for me to scratch her belly. Things had been simpler when I'd been younger. Edmund, Isis, and I had been roommates for a year while I was in school. That was then, and this was now, when I had vampires to worry about and wondered if I'd be living the rest of my life in only a few short days.

The front door closed again, and I heard the elevator go down. Joshua, Edmund's boyfriend, must have dropped off the dogs and gone back out. Joshua used to go to school with me as well and worked at the Tearoom while I did. It was there that he became involved with Edmund and had been one of the reasons I moved out of Edmund's after only a year.

"You weren't supposed to be in Boston until Samhain," he said while standing at the bar that separated the kitchen from the living room.

I shrugged, thinking of Samhain, the Celtic name for Halloween. It was true I hadn't planned on coming to help him with the annual séance the Tearoom held until then. When he called asking me to help with the ghostly gathering, I thought it a little odd. It was unlike Edmund to call anyone to come and visit him, let alone ask for help. His abilities kept him cloistered as the emotions of others pressed on his mind. Even though he had the same abilities as me, he was more powerful than I could ever imagine. While I'd been living with him, he'd only ventured out once or twice a week. He employed dog walkers and couriers to do his grocery shopping. The world was just too much for him to deal with. I, on the other hand, learned to drown out the static of others' feelings. It was easy. I imagined a volume control and turned it down to a reasonable level. It shut out much of the din, but there was always static lingering in my mind from all the bustling minds.

"Yeah, well, things change. Life changes. It's funny you know. Who would figure after all this time I'd end up right back where I started."

Edmund took a sip of his soda and stared at me. The pressure of his thoughts descended on mine as he read my mind. I didn't care.

"You shouldn't have brought her here. She's not...normal."

I laughed at the word. No, Veronica was anything but normal. "You're right on that one. Why not bring her here? Just because she's—" I paused, not being able to say the word vampire in front of Edmund. He had always known my fascination with the creatures of the night. Now bringing one to the meet him was a little strange. Admitting what Veronica was, confessing her existence to him would make the past two weeks real. "She's different, yes, but she has the right to know her destiny."

"Raven, she's a fucking vampire. Only you would find something like her and bring her here. It doesn't surprise me in the least. You've always had a fascination for the dark. You're right—I guess she does deserve to know her future. I couldn't tell her what path she walks on. She had a hand in choosing her own destiny, just like you and me, before she incarnated on this earth. And now, like you, she faces a huge decision."

"We all face decisions. She's trying to keep us away from her bastard of a master. That was why I brought her here. I thought you could help her. I need to know why she came into my life the way she did. Why now, when things were going great? Was it Fate, or just my luck that a real vampire would walk into my life, considering I thought ghosts were the only things that defied death?"

"Raven, you and I both know there are many different kinds of beings that lurk in the shadows. What do you think the beings are that give you information? You just don't pull the readings out of your ass. They come from somewhere, the Divine maybe, angels, devils, whatever they are. That isn't the point. I can't give you the answer you're looking for."

"I'm not asking for a reading. I'm asking a question. Damn it!" I propelled off the couch, turning my back on my one time employer. I examined his windowsill, noticing all the different types of candles. Some had burned together forming rainbow pools of wax. The faint scent of smoke lingered in the air as if he'd just blown them out before coming downstairs. It wouldn't surprise me.

"Sit down, Raven, and I'll answer your question." I sighed and joined him again. "One thing, you're here a month early. I had a feeling you'd come unexpected, but it's probably for the better. I didn't think you'd have a guest. She throws a wrench in things somewhat, but in the end it will work out. What matters is that you're here, and I believe it was Fate that brought you here early. Now both of us believe in Fate and that before we are born we pave a path for our own destiny. Right?"

I nodded. Edmund and I had had this talk many times in the past. It was a general belief among the psychics in the Tearoom that before being born as humans, we chose the main outcome of our life. The specifics of choice and free will, and the sequence of events were left up to Fate, or God, or whatever one believed in.

Many of the psychics at the Tearoom were Wiccan, worshiping nature and God as two separate, but equal entities, the God and Goddess. While there, I adopted some of their beliefs, like calling Halloween Samhain, but only because the distinction was made that Samhain was not the compromised version of Halloween, when children went house to house to get candy and witches were green skinned women riding brooms or hovering over bubbling cauldrons. Instead, it was a night when the lines between the worlds were thin. It was transparent enough to have ghosts come back from the grave to reach out and contact their loved ones. It was the night the New Year began in the Wiccan tradition, when people stockpiled for the oncoming winter. I believed in this, and the only reason children dressed up was to frighten away evil spirits that floated around on the fright-filled night. In terms of a god, I acknowledged something floating above us, and no matter what sex it was, all that mattered was that it had acceptance for everything.

"What does Fate have to do with all of this, Edmund?" I asked, trying to avoid looking at his teeth, stained brown from all of the clove cigarettes he inhaled.

"Fate has everything to do with it. Why do you think you're here so early? It's not to talk about the séance. It's about your destiny. You need answers to questions you've already got the answers to. All you have to do is think about everything you were before Veronica came into your life. That is the answer."

I started to speak, but he glared at me. He had spoken his piece and wouldn't say any more. My irritation rose. I wanted to kill Edmund; he always spoke in riddles. It was better to drop the subject and move on. I'd figure out the meaning later, and then realize that whatever he said was right anyway.

"So how's the Tearoom going? Business been good?"

He smiled sadly. I tried sensing his thoughts, but like always I couldn't get past his barriers. He was impossible to read, but every once in a while when he wasn't expecting it, I slipped in. This was not one of the times.

"It's dying. Slowly, of course. I'm sure once some new life has been put into it, it'll thrive again. The Tearoom has an energy of its own and will outlast all of us." Edmund paused and lit up a cigarette. He gulped a quick puff and then continued. "How's business for you?"

"Fine. It's been good." I stopped as Edmund erupted in one of his coughing fits. This time it was a deeper cough than the one I was used to hearing. I wondered how his health was. I hoped his infection hadn't caused his immune system to fail. "Are you okay?"

"Oh, yeah. Just peachy. I'll be fine. I just gotta stop smoking these damn things. Or maybe even the pot. Yeah, right!" He laughed.

I smiled at the comment, though I knew he was hiding something. Of course, I knew if he didn't want to talk about something, he wouldn't.

"You should go back and get your friend. I don't like her much, but she'll figure things out. Trust me, she means well, so you can trust her no matter what. I'll see you next week when you stop in. I'll have something for you by then. Now, give me a hug."

I leaned over, sinking more into the couch as I got to him, but that was okay. I wondered what he meant about me stopping in and something for me. Knowing Edmund, it was probably a crystal. I didn't think I'd be staying that long. I yearned to get back to New Orleans so I could get on with my life. I hoped Veronica would come with me, but I didn't know. I had clients waiting, and the chill of fall hung in the air of Boston. I didn't want to be in the city as it got colder.

"It was good to see you. And thanks for everything."

I got up and out of his bear embrace, looking at him one last time, remembering how much he'd done for me over the years I worked for him. He really was a big brother to me, and I never found the right way to repay him for his help in developing my abilities. He looked the same after all these years. His head was still bald with spikes of black and grey hair protruding from it, but he had lost a few pounds from his hefty frame. He seemed healthy aside from his cough, but then again, he'd had that all the years I knew him. I shook off the thought. Yes, he just had to give up smoking.

"If you think too much, smoke'll come out of your ears. Now go downstairs," he urged.

"See ya, Edmund." I gave Isis a final pat and walked out of the apartment, closing the door before pressing the button for the elevator. I waited and then rode the elevator back to the Tearoom. Veronica was nowhere to be seen.

"She went downstairs, Raven," Peter called from the back, where an old couch still survived, where all the psychics sat and got a clear view of the door.

"Thanks, Peter. I'll see you later."

"Bye," he yelled down.

The elevator jerked to the ground floor. Veronica stood outside, leaning against the glass front of the building. Observing her, I wondered what she thought about while she scanned the people. Did her hunger linger underneath the surface of her thoughts? I now knew how hard it was for her to be what she was, and it hadn't been her choice. My thoughts of becoming a vampire had been romanticized, and the harshness of the bloodlust never entered my mind. Even though I didn't want to be a vampire anymore, I wondered if I could still hypnotize her, fooling her into thinking I was.

I pictured the purple in my aura growing outwards, expanding until it encompassed all of my senses and touched the humans in the building and anyone who came in. A cool chill zapped through my spine as the familiar feeling I had become something removed from society descended over me. My gums tingled as if I anticipated the call of blood, but really it was the thought of overcoming her. Smiling, I opened my eyes, unaware of the people who didn't notice me walking in. I willed them not to see me, and they didn't.

My aura rubbed against Veronica's. The muscles in her back tensed. Her hands clenched and her fingers stretched an inch or so. Placing a hand on Veronica's shoulder, I made her jump. It reminded me of what she had done when I thought her to be human and she thought me to be a vampire. The ability to fool her was still in me.

Veronica recovered quickly. Her hand came within centimeters of my throat as she spun around. Anger flashed in her eyes when she realized it was me, but she relaxed, allowing her fingers to shrink back to normal.

"I could have hurt you," she growled. "Why did you do that?"

"To see if I could and to test a theory," I said, crossing my arms over my chest.

Veronica ran her hands through her hair and peered into my eyes, contemplating something. Probably whether or not to scold me or to just let the matter drop.

"Do you think you could fool other vampires?"

I nodded, understanding her train of thought. She assumed if I deceived her we could fool Devon into thinking I had become a vampire and he would leave us alone. I assumed even if we did mislead him, he would still come after Veronica and me. Even if we couldn't fool him, I knew I had tricked others of her kind in the past. I remembered the vampire in New Orleans the first time I met Veronica. He assumed I was like him and let me pass unharmed.

I smiled. "Sure. You want to test an idea?"

"Yes, but I don't know where my kind gather around here."

I knew exactly where vampires congregated in the area. "There's a club in Cambridge. Goth night is every Wednesday. And on Fridays it's either fetish or goth, depending. Considering it's Thursday, we can go tomorrow, or even next week. It's up to you."

"I'd rather go on a less crowded night, just to make sure. And besides." She paused. "We'll have to dress the part, so we need to go shopping."

I laughed, wondering how she could go from being pissed to being in a great mood in a matter of seconds. It didn't matter because even if she didn't have typical PMS, I was sure there was some type of vampire equivalent. I was not about to ask her, though. If she wanted to shop, then I knew just the place.

"Sure, when do you want to go?"

"How about tomorrow, in the afternoon?"

"Sounds great, but there's one thing I've been wondering. How come you can be in the sun? Vampires are supposed to fry in the daylight."

Veronica laughed. "Don't believe everything legends talk about. Some of my kind can't go into the sun. Those that indulge in the beast can't stand the light, but those of us who fight our nature can be out in the sun for hours at a time. We are not immune to it though. Eventually, the rays will eat away at our skin like acid. I can go in and out of the sun for almost a whole day, taking an hour or two inside to look at clothes or something, but after three hours of direct light, I'm toast.

"I was at my limit when I brought you back. What you saw was nothing. When I placed you on the bed, my wings had burnt off. There wasn't any skin on my back—it was all gone and had eaten away to the bone. I almost died bringing you here."

"Oh!" I couldn't think of anything else to say. All of my anger and mistrust drained away. It didn't matter what happened before. Veronica would always protect me, and she'd proven that.

I smiled, noticing the beauty of the night. It was a wonder she was alive, considering she'd been born in the late eighteenth century. I couldn't imagine her in those times. She was a creature that transcended time as she held me captivated. Veronica was something special that walked into my life, and I would keep the promise I made to her in New Orleans. I'd bring her back into the light as well as discover the true meaning of the night.

20

CHAPTER TWENTY

My name is Brenna.

We stood outside The Black Rose in the new clothes Veronica had purchased last week. Once again I adjusted the red corset as it conformed to my body.

"I hate breaking these damn things in. It takes forever," I bitched.

"It looks wonderful on you." Veronica reassured me.

"Thanks."

I glanced down at the rest of the outfit. I wore a black mesh ballroom skirt and a black velvet top. The red corset went over the whole thing. Veronica chose to buy a white vinyl ball gown, which clung to every curve of her as well as squeaking when she walked.

Both of us wore flat black shoes. She wanted to get boots, but I talked her out of it, considering if she got blisters she'd heal, but I'd be stuck with them.

"Veronica, how are we going to get in? My ID is in New Orleans. It's not like I planned on coming to Boston."

"Not to worry," she grinned, her teeth elongating.

"Can we see some ID?" one of the three bouncers asked. He was shorter than the rest, pockmarked and had red curly hair. The look he gave us made me feel like dinner.

Veronica glanced at me, her eyes burning red a moment, and she giggled. She turned back to the bouncers and stared each of them in the eyes. The air grew thick as she took hold of their minds like fishes on a hook. The energy around her contracted. As she let them go, the atmosphere returned to normal.

"You don't see us. We're not here, just ghosts."

The bouncers went blank and let us pass. The redhead even opened the door as we strolled into the club without paying. I glanced back at the cashier and saw her vacant expression as well, and then she snapped out of it, asking the next customer for money. Veronica tugged on my arm, pulling me into a room off to the right, which had a dance floor with rainbow strobes lights and Industrial music playing. A few people jumped up and down to the beat. I curled my nose at it, hating the type of music the room played.

"You need to change now," Veronica said.

I laughed as if reshaping my aura were as easy as changing clothes. I didn't think Veronica understood how much concentration it took to get into the part. Once there, I could hold the ruse easier.

I nodded, focusing my aura. The energy expanded around me so I got a full sense of the room. I was in every corner at the same time. My nostrils flared as the familiar energy surged through me. The thrill of the hunt ignited in me as I realized how much I missed the façade. If there were any real vampires among the mix, they'd never suspect a thing. I'd entice the humans, making them my prey. Each one would love me, coming into my waiting arms, until—

"Brenna!" Veronica shook me out of my haze.

A snarl formed on my lips, but the urge left me as the coolness of Veronica's hand fell against my shoulder. The thoughts cleared from my mind, but the old longing to hunt still rippled through me.

"Are you all right?"

I nodded, scanning the incoming customers, wondering if they were vampires. It was strange because now that I deliberately projected the vampiric ruse, there was something missing, but I couldn't put my finger on it. Veronica had to be my guide in the situation.

"Are there others in the club?"

She looked across the main entryway and into a small salon where the dancers sat and drank. I followed her and took in the scant clothing of some of the patrons. One guy with frosted blond hair wore vinyl pants held up by leather-spiked suspenders. His nipples were pierced with inch long barbells. Next to him was a woman with long, braided brown hair. She wore a red velvet cloak that covered a red vinyl nurse's uniform. It was the third companion in the group Veronica pointed to.

"There, the one in the red miniskirt. She's one, and very old."

I spotted the vampire who faced us. The woman looked to be no older than twenty. Her hair was the color of a streaked sunset. She had a drink in her hand. I wondered how old she actually was. My shields wavered a moment as I lost my concentration, and it was then she stopped in mid-sentence and stared at Veronica and I. My breath caught in my throat. This was the test. If she found out, then I'd be bait, and Veronica would—well, I didn't know what would happen to her, but it'd be bad.

The other vampire raised her glass and motioned for us to join her. The gesture reminded me of the very same one I had used to acknowledge Veronica just two weeks ago. How fast things had changed.

Veronica looped her arm through mine as all the muscles tensed in my body. I felt like I had been spiked into the floor and there was no way anyone could move me.

Just relax. Don't let her sense your fear or she'll be curious. Let her think you're my child and just learning to be what you are. It'll explain a lot. Now smile, Veronica whispered in my mind.

I nodded internally, allowing my muscles to relax as we crossed the room. I plastered a huge smile on my face, hoping it would hide the uncertainty that burned inside me. I had no idea how long the ruse would work and my energy would remain smooth and not falter, revealing what I truly was.

"You must be new in the city," the other vampire said. Her voice held no hint of an accent. Her lips were as red as her miniskirt. The lipstick contrasted with the olive tone of her skin. The energy around her was ancient, older than Veronica. Outwardly, she was younger than I first thought—eighteen, sixteen even. Her eyes told a different story. This woman had seen centuries, millennia even.

"Yes," Veronica answered. "Raven thought this would be a good place to observe the meat."

The ancient vampire's gaze fell on me. Her mind sliced through mine. She knew everything about me in a second. I didn't think she sensed I was a phony, but assumed I'd just been turned because of the human-ness about me that she couldn't stand. She hated the cretins she fed on, fucking and playing with them. The image of the beast within her flashed in my mind. It was twisted, everything Veronica was not. This ancient one could not stay in the daylight more than half an hour or she'd ignite like dried wood. Her mind left an imprint as she withdrew from my thoughts. I assumed I'd passed the test because I was still breathing.

"Yes, this place has a certain atmosphere that draws many of us. It's neutral territory. We do not fight here, and many mortals are already marked, so you must be careful not to take one that is."

"We'll be careful. Come, Raven." Veronica tugged on my arm, steering me through a small passageway and into another dance room. This one played music I was more used to. Good old-fashioned goth.

Veronica grabbed a stool at a side bar and I sat next to her. She gazed around the room and then back at me. The muscles in her face relaxed. I could almost see the tiny hairs along her arms lying down.

"She's old. She's a bitch. She almost didn't buy you were just a youngling. I thought she'd tear you apart for a second."

"Maybe we should go then. I mean, if you think it's not working?"

"Nonsense. I think your disguise will work on many. Most others don't inspect minds unless you're considered a threat. I don't know why she did that to you. Those that are possessed by the beast can do strange things. Especially vampires that only crave power and domination. I didn't expect that she would do that. Most of the others couldn't care less about you.

They just want blood. She's right; this place has an atmosphere that draws others of my kind here. I wonder why? How did you know about this club, anyway?"

I grinned. "It was a frequent hang out of mine in college."

"I'm surprised you weren't picked off."

I hit her hard on the shoulder. "Hey!"

She laughed. Her laughter was genuine. It was the first time I'd known her to be completely comfortable in public.

Her hand came to rest on my knee. I glanced down at it, hoping there was something more to the gesture.

I traced the veins of her wrist, admiring all the differences about her, remembering when I first met her. The attraction I held for her was nothing sexual. She intrigued me more than anything. I deeply wanted to help her, but after seeing inside her soul, things had changed. I had changed. I caught myself falling in love. Veronica caught my finger with her other hand, applying some pressure to my knee with the other. Her eyes swirled, going from black to red to something in between. They pulled me in. They weren't hypnotic, just alluring. At first I assumed it was her other half close to the surface that made her eyes dance, but it was all the emotions surging through her. They overwhelmed her senses now that many of her walls had come down. So much had changed in such a short time, I didn't want to hurt her, but I wanted her.

I leaned in for a kiss, her breath hot upon my lips, but a song came over the speakers that drew my attention away from her.

The lyrics were about vampires dancing in a moonlit garden. I smirked and watched as people gathered on the small dance floor. I grabbed Veronica's hand, pulling her from the stool before she could protest. If she didn't want to dance, she'd have stopped me with a minute portion of her strength. She didn't. She came with me, joining the small throng of people. She looked at the others dancing, not knowing what the moves were. I laughed and gave myself over to the beat.

The fogger filled part of the club with smog as it mixed with the already thick cloud of cigarette smoke and sweating bodies. I twirled, ignoring the boning in the corset and the fact I wasn't able to breathe. It had been a long time since I just enjoyed the music. Opening my eyes, I checked on Veronica and saw she had also fallen into the beat.

Dancing in a goth club was not the bump and grind of regular clubs, nor was it the jumping of the rave scene. It was melodic and slow. The hands and body told a story as music filled the senses, caressing the insides, infiltrating the brain, and ruled for the duration of the song. I lost my balance a few times, but caught myself, falling into a belly dance step. It didn't matter what I looked like. No one watched me.

I shifted through one song and into the next, as the number of people dwindled from the dance floor. The beat of the next song moved up a notch. It was harder to find a rhythm in it. Some dancers decided to take their one-man show to the top of the stage or inside a small cage on the outskirts on the dance floor. The ancient vampire set her drink down and came to the floor, her movements pointed and exact. She'd heard this music before and knew how to manipulate it and those around her. She pulled the tune into her, drawing attention to herself, and drew focus from those humans in the crowd who might become her next meal. I was spun into her web, but Veronica grabbed my hand and gave me a sharp yank. I looked into my companion's eyes, finding the strength not to lose myself again.

I stretched my arms out to her, welcoming her into my dance space, but she shook her head. I wasn't going to let her get away. I moved within the beat until I was inches from her, encircling my arms around her waist and then pulling her to me so our breasts touched. The coolness of the vinyl slipped beneath my fingertips, as I struggled to get a grip on her. Veronica tensed a moment, but I never took my eyes from hers until our bodies moved in time.

One of her hands traced my shoulder blades, igniting my hunger for her. Her nails traveled along the back of my neck, then the side, passing over the punctures she'd given me. It seemed my immune system had taken to healing them fast. Maybe some of her ability rubbed off on me. More likely the wounds were never bad to begin with. We danced together through the rest of the song and into another. I was losing my breath and about to suggest that we stop or at least I sit down, when she tensed against me. This time it was not because I had touched her. It was something else. I heard a low growl building in her throat. Her other half had broken free.

Her nails cut small holes through my corset. The sharp pain of flesh tearing as her claws went into my skin seared me, but I held my tongue. I tried to turn around, but she wouldn't let me go.

"Veronica," I whispered.

She didn't hear me. The muscles in her face twitched.

"Veronica!" Still nothing.

I sighed and gathered my mental strength. I hoped she was distracted enough not to have shields in her mind or I would never be able to get through. I would be torn to shreds before she realized what happened.

Veronica! I yelled, finding a small opening in her barriers.

Her beast jumped once my thoughts penetrated her mind. Then it retreated and Veronica let me go, realizing what she had done. She backed away an inch or so, and I was able to turn and see what had set her off.

A man leaned against a pole wearing black skin-tight pants and a black leather vest that exposed his pale chest. He had short spiked black hair and a silver cross dangling in his right ear. He was familiar somehow. I had seen him before, but not in Boston. I thought a moment. I had seen him in New Orleans, right before I spotted Veronica. He had invaded my thoughts, demanding my attention. I knew when I looked at him. He was something different, and he had let me have Veronica. He was another vampire. That was why I recognized him.

"Veronica, he's okay. I'm sure he means no harm."

She took a step forward, not taking her eyes from him. "That's Devon."

I stared at her in disbelief. He was not the same man who had seduced me. The man I had fallen for was blond, all-American looking. It couldn't be him.

"How could it be Devon? There's no way. The man I slept with was beefier, had blond hair. How could he change into, well, thirty pounds lighter, shorter hair, all in a matter of a week?"

"You know we're shape shifters. Did it ever occur to you we could change our appearance as a matter of will? Damn him!" Veronica walked past me and headed for Devon.

The temperature rose in the room as her anger seethed into every corner. Tension ignited in the club. I caught a look on the face of the ancient vampiress. She was salivating, waiting for a fight, but I remembered what she'd said. This place was neutral ground. Devon was only here to provoke Veronica. If she made a mistake, it could be fatal. I threw up my hands, not wanting to get between two vampires, but that didn't matter because I already was. I ran over, trying to block Veronica's rage from my head, but it came, pounding on me like a man ramming a hammer onto a railroad spike.

"She'll be mine, Ronnie. Just you wait," he smirked as I walked into the conversation.

I glanced down and saw Veronica's hand ready to slash his face. I threw on a smile and joined the discussion. "It's so nice of you to come by, Devon. If you don't mind, we were just leaving," I said while staring at Veronica. "Remember this is neutral ground," I chided her.

She stopped her hand in mid-swipe, centimeters from his face. She looked at me and then back at him. She fought to gain control. After a moment, she took in a deep breath and regained her composure. "You're right, Brenna. This place is a little too crowded for my liking. Shall we go?"

I nodded and took her arm. We got a few steps before I heard Devon say something to me. I turned back to him. "What did you say?"

He grinned, exposing his fangs. "I said it's a great act, but I saw through your guise even back in New Orleans. You tried so hard to be one of us, but all you are is her lackey. She doesn't love you. She's incapable of the emotion. Besides, we both know she isn't a good fuck."

I launched myself out of Veronica's grasp and hit Devon hard across the face. My knuckles impacted with his nose. Blood appeared in a trickle on his upper lip. He looked at me with a shocked expression and tried to come after me, but Veronica turned around, confronting him.

"Now remember, Devon. This is neutral territory. No attacking others of your own kind."

Devon's pale complexion grew blotchy as he tried to hold in his anger. "She's not my kind. She's just meat."

Veronica looked at him. "There are others here who would tell you different."

She pointed to the ancient vampire in the back. Her arms were crossed over her chest. Everything about her was calm and collected, except her index finger on her right hand tapped impatiently against her wrist, one long black nail turned into a talon. When Devon noticed the ancient vampire he backed off. I looked and knew she'd helped both of us, but now she wanted us to leave. I nodded my thanks, and Veronica and I both walked out of the club and down the street, waiting for a cab to stop and take us back to Boston.

Once we grabbed a cab, we both sat silent in the back seat. My vampire wasn't mad. She was lost, brooding, wondering how Devon had found us, what he was going to do next. I tried not to think about it. All I wanted to do was get out of the corset and take care of the seeping wounds Veronica had inflicted. Blood oozed down my back and stuck to my shirt. I didn't care. I just wanted to wash up.

Finally, we returned to the house. Veronica used her mental powers on the cab driver and got out of paying the bill. I waited as she pulled up a loose brick and got a spare key to unlock the door. Once inside, I went up into the bedroom to change. I found myself staring into the night as cars moved by on Beacon Street and college students talked amongst themselves as they came back from clubs or bars. I realized what kind of a world they lived in and what type of situation I'd stepped into. No matter how long I lived my life, I was never going to be the same. I was always going to be on the outside looking in because I truly knew what the other side of reality was.

21

CHAPTER TWENTY-ONE

My name is Veronica.

Brenna walked up the rotting wooden stairs and into the bedroom, but all I could do was stand in the doorway, a slight breeze licking at my back, chilling the vinyl outfit I wore. I ignored the chill, letting my body temperature adjust itself. It'd been a shock to see Devon, his looks intact even after I had nearly taken his eye and half his face. Even as I thought of this, the anger creaked in my bones as the beast in me struggled to break free from its resting place, but it was not going to get out this time. When I brought Brenna up here, I had known that it was inevitable Devon would eventually find us.

We could run, each of us going our separate ways, trying to stave off my Master. Devon would find both of us, and he would force the other to watch as we were tortured. No, it was no use to run. The standoff had to be here and now.

Cocking my head, I heard Brenna moving upstairs. I listened to her steady heartbeat as it raced life through her fragile and tiny veins. I yearned to take her into my arms, but I didn't want to feed on her. I just wanted to hold her so she could warm my frigid heart. The thought of anything happening to her turned my brain cold and drove me into a frenzy. I didn't know when Devon would strike next, but it would be soon. I sighed, thinking of the ancient vampire at The Black Rose.

She knew Brenna was not a vampire. She knew that from the scent of her. I had to say something to ease Brenna's fears. I did believe her camouflaging worked, but the ancient vampire was too old. I thought maybe it would work on Devon, but he already knew she was mortal, so he would have made the effort to penetrate her facade. I couldn't be sure if he was too old as well.

I mounted the stairs, thinking of something to say to Brenna. She'd reaffirmed my heart wasn't dead. She gave me the hope I could still go on living, finding some type of beauty in a human world, considering I was no longer part of it. I climbed halfway up the stairs and suddenly wondered how long it would be before the old boards would not support my weight. I glanced up at the ceiling, noticing the chipping flakes of paint, and the little sag underneath the light fixture. How long would it be before it all came crashing down? I didn't care. Edmund had been right, this place wasn't haunted. The only ghosts it held were in my memory. I was the haunted one who needed to be free of an old memory. I didn't need this place anymore.

I smiled as I reached the top of the stairs. I'd put it on the market. I didn't need the money, not really. Maybe then this house could see life back in it once again. Brenna and I would go away, probably back to New Orleans, where I knew she was happiest. I didn't care where we went. I'd spend the rest of my days with her, even as she grew old and then finally died in my arms.

I walked into my old bedroom, no longer afraid to think of the awful things that had happened so many years ago. Brenna peered out the window down at the street. The streetlights caught her hair. It was dark and luxurious as it fell across her neck. I moved slightly, admiring her beauty when she turned and noticed me.

I smiled at her and waited for her to decide what to do. She was so peaceful, her expression so serene, I didn't want to break the fragile moment. I wanted it to go on forever until there were no more nights and no more days, just time blending and stopping. Until

Devon was just a memory and there was nothing else left between us except the space in the room, and then she would be in my arms.

22

CHAPTER TWENTY-TWO

My name is Brenna.

Veronica stood in the doorway waiting for something. Brought out of my thoughts, I knew someone was there, but I couldn't sense who it was at first. My energy had been drained from keeping my shields up at the club and having the ancient vampire rifle though my thoughts. I imagined if I'd been like Veronica my energy would have remained intact, but I was only human.

"Are you all right?" Veronica asked.

My forehead wrinkled as I realized how she kept asking me that question. She seemed to think I was some type of porcelain doll, when only I knew how breakable I was. Combined with my mental exhaustion and the events of the night, I didn't need her doting on me as if I were a needy child.

"I'm fine," I muttered. "Can you please leave me alone a while?" My voice contained a coldness I didn't feel. I wanted it quiet so my mind could have time to recharge. Veronica's presence vibrated against my brain like an insect in a spider's web. I knew how I felt and I didn't expect her to understand. I couldn't keep her out any more than I could block out my own thoughts. She was everywhere.

I stayed, staring out the window and not knowing what else to do. I couldn't see her because it was too dark, but I knew she left. The floorboards groaned as she retreated somewhere else in the house. I sighed as my heart sank into my stomach.

Damn it, I thought and went after Veronica.

I might be in a bad mood, but I shouldn't be taking it out on her. I checked the other rooms upstairs and then downstairs, but she was still nowhere to be found. The door wasn't open, and the house was silent. I didn't have the strength to expand my mind to see if she was in the basement or even some hidden attic. I was not going to go exploring anymore. It was old, and normal houses and old sites didn't creep me out, but this place did. I didn't know why. I shivered at the thought of being left alone here. It was so lonely and deserted. One could tell no one had lived here for a long time.

The house had become an entity unto itself, holding sadness I had never seen in an abandoned building, and I had been in plenty. The whole place needed life, and in a bustling city like Boston, I was surprised the homeless hadn't decided to find their way in here and make a home. But no, there was no one, just the occasional visit from Veronica, and it seemed she rarely came to this part of the country. I assumed the only reason she brought me here was to get away from Devon, and it was the only place she could think of. An instinct to go home. My instincts told me that whenever she came here something in the back of her mind told her there would be a warm fire and a family to greet her. But whenever she opened the door, all she was met with was a looming emptiness. She thought this place to be haunted because it held so many bad memories. From the first moment I woke here, I knew there was nothing in the building save a few termites gnawing away at the wood. Even they were scarce. All that lived here were ghosts of the past.

I sighed and sat down on a sheet-covered couch. A cloud of dust engulfed me as I did.

Poor Veronica, I thought.

She had no one, didn't know who to trust in a world that was a lie to her. Now I had told her to take a hike. I really knew how to make things right.

I don't know how long I sat there, but I finally decided to lie down and the next thing I knew someone tapped me on the shoulder. I opened my eyes and saw Veronica smiling down at me. I smiled back and got up slowly. This time as I moved the sharp pains from the wounds she gave me ran up my back. I cried out, holding my back.

"Are you all right?"

That question again. My gaze hardened. I didn't need to hear that at the moment, but I didn't want her going anywhere either. "No, I need to get this damn corset off."

"I thought you would have had it off by now."

"Yeah, well, I went looking for you after you left the room, and you were nowhere to be found. Just the empty house. I came down here to wait, but I guess I fell asleep."

"Here, I'll help you. Stand up."

I did as I was told, the mesh material of my skirt scraping against my legs. Veronica's arms came around me, as she began to unbuckle the front. It was too tight, so she had to move to the back and undo the lacings. She had a hard time undoing the knot. Each time she pulled on it, it drew me closer to her body until I was only inches from her. As each string came looser more oxygen rushed to my brain. Finally she was done, but I lost my balance and fell back into her. She caught me, her arms coming up under mine. Her fingers brushed against the sides of my breasts.

My nipples hardened as she removed her hands from my chest. I caught her hand and held it over my breast, so she could feel the nipple underneath it. Her fingers lingered a moment too long, and then she backed away.

I turned to her, wondering what she was doing. She could read my emotions, just as well as I could read hers. She knew how much I yearned to be with her.

"Don't tease me," she said, her voice husky with hunger of some kind.

I took a step forward. She didn't know if she could trust me. She assumed I was manipulating her just as Devon had. As the space grew between us, some of the walls she had torn down were thrown back up around her mind. She didn't want to be hurt again. I wasn't going to hurt her. I wanted to show her how sorry I was, wanted to indulge in the desires which had been rising between us, and for the first time give myself to someone without having to worry about what they thought of me. She knew who I was, what I was.

I crossed the few feet between us. I raised my hand and traced the line of her jaw. I leaned in, touching my lips to hers, feeling the softness of them as if they were silk. I kissed her, but she didn't respond. She was as a statue next to me, and I couldn't seem to raise her passion. I separated my lips from hers, cupping her face in my hand, all as she looked at me with a dead stare. The thing on the outside was just an automaton as she assumed I would take my pleasure out on her body while she retreated inside her mind. I didn't want that.

Trust me, please, I whispered inside her mind.

I poured my feelings into the plea as I let it reach all throughout her thoughts. I let her see my pain and regret for pushing her away earlier that night. I only wanted to be alone for a little while to sort things out in my head, to recharge. I needed her.

She stirred, blinking, seeing me in front of her instead of being the robot she had been before. Applying pressure to her breast, I massaged it in a circle through the vinyl. I pressed my lips to hers and this time she reacted. Her other hand came around my back, pushing me into her, until my skin stuck to the vinyl. My tongue snaked in between her lips as my hands moved at the back of her dress trying to find the zipper. Heat rose in me as I found myself getting wet, dripping. My tongue traced the outline of her teeth. They were like mine and then my tongue wrapped around her canines as they extended. I pressed my mouth harder against hers as they descended, only to show her I wasn't afraid. With this I heard the stays in the corset rip and it fell down around me feet. I disengaged myself from Veronica and looked at her. Her hand had become a talon and shredded the laces.

"Oops," I giggled.

She laughed and caught the underside of my chin with one of her claws, tracing the side of my face as her finger went from bone to flesh in a matter of milliseconds. The sensation of her morphing skin against mine was peculiar, more like a moth's wing against my cheek. She moved down my chin and then traced the neckline of my shirt, teasing, before slipping her hand underneath the garment and cupping my breast. The nipple firmed immediately, growing harder than it ever had before as she tweaked it between her thumb and index finger. I closed my eyes, moaning, growing wetter with each simple caress.

I pushed against her, finding her slender neck and began nipping at the skin, bringing it between my teeth. Biting and sucking, I traced small circles on Veronica's skin with my tongue. My heartbeat quickened until it was in tune with hers. I lingered at her throat a moment as my hands found her zipper and unzipped her dress, and then I found her flesh, her bare ass now exposed. My hand moved over her cheeks, feeling the firmness of the tissue. Her fingers were now at the waistband of my skirt, and as one hand worked my nipples, the other found my moist, warm clit. The coolness of her fingers caused me to jump, moving against her. And then she had me, massaging my clit in a circle while all I could do was hold onto her ass, clenching the firm flesh as I waited for release. That did not come, as she worked me to the point of orgasm and let me go. I licked at her neck, working up to her mouth once more, letting my tongue caress her fangs. Her lips were waiting to be used. I wanted them used on me. I yearned to feel her fangs cutting into me, anywhere. I wanted her to go down on me, licking and nipping at me. I desired pain and pleasure all rolled into one. I craved sheer abandon and loss of self, and she could give it to me. All I had to do was give myself over to her.

Her hands moved up and came under my shirt, lifting it off of me. The chill of the room hit me as I stood half naked. She moved behind me, her nails scratching along my flesh as she did, sending shivers racing along my already heated skin. Her hands traced my shoulder blades, lightly pinching the skin as she massaged my muscles and bones, easing the tension out of them, moving down each vertebra until there were no knots left to speak of. Her tongue tickled the back of my neck as she traveled along the ridge of my shoulder blade, working down as her hands pushed down my skirt. Her hands came around me, gripping my breasts. She squeezed them hard enough to leave bruises, enough to elicit a moan out of me as I pressed my ass into her cunt. She was as wet as I was.

Her hands sought entrance as she applied pressure for me to spread my legs. One hand found my hard node. The other grew longer, but retained its fleshiness and moved inside of me. First one finger slid in, and then two until she had three fingers inside of me. She nipped at my shoulders and the base of my neck while all I could do was hold on for the ride as she took me to release, to a point where everything flooded over me and I didn't know where the world began or ended. Sensations like crashing waves pulled me under and drenched my brain. It was only she and I, her cold hands inside of my warm, wet walls. I lost myself to the pleasure of moaning and writhing within her grasp, but even as this happened I felt incomplete. I needed more of her.

She worked me for a few more moments and then let me go. I turned around, gazing at her breathlessly. My body glistened with sweat, and I only craved to bring her the same kind of pleasure she had brought me.

She released me and I knelt down, parting her with my hands, finding her clit with my tongue, licking and suckling on her like a kitten, tasting her salty juices, using my tongue to work her. She bucked against me as my fingers pressed the walls inside of her. They began to contract around me, as she came, and I kept her there. Waves of ecstasy moved from her into me as my mind was open to her feelings. It doubled the pleasure as well as the fun because I tapped into her emotions. The echoes of her pleasure rode my mind, but still an emptiness remained inside of her. I didn't know what it was.

"Brenna. Enough. Please," she groaned.

I didn't stop. I kept her going. Redoubling my efforts my tongue flicked faster over her hood. Her fingers wrapped in my hair, keeping my head locked to her until finally she pushed me away. I landed hard as my tailbone connected with the floor. I looked up at her. Not a drop of sweat was on her body, but her eyes showed how much she had enjoyed my manipulations. She slumped to the floor, and just stayed there, the coolness of the wood having no effect on her. Her hair hung over her face and hid her expression. I crawled to her, wondering what profound sadness still lived in her as my mind caught the emotion.

I moved the hair out of her eyes and saw thin red tear streaks on her cheeks. I wiped one away and brought her into my arms. She sobbed, wetting my shoulder.

"You're crying, love. Why are your tears red?" I whispered.

"Because I'm a vampire who sacrificed her soul. My kind is tainted. And you're so pure." Veronica touched the side of my cheek and smiled. I saw the pain in her eyes and the hope. This had been the first time she'd given herself to a partner. I was the one who had shown her that love didn't come from a man ramming a dick into her cunt. I nodded and let her cry until she looked up at me and smiled.

I leaned in, kissing her soft mouth, cupping her face in my hands again. In that moment, I wanted her to know how much she meant to me. The feeling couldn't be expressed in words, even with me touching her mind. Veronica needed something to warm her from the inside out, the ultimate thing she could get from anyone.

"Take blood from me," I whispered.

Her eyes grew round at my suggestion. "No."

Tracing her neck, I felt her almost non-existent heartbeat underneath. "I'm not afraid."

"You should be. I could rip you apart if I chose to."

"You won't. Besides, it'll show you how much I care for you, making this a more memorable evening."

"What we just did? Fucking each other to release anxiety! I mean, it was great, but I'm not going bite you because you want to experience the thrill."

She got up from the floor. I followed.

"Is that what we were just doing? Rutting like animals? I thought it was something more than that. I thought it might be more enjoyable if you had your fangs buried in my neck. I'm not looking for some fucking thrill. If that were the case, I would have stayed with Devon and let him rape me, using me over and over again until I didn't know the difference between surrender and love. Does that sound familiar, Veronica?"

I couldn't believe she thought I was some groupie just wanting to have my blood drawn like it was some big thing. I suggested it only because I wanted to make her happy. She clutched her head and screamed in frustration. She turned and came to slap me, her fingers turned into talons. Veronica stopped inches from my face. I didn't flinch as she came at me.

"Go ahead, Veronica. Become just what Devon wants you to be, a killer without a conscience, a thing unable to feel love or pain. Go ahead. I won't blame you or haunt you as the memory of your sister does. If you do, remember one thing. I'm not like Devon. I never put any demands on you. All I wanted to do was to help. And if you kill me, you'll kill the only semblance of salvation you have within yourself. So go ahead." I turned my neck so her talons could have a clean shot. I waited. Nothing happened.

Instead, I found myself in her embrace. Her fingers returned to normal as she stroked my flesh as if she truly cherished me, or like I was an object she had not seen in many years.

"I'm sorry," she whispered.

"It's okay. I'd never hurt you intentionally. You know that."

"I know."

I held her and in that instant she was not the vampire I knew, strong and proud, she was the frightened girl who had been seduced by a fiend so many years ago. She was the girl who had been thwarted out of a loving marriage by a monster and had given up her life in blood and pain. In that moment, she and I would never be separated, no matter what happened to me. If I died tomorrow she would be at my side. She would protect me, always. It would be she and I until I drew my last breath.

Her hand came up and held the other side of my neck, pushing it to the side, so she could have a better angle. I held my breath and waited for the pain, but it wasn't bad. She took great care in making sure her entrance was swift and painless. I drew in my breath through my teeth and then I felt her suckling, heard the sucking sounds as she drew in my life. My hands traveled down to her nether region and began to work her once again as she bled me. Each of us began to move in time, our breath quickening along with one another. At the moment of her release, I was lightheaded and growing slightly cold, but it was then as she withdrew from me that we came in each other's arms.

23

CHAPTER TWENTY-THREE

My name is Veronica.

The smell of blood drew me into consciousness. Shock hit me when I opened my eyes. The once stark white sheet that used to cover the couch was now stained red. The smell of familiar blood wafted into my nose. I'd tasted it before. It was Brenna's. Droplets of it had dribbled on the floor as if a child had run rampant with a bucket of paint. My jaw hardened. My teeth sharpened all at once, leaving me with a furrow of fangs. The edges shredded my gums, and blood welled up inside my mouth. Unconsciously, I licked my lips as the thick liquid slid down my throat.

My fingernails hardened into black talons until they were six inches long, the full extent of their length. I got up slowly from my resting place listening, for any sound of Brenna, but I was met with utter silence. Nothing breathed inside the house, except the ghosts, which lingered within my mind, but even those past whispers were silent now. I scanned the room with all my senses for any sign of Brenna but found none. I looked down at the dribbles. I touched the tip of my tongue. I tasted Brenna and caught a whiff of her fear mixed in with the crimson liquid.

An image flashed in my mind as the blood hit my system, and I experienced things from Brenna's perspective. Something grabbed me around the throat so I couldn't scream. I looked up into Devon's deep eyes, my will paralyzed as he clamped down on my throat. His grin was wicked as he picked me up and brought me to his lips. Twin surges of fire erupted in my neck. I flailed against him, kicking him. He continued to drain me, and as I struggled against him his talons raked across my arms and he snarled, digging further into my throat, taking in my life. I was cold and blackness descended.

I caught Brenna's fleeting thoughts of me, but there was nothing she could do to wake me, even though I was feet away, because I was wrapped in the sleep of death.

I growled low in my throat, allowing my vocal cords to constrict so I became more beast than human. I blamed myself for not protecting her, not even with my strength could I save her. Edmund had been right. Devon knew where I was, and now he had the one I cherished more than my own life. My form shifted, able to support me on all fours as I ran through the house. I was neither wolf nor large hunting cat. I was something in between, something that only could be compared to a hellhound. I ran into the kitchen, following the trail of blood. It stopped at the edge of the counter. I flicked my now forked tongue out, catching a drop. Devon had only been here within minutes of me waking, probably just stirring from his own death trance a half an hour or so before mine.

On the counter was an object. Momentarily I reverted back to a standing position and saw a knife dripping with blood stabbed through a tarot card. I gave the knife a yank, but it wouldn't budge. I tugged again and the blade broke. The other half stayed embedded in the wooden countertop. I looked down at the thing it had pinned. It was a tarot card from Edmund's deck, which I had shuffled a week before. Through the blood I saw the image underneath. It was not just any card. It was the Death Card.

I growled again at the thought of Devon touching Brenna. I looked at the card once again and knew where he had taken her. I didn't know how he had achieved it, but the one place I thought she would be safe from him had become her crypt when it had once been her haven. I tossed the remnants of the knife aside and ran out of the house, not bothering to open the door. Rather, I crashed through it. I didn't feel the two-inch oak splinters that embedded in my skin, nor did I care that the four-inch thick wooden door would have to be replaced. I raced up Beacon Street, past all of the college dorms and Boston Garden, and then across Charles Street, uncaring of the honking horns, or of the metal contraption I hit. I later learned I'd dented the side of a garbage truck. None of these things could stop me as I made my way toward Winter Street, toward Brenna. I shook off the daze the impact had given me and moved quicker than I cared to think about, growling at unwary humans as they crossed my path. I splashed through the Frog Pond in the middle of the Boston Common and came to Park Street Station.

I stopped at the edge of Tremont Street as I heard the screams of those passengers just coming or going down from the subway. Baring my teeth at them, I knew they'd never seen the likes of me except in their nightmares. I caught the scents of all of them: one had just had sex, one was close to death, and another young redhead had her period. All of their perfumes mixed in my nose, but I didn't care.

I looked both ways, noticing there was no traffic, and leapt across the road in one fluid movement. Landing on the brick lined street, I kept on going, running though the already broken glass doors and toward the elevator. Then I stopped.

Devon would be expecting me to come through the main door and maybe he had set a trap. No, I couldn't go that way, as it might endanger Brenna even more. I regained some of my composure and calmed a little. My anger still boiled under my skin, and my muscles rippled as I changed form. Taking my human appearance, I kept the talons and sharpened maw. I backed out of the hallway and pushed open the broken front door, the tinkling sound of glass reminding me of church bells as it hit the brick sidewalk. I walked backward out of the building and surveyed the surroundings. There was an alley, but it was not on this side of the building. I raced back up Winter Street onto Tremont Street when I saw a small alley hidden next to a church. This was how I could get in. I saw the fire escape leading up the side of the building.

My claws sank into the bricks and I hurdled over the gate, allowing my wings to shape, as I was airborne. Then I flapped up along the building until I was at the fire escape of the Boston Tearoom. I landed as softly as I could, pulling my energy around me so Devon would not sense my arrival. I placed my hand on the door and pushed. Wood splintered on the other side as I broke the bar that kept it sealed.

Shit. He must have heard me. My surprise is ruined, but it doesn't matter. I have to get to her in time.

I rammed into the door. It opened and I tumbled down the stairs, landing hard on my ass.

I got up slowly, catching the faint scent of sage. I tasted the remnants of it on my tongue as the ashes lingered in the air. This place had been cleansed recently to keep evil things out. I snickered. Little good it did. My ears perked up when I heard a faint moaning, a slight beating. I recognized the sound of that drum. It was Brenna and she was still alive, but barely. I didn't have much time.

I moved down a narrow hallway and found Brenna and Devon in the main room where I had my reading done the week before. There, in a pool of blood, was Brenna. Devon leaned over her, still in human form. He sucked at her neck greedily, trying to lap at the little blood left in her body. The pallor of her skin reflected the candles, which burned next to a small shrine to the Virgin Mary in the corner of the room.

"Get off of her," I growled, my vocal cords shifting to normal once again.

It took Devon a moment before he acknowledged me. He stole one last sip and then looked up at me. His eyes were black, burning red in the middle. There was no humanity left in him. He held Brenna close while wiping her blood off his mouth with the back of his hand.

"I knew you'd come just in time," he purred.

I took a step forward, but he stopped me as one of his talons curled around her throat.

"Tsk, tsk, Ronnie. One more step and she'll die forever with no hope of being brought back. I'm sure you wouldn't want to see that, now would you?"

"No," I whispered.

I looked down at Brenna and saw how fragile she was. How innocent. She wanted so much to be normal, but it just wasn't in her to fit into a world made of stupid rules. That was why she pretended to be a vampire. She thought she could get away from the rules, but not everything is breakable. Her fate caught up to her, and she became tangled up in the web of my life, my destiny. Tears poured from my eyes as I looked at her, wanting her to be so far away from here, back in the heat and heaviness of New Orleans where she could still pretend to be whatever she wanted. My heart broke as I saw her there dying on the floor, her life now imbibed by Devon.

"You love her, don't you?" he asked, completely baffled by the thought that I actually felt some emotion. He never truly loved me when he thought to marry me years ago. I was just another conquest. "This just gets better and better."

"Why? Do you find it so hard to believe? Just because you don't have a heart doesn't mean I don't." I hissed.

"Oh, I could not care less about my heart. No, Ronnie, I was just saying this gets better because if I had known how much you cared for this mortal then I'd have done this ages ago just to torment you. As it is, this whole time has been wonderful. And Brenna, she's delicious, but I'm afraid she's dying, and I'm late for a dinner date."

He glanced one more time at Brenna and then put her down, letting her head thump against the hardwood floor. Her skull cracked from the impact. I moved then and gathered her up in my arms as she grew colder.

"You're going to let her die? You can't just leave her."

"It's not up to me anymore. It's your decision. You can let her die or bring her back. Either way you'll have the guilt of her demise on your conscience for the rest of your indentured life, and then you'll realize everything I told you was right and you'll beg me to take you back." He paused and fingered a few of the cards on Edmund's table. He drew one and looked at it, smirking. Then I felt his hot breath on the back of my neck as his cold talons encircled my throat.

"Then, you'll wish for the mercy I'd have shown you if you had come back to me willingly. All of these games try my patience. The next time I won't be so fooled as to let you out of my sight. You'll be starved, emaciated, your blood eating away at you before I let you feed. And then in between I'll make sure you never have enough to heal properly. In time these pretty features will be scarred, with maggots and worms crawling inside of your skin, and not just your face and neck this time, this time inside your whole body. Oh yes, you're not going to get away from me that easily." He breathed in my ear and his forked tongue caressed the side of my face. I tried to pull away, but he held me in place.

"Remember, I'll be seeing you."

With that, he was gone. I assumed he went out the way I came in because I didn't hear the elevator nor did I hear any doors open. He just vanished. And I knew it wasn't over. No, everything had just begun.

I held Brenna close to me, pressing my fingers to her seeping wounds. Tears freely flowed from my eyes. For the first time in a long time they came, as I had no walls encasing anything in me. Everything I was, beast and all, cried out for the rape of this innocent, for the taking of a life. Ronnie surprised me and I even felt her sadness. Strange, because I thought she didn't feel any kind of positive emotion. I wondered what had changed. I posed the question.

This human sees us for what we are. She has grown on me, my beast answered and then retreated. I dared not ask anything else since I doubted I would get an answer. Still it was something to ponder.

My hand hovered over Brenna's chest as I felt for her pulse, but my hearing wasn't wrong. With each beat her heart struggled to pump the last trickle through its arteries. Her skin grew colder, losing body temperature as she plunged into death. I swore to myself I wouldn't bring her into the life I had led. She would not become a monster. She would not end up like me.

"Who says she'll be a monster?" I looked up at the voice and found Edmund standing in the doorway. Through my tears I wondered how long he had been standing there. The more I looked at him, the more I realized I saw the hallway right through him. I hugged Brenna close to me as if trying to protect her from the specter, but she was already beyond my protection.

"Why do you say that?" I asked Edmund, the ghost or whatever he was. I didn't care if he read my mind. I needed to know what was in store for Brenna.

Edmund walked into the room. I noticed the energy around him rippled as though he were coming through space and time to be here, to help. As much as I wanted to know how he did it, and what he truly was, at this point I didn't dare ask. Brenna was slipping away.

Edmund passed his hand over Brenna, seeing when Death would claim her.

"She's not gone, and you know she made her choice the moment she came onto this plane. If you think meeting her was an accident, you're wrong; just as you meeting Devon, or meeting the old gypsy in the park, were not accidents. She knew when she came this was going to happen. We even discussed it when she was here. She knew something from the dark would bring her into the light."

"I'd be condemning her to darkness. To live like I am. Forsaken by God. Forever to be a demon."

Edmund shook his head. "Have you ever asked her what she believes? Maybe she doesn't believe in God the way you do. Maybe she sees the world through the eyes of one who accepts all creatures. Maybe a Goddess, even. You've seen this representation from the painting on the wall, of one who accepts. She sent you love the day you walked in here." Edmund gestured toward the painting on the wall.

I followed his outstretched hand. The woman was no longer on the wall, but standing in front of me with her arms outstretched.

"It's not possible," I whispered.

"You're not possible. Vampires are only in books, yet you're here. Why can't she be real? Why can't a friend reach out from beyond the grave to help a person he cared about? Maybe even angels and devils are one and the same. Anything is possible. Even a condemned vampire finding the light, turning away from the darkness. Try it, and save both of you."

With that, Edmund started to vanish.

"Wait, you're dead. What will I tell Brenna?"

He smiled faintly. "She'll know. Besides she'll find arrangements have already been made. She'll be able to keep the Tearoom running far longer than I can. Besides, she'll have a good business partner. Take care of her for me." With that, he was gone.

I gazed back over at the mural and the robed Goddess was back among her pillars of stone with a saddened expression on her face, as though she knew Edmund had passed on. I shuddered and then looked down at Brenna. What did she believe? Was Edmund right: was this her destiny? Did she know? I couldn't answer those questions without being able to talk with her and to do that I had to bring her back to life. I had no choice. How could I give up the one I truly loved?

"All right little one, if it's what you came here for, then so be it." I repositioned her so her lips touched my neck. Praying it wasn't too late I opened a gash in my throat. The warmth and stickiness of my blood welled up, seeping out upon her lips.

I locked my eyes with the Goddess on the wall and begged with all my might for her to send Brenna back to me. I needed her with me forever. I prayed for forgiveness for all of the sins I had committed over the years, for killing my sister and my parents. I asked for all their blood to be washed from my hands and for their ghosts to leave my house. I kept the house because I thought it was my obligation, but now I realized it was just a thing I didn't need. It was a place of wood and brick that held old memories. My family had moved on and had already forgiven my sins. It was I who had to forgive myself. Just because I had become the thing I was didn't mean I had to live my life in the shadow of that evil. That was what everything boiled down to: the final revelation of self, when all masks were off completely. It didn't matter if it was a god or a goddess on a wall, as long as it was something above that forgave.

Brenna's lips moved slowly against my neck, suckling like a newborn kitten.

My prayers had been answered. I had not lost the true thing I loved. She was going to be with me forever and always. I sighed as she began to tug on me harder. Her hand came up, encircling my waist, the other pushing against my neck to latch onto the wound more securely. She took mouthful after mouthful of what I had. I didn't care that I grew cold, that my heart slowed down, that she was taking too much. I didn't care because all the weight lifted off of me. I was free to fly with her beyond the mortal coil, and be with her in whatever realm she chose. Soon, I realized that to do that I had to teach her and show her the ways of our kind. I had to pry her off of me.

When I did look into her eyes, they were not black from hunger like all newborns of our kind. They were the clear, human eyes she had died with. The only things that hinted at her otherworldliness were the silver flecks dancing in her pupils like a kaleidoscope. I smiled to myself as I looked at the newborn, for a miracle had truly happened. A new vampire had been born this night, and she was like none the world had ever seen.

24

CHAPTER TWENTY-FOUR

My name is Brenna.

I took a breath, forcing myself to inhale. Somehow I had to prove I was truly alive, that nothing had changed, but everything was different. The air in my lungs tasted funny, particles of old sage lingered in the air as they stuck to the tiny air sacs in my lungs. I distinguished between the particles of dog dander as well as the regular household dust built up in the environment. All of this by taste and smell alone.

Opening my eyes, I tried to rid my mouth of the taste of stale blood. Then something caught my attention. My heartbeat was off. It was slower than it had been before. As I thought about it, it sped up and returned to its normal rhythm. My eyes focused, taking in the light. Everything was a myriad of colors, rainbows reflected off the pictures on the wall. I scanned the room, my gaze settling on the Saturn mural on the ceiling. Suddenly the mural was in 3-D with the shooting stars grazing the other planets and the rings of Saturn actually rotating. I blinked and the mural was flat, just paint on plaster.

I looked around the rest of the room and saw the transparent figures of ghosts leaning against the walls. Most of the spirits I didn't know. One I saw wore a leather apron and held a hammer. I surmised he was the shoemaker who once inhabited the Tearoom. He looked upon me and smiled, then walked toward the rear of the Tearoom and vanished. I thought it odd to see him, but it was the other specter sitting in Edmund's leather office chair who made my heart stop beating as I stared at it, or him, the ghost of Edmund. He was transparent at first, but then became solid. I smiled at him and knew somehow he had saved me. He nodded, still reading my mind, and then turned in the chair, picking up his deck of cards and pulling one out. He held it up. It was the Universe, a card that showed new beginnings, that anything was possible, that there was a world beyond this that both of us had stumbled into. I nodded, understanding the implication.

I'll be with you always, he whispered in my mind, and then he was gone.

My old friend had died, but he would be there if I needed advice or just someone to talk with. Even though I had crossed a different threshold of reality, I had not lost my psychic abilities. In fact, they had been enhanced in ways I wasn't used to, but I could still see spirits and predict the future. Closing my eyes, I took a moment to compose my scattered emotions. Then the pain hit me.

It started in the pit of my stomach, working into my veins like molten lava burning through me, and I got the worst cramps I'd ever experienced. My thoughts, my rationality were breaking down. Something deep in the back of my mind stirred like a bat stretching its wings before taking flight into the night.

My awareness shifted, bones elongated in my hands, stretching the skin and muscle, turning my fingers into talons. My teeth grew, giving me a maw a lion would envy. My ears moved and the muscles danced in my back as something wanted to break out from under my skin. My face flattened and my jaw stretched, allowing room for all of my teeth. Pain coursed through me. I wanted to give myself over to it, to let the waiting beast into my psyche, but I heard a voice through the haze. Something I latched onto to save me. It was Veronica.

"Fight it, Brenna."

Her voice was a light that gave me strength. The beast came out of the cave in my mind. I saw what it was we vampires truly were. Veronica was right. We were angels fallen from grace, shunned to embrace the darkness. I saw a beast with twisted horns, a maw of sharp teeth, and a furry black tail with wings of old leather. I didn't believe in demons; I believed in acceptance and Fate. I'd chosen my destiny before I was born. Edmund knew this, just as I did. I stretched my hands out, taking a step forward until I had the demon in a lover's embrace. Its claws ripped furrows in my back. It howled and screamed, struggling against me, but I held tighter as it thrashed, afraid of me, afraid of the emotions and the purity of my soul. I held fast, and after a moment it looked into my eyes, knowing I would not give up, and it bowed its head in acquiescence and then shattered. The beast disappeared, going back to where it had come from. The seed planted in my soul by Devon died. Even though I accepted the beast, it was still in my personality; I could control the demon. I had control over my own actions and didn't have to listen to an alternate personality like all the other vampires. All my thoughts were my own. The space where it had been was occupied by both parts of my psyche. I had overcome my nature, while all other vampires embraced it.

My muscles stopped rippling, and my teeth returned to normal, except for my canines. My face shifted back to its original state, and my fingers and hands returned to normal. Yet, I knew I could draw my talons or the wings in my back at any time. I could even change my shape if I wanted to. The demonic blood had reshaped me, even though I didn't answer to its call, so if I wanted I could take on the shape of the vampire. I was in control. I had the decision of who I would kill. Even as the beast had disintegrated, my hunger burned fiercer, seeping into every part of my body.

I untangled myself from Veronica's arms, noticing how pale and lank she was. I had taken much of her blood, and she needed sustenance more than me. We both got up, but she stumbled.

"You have to feed," I told her. My canines vibrated from the hunger pain.

"What made you the smart one all of a sudden?" she asked, trying to relax, but I saw behind the façade.

"I'm the psychic, remember?" I teased.

"Very funny. Let's go!" Her voice grew hoarse as she let the beast into her nature. She began to walk out of the Tearoom when I grabbed her. She turned, growling at me, her eyes turning black as the hunger inked into them. I knew she hated her nature, fought against it for so many years, and just as she had given me strength she could embrace her beast as well.

"Wait."

She took a breath. Her eyes brightened from black to midnight purple.

"What?" Her voice was garbled because her vocal chords had shifted.

I took her face in my hands, feeling the waxy texture, the coolness underneath, knowing this moment my flesh felt the same. With the same hunger rampaging its way through me, I pushed it aside to focus on her.

"Do what I did. Embrace your nature."

She shook her head. "We're different creatures, believe different things. We have been in blood and pain, but you accept this demon. It's my punishment." She wormed her way out of my grasp, but I caught her again.

This time when she faced me she was fully transformed, just in a matter of milliseconds. This was her true other half, Ronnie, birthed by Devon. Her hand wrapped around my throat, her talons cutting into my skin. She lifted me up so my toes brushed the floor. Her nostrils flared as she took in my scent. Looking into her eyes I knew this was the thing that had attacked me in New Orleans.

It licked its now black lips with a forked tongue. It didn't matter if I was a friend, a fellow vampire. It only smelled the remnants of human blood on me. I was not going to let my existence end in its embrace. I had to get to Veronica's buried personality. Gathering my dwindling mental strength, I threw my mind into hers. The beast was not expecting the attack so it dropped me, its hands flying to its head. I worked through the madness of its personality and hunger. I sensed something else in its twisted mind, emotion for me, which was strange. I didn't linger on it and found Veronica huddled in a corner of her mind.

Help me, I whispered.

She didn't respond and the beast fought my invasion. It didn't like being tested.

Is this how you want to look forever? You want me to die by this thing? I took the image of her in bestial form and threw it back into her mind.

I shook my head, coming out of a daze, watching as the creature smiled and wagged its finger at me as if I were a child who'd disobeyed its mother. Then something happened.

The thing stopped. Its whole body writhed as if a thousand bolts of electricity ran through it. Muscles rippled and contorted. The features of the face went from human to animal to something in between. The wings withered like deranged flowers. And then it all stopped. Veronica crumpled to the floor and lay there. I crawled over to her and put my hand on her back, running it along her spine, feeling the tension of her muscles. As I took her into my arms, she relaxed and it was then she finally looked up at me.

Her eyes were not like they had been, not purple or totally black. Her pupils were dark blue, the irises dotted with purple and the whites of her eyes were gray, almost silver. Her face changed shape and was not as pointed, but more rounded, fleshier, more human. She looked into my eyes as tears moved out of hers, and she smiled.

"It worked!" she whispered. "It really worked." She gazed at her fingers and felt her face, examining the changes. "You're okay?" she asked, the innocence in her voice as sweet as any child's.

I nodded. I knew it would work. I knew she could overcome her own fears and demons, no longer punishing herself for what was done so many years ago. She was so happy. She and the beast had accepted one another. Hopefully it would be for the better. Her joy radiated for now she was in control and no one could take that from her. Devon could no longer manipulate her. Even as we both shared in her joy, the pain and hunger I had suppressed overwhelmed me and I fell into Veronica's arms, moaning. The look of joy was replaced by one of dread.

"Come, we must get you fed."

Veronica helped me up and out of the Tearoom. She pressed the elevator button and hauled me in and out of it. I tried to move, but my legs weren't functioning, just dragging along. She finally got me up and told me to stay, leaning against the cool glass front of the building. I closed my eyes, trying to let the temperature ease my burning veins, but no. I stood there, my vision blurring and my hearing becoming muffled.

"Here, little one. You must take her, or you won't have enough strength to complete the change."

I didn't argue, even though I wanted to. I wanted to be the one to choose my first victim, but my body called out for food, something to keep me going, so that my dead cells could rejuvenate and kick start my system. I needed blood, and even though I had reconciled my nature, I had plenty of time to learn the ways of the hunt and to taste blood. Now all I wanted was the girl in front of me. I opened my mouth as Veronica pressed her against me. My teeth descended and I pushed them against the girl's flesh, feeling her heart through my canines. I stood there a moment, hypnotized by the beating of life as it vibrated in my mouth. I knew this was what I wanted, what was underneath the surface.

My teeth pierced her flesh. I swallowed the first mouthful and the warmth spread throughout my system. As I tasted her blood I noticed there was an odd flavor to it. Almost like decay. I realized my prey was dying even before she came to my lips, but her life was better than coffee or hot chocolate as it warmed me. All of my nerve-endings came alive. The oily texture of my meal's perfume clung to my upper lip and went up my nose, overwhelming my olfactory senses with a hint of musk. I almost sneezed, but my body processed the smell and evaporated it. The tiny fibers of my clothes dug into my skin. I longed to rub against the glass to scratch my back, but I knew it would do no good. Ducks flapped their wings on the water in the Boston Gardens about a half-mile from where I was, settling down for the night. I heard cockroaches scrambling though the walls in the building, trying to find places to lay their millions of eggs.

This was the life I had chosen before I had been born into the world as a human. Edmund had been right. Fate played a part in everyone's life. I was destined to become a psychic, to feel compassion for humanity and understand their emotions. In that skill I could make a living in the enchanted and haunted city of New Orleans. With it I attracted and hypnotized Veronica while pretending to be the thing I craved all along, and she brought me into the life I had already set up.

The tarot card Edmund pulled had so much more meaning than I had anticipated. The Universe had given me a chance to plan my life, and now was my time to take my place in a universe created just for me. I had the time and the opportunity to do whatever I wanted, to go anywhere, to be with anyone. It didn't matter because I was alive, or undead at least, and I had everything I needed.

The girl underneath me grew colder with each sip. My newborn hunger demanded I finish her, but I sensed that my body didn't need all of her blood. There was something else, too. I couldn't kill her. It didn't seem in my nature to kill. I pulled away from the prey.

"I can't," I whispered. "I can't kill her." I looked up at Veronica for her approval.

"Why?"

"It's not who I am. I can't. You, you finish her." I moved aside, knowing that Veronica had to feed as well.

After a moment of indecision, she acquiesced. She took up where I had left off. After a few moments, she had drained the girl. I picked the body up and scanned the streets, noticing the trash bins across the way. I stuffed her into one. If any passersby saw me, they thought I was a tenant dumping a bag of garbage. It was the image I projected, so they paid me no mind. They assumed I was going on about my natural business. I liked my new powers very much and would soon learn to love them even more as I grew into my existence.

I smiled, but now that my mind had cleared and my body was sated, something else bothered me. A tingling started in the back of my brain, just like those I used to have when I was human, letting me know something bad was about to happen. I tried to shake off the feeling as we walked down the street. That tingly feeling in the back of my head remained as I thought about the events of the evening. It was not going away, and soon something bad was going to happen. It had something to do with Veronica and Devon, as well as me. No, he was not done with us yet. Soon we would have to confront Devon once again, this time to rid the world of his evil. Looking back, I didn't understand how I didn't see him for the con he was when I had fallen for him in New Orleans, but then again, it was a city of mystery and anyone could wear a mask. It seemed that all three of us did. Now I had Veronica to myself and the night called for me to explore it so I could discover my new powers and be with the one who truly loved me.

PART FOUR
THE DEVIL

25

CHAPTER TWENTY-FIVE

My name is Veronica.

She was my blood, forged from my own image, but there was something so alien about her. There was no beast nestled inside of her, as there was in me, because she had been born embracing it. Brenna had forced me to face my other half to stop it from hurting her. And I did. Ronnie and I squared off. I told her I didn't want Brenna harmed. She was going to be our child. If Ronnie cared for her as she said she did, then we had to work as one. We argued, and then finally agreed to merge our personalities. We became one. Now it was as if there was a part of me missing, and yet it was still at my calling. I didn't know how to share this knowledge. I didn't even know how to absorb it myself. As Brenna walked beside me in the fall breeze, her cloak billowing behind her, I wondered if she would ever fit in with other vampires. The ones we'd encountered so far hadn't detected anything different about her, except a softness of her aura. Part of her was still human. Something I was not.

I sighed, letting the breeze play with my hair. I had showed her how to use our powers. She was stronger than I, and her tolerance to the sun was unheard of. The first day she woke, she patrolled the streets, taking in the sights and sounds with her heightened perception. When I woke and found her gone, I panicked by the time the sun had set. I followed the invisible thread between us and found her standing in the Garden gazing at the ducks in the pond, marveling as she saw the mites jumping in their feathers.

I noticed how flushed she was. A faint blush adorned her skin. I asked her how long she had been out in the daylight. She said she'd been out since eight that morning, just wandering around. I couldn't believe it at first because that meant almost ten hours of sun exposure and there was nothing, just the slight irritation on her hands and face, the beginnings of a more severe reaction. I asked her if the sun made her uncomfortable or if she had begun to burn. She looked down at her hands, noticing the color, and replied that she had been itchy for the past three hours, but it wasn't anything that bothered her.

This tolerance was unheard of, even among the Ancients. They could go out, but some type of degradation happened in their cells. The newest ones had the greatest aversion to the sun. One would think it would be the other way around, the youngest still close to humanity would have the highest tolerance and the older ones would have no immunity because they were decaying inside. But no, it all depended on the beast inside of us and how much we indulged it.

Brenna had no demon, but I surmised if she had not fed, and had consistent exposure to the sun for days on end, eventually she would die because of it.

But now, a week after her changing, I wondered how she truly adjusted to her new life. She had become quiet and withdrawn and we had not shared the same bed since before her turning. I missed the closeness of her pressing into my body as we slept, even the scent of her hair. When I woke and found I had lost her that morning, I didn't know what to do. Now it felt as if she was a stranger spending time in my house while I walked her through the nuisances of our existence; the woman I fell in love with had vanished. I hadn't brought it up because I didn't know how to broach the subject. How could I tell her she had changed and we were two separate beings?

Even when I tried brushing her thoughts, they were lost to me. I couldn't penetrate the walls, and even her expressions were unreadable. The more I tried to bring us together, the more she separated herself from me. Everything in me wanted to take her into my arms and comfort her. My heart cried out to be wrapped in her very being, but she was so distant it seemed she survived on a desert island.

I couldn't let her out of my sight. Devon hadn't returned, but I knew he would. I had to care for Brenna until she was strong enough to go out on her own. She was too interested in the wrong things, obsessed with staring at candle flames instead of planning the future, but then again, I couldn't read her thoughts, even with the bond we shared. My blood should have made it possible for me to go within her mind. I should have even been able to control her if I wanted to, forcing her to obey me, but I would not inflict the same lifestyle that Devon imposed on me. Every time I tried to look into her mind, she knew. She would look at me funny and then smile.

I smiled to myself at that thought. I was proud of her on that front. Some things I couldn't teach her. Other things like how to hypnotize, move within the shadows, and how to tone down our senses were harder. She began adjusting to her life well and wouldn't need my help for much longer. When that happened, I would disappear from her life, letting her make her own way, as it should have been with Devon and me.

I shuddered, wondering what his next plan would be. He sought to destroy me when he left Brenna for dead, but he hadn't succeeded. I fought and overcame the beast inside me. Now I was something different, something even different from Brenna. I had combined the two elements of myself and didn't know where I stood, but I figured over the years they would mesh completely. Things were still shaky in my mind about the demon, the cement of the combination of my two personalities still drying. I didn't feel the regret of my sister's death anymore. I didn't feel the remorse of killing anything, but I would still only prey on the dying. Brenna had fulfilled her promise to bring me back into the light. She kept me intrigued long enough to let me bring her into my life, and now this was where I was.

"Veronica?" Brenna brought me out of my thoughts.

"Yes?"

"Let's go back to New Orleans. I need to get out of Boston for a while. There are things that should be done before I can truly figure out everything. Can we go back?"

I nodded, thinking it was a good idea. The scent of our kind lingered in the air, growing stronger in the past few nights, and I wondered if this prompted her decision, but it didn't matter. I had the urge to travel and now was as good a time as any. I figured I would help her to resettle back in New Orleans and then I'd disappear into the night and let her be on her own.

"When did you want to leave?"

"Now. I mean, it'll take most of the night to get there, but I didn't know if you would be up for the long flight."

"I brought you here in a few hours, so I think I can manage, but you, you'll need help getting your wings out. You do have them, don't you?" I glanced at her, not sure if she even retained any of the shape shifting abilities all of our kind possessed.

"Of course. Why wouldn't I?"

"I didn't know. You're not like the rest of us in so many ways I just assumed, but it doesn't matter. Let me show you how to unfurl them." I reached out my mind and brushed it against her, but recoiled when the lash of her psychic abilities slammed into my tether. It was obvious to me she didn't want my help.

"No thanks, I can do it."

She removed her shirt, her face knotted in concentration. The muscles in her back danced and grew and the skin turned black as her wings emerged. They were the same size as any of the others I had seen and the same texture, something akin to old leather. The mucous on them broke off into crystallized pieces as they emerged from her skin to be blown apart as soon as it hit the ground. She extended them, stretching them as a bird does after being in one position for so long. Her wingspan was over eight feet, impressive. If anyone saw us they might think she was some kind of fallen angel and I might be the inevitable prophet.

"See, I did it."

She took to the air, her wings fluttering against my hair, as she cloaked herself from human view. It would not be good for any mortal to see us. I shrugged and removed my shirt as well, not caring if a passing human saw my tits, and then like her, I became invisible and I was airborne, off to New Orleans, wondering if I was running from something or if I was going to rediscover my destiny this time.

IT TOOK US six hours to fly from Boston to New Orleans. We were not as fast as a plane, and as we landed in the muggy environment, both of us were exhausted. Flying took much out of us, and I longed for the emptiness of sleep to restore my weary spirit. We set down in a darkened alleyway of the French Quarter and began to blend in with the tourists still partying even though most of the bars had closed. We went back to her house and climbed up to one of the balcony windows.

As we entered into her bedroom, I caught a whiff of Devon, as she had slept with him in the weeks before. I crinkled my nose at it and put him out of my mind. Sleep was the most pressing thing. I noticed the bed and a deck of tarot cards sitting out on the bureau. I smiled as I thought of those cards. In the end they had predicted everything that happened to me. What Edmund had told me was just as veiled as what the old gypsy had said. How right she was, how I wished I had listened to her back then. She had been right about being able to save my soul. I guess I owed Fate a lot. I contemplated choosing a few cards about Devon, wondering what would happen next with him. I didn't want to push my luck, so I left the cards where they sat.

The whirring of a fan started overhead. It cooled my flushed skin and helped to adjust my body temperature. At the thought my body regulated itself and the fan was now nothing more than something to circulate the air.

"Do you want something to drink?" Brenna called from the kitchen.

"Sure, whatever you're having," I yelled back and moved to inspect her open closet.

I pulled out a few dresses and saw that all of them were gothic. I held up a few of them up to myself and looked in the mirror, admiring how they would look on me. It helped that Brenna and I were about the same size, but if I wanted I could change my physical shape and appearance for a few hours, becoming taller, shorter, fatter, it didn't matter. I never used that part of my power; I liked my own image well enough.

"You can keep it if you want. I have others in the closet and don't wear that one much. Here." She handed me a glass of red wine.

I took a sip and puckered at the tartness. I normally drank something sweeter.

I threw the dress on the bed and sat next to it, waiting for Brenna to say or do something, but she set her wine down and began peeling off the rest of her clothes. Her pants fell to the floor, revealing smooth, now hairless legs. I held my breath as she turned back toward the closet, revealing the curve of her ass. Passion rose up in me, and I wanted to fuck her until she moaned for me to stop, but I didn't do anything as she opened up her bureau drawer and pulled out an emerald nightgown and slipped it over her lithe body. She picked up her wine and downed it in one swig. Then she stretched out beside me.

I yawned. The sun would soon break over the horizon, weighing down my bones as it always did when it was high in the sky, but instead of ignoring the pull to sleep, I decided to give into it.

I set the glass of wine on her vanity and pulled my pants off as well and left them on the wooden floor. I glanced down at Brenna, who now had her back to me, and slid under the covers. The coolness of the satin leached into my skin and I wanted nothing more than to turn over and take her. Images of how I would ravage her entered my mind, but I held my spot.

"Brenna?"

"Ehh?" she asked half in sleep.

"Nothing," I whispered, knowing in my heart that there were no sparks between us, except master and child. When she had been turned everything about her had changed, including how she had felt for me. My heart broke and sadness leaked onto my pillow as the sun moved over the horizon, bringing me into sleep.

26

CHAPTER TWENTY-SIX

My name is Brenna.

Veronica still slept as I watched the slight rise and fall of her chest. The movement was so subtle I almost didn't see it. I swept a piece of hair that had fallen across her mouth and brushed it aside, feeling the softness of her lips. The mouth I had kissed when I was human. I remembered the night we shared, before I had lost myself, and longed for everything to be right between us. Veronica thought I didn't need her anymore, thought I didn't want her, and that crushed her. She assumed since I had become this new kind of being, my feelings for her had died, but none of that was true. On the contrary they had grown, so much I didn't know how to contain them in my heart, but I didn't know how to show her either. I was afraid of the intensity of everything.

The newness of my lifestyle overwhelmed me and I absorbed all of it, retreating into my own world. I hadn't noticed, until recently, how much I hurt Veronica. I should have listened to her more carefully, felt the emotions in her heart, but the littlest things held my attention. Even now as I watched her resting, I knew how hard she fought against the beast inside her soul. It was in the way she walked and held herself. She was different. There were times she thought her hard won freedom would fly apart, and she would be two separate things again.

Both of us were different creatures, each born of the same strain of blood, but molded differently. I knew this by reading her thoughts, which she assumed were veiled. To most of our kind they would have been, but my mental abilities were three times that of hers. My tolerance to the sun was high enough it almost didn't bother me, but if I didn't feed, the sun would begin to peel the skin from my bones; as long as I didn't let that happen I was fine. There were many other things I had discovered in the past week or so since I had become like her, or should I say similar to her.

I was something outside the race of vampires. I needed blood to survive, to allow me to live through the years while my body molded itself into something that lived forever, or close to it. I had the physical strength of other vampires and was stronger than a human, but I was not the strongest among my kind. The thing that set me apart from all of them was that I had no beast inside of me. In a sense, I retained my humanity. I didn't have to kill to survive. I could take what I needed and let my victims live where all the others had to kill.

With Veronica—I didn't know what to do with her. How could I tell her my feelings when I knew she was going to leave me, abandoning me to be on my own when now was a time I needed her most?

I stretched and got out of bed, knowing my movements wouldn't wake Veronica. It was three in the afternoon and she would sleep until the sun set. I threw off my nightgown and went to my closet, slipping on a black dress that clung to my form. I caught a glimpse of myself in the mirror and thought of the last time I had been before the glass. I glanced down at my bureau and saw my fake fangs sitting in an empty contact case. I picked up one of the acrylic teeth, wondering what I'd been thinking when I first put them on, pretending to be the creature I was today.

I noticed for the first time how different I looked. My eyes had become darker. They were now truly black, with a faint ring of silver separating my irises and my pupils. They expanded as the sun shifted to the other side of my house. The whites of my eyes were almost luminous, the red veins no longer there, and when I turned my head they flashed rainbow color like a fish's scale. My skin had lost any imperfection, no more scars or freckles. I no longer had to worry about any unwanted hair on my face or legs. My muscles were more defined. I saw their outlines under my skin. I had become something better than what I was and had retained my humanity in the bargain.

I spied my tarot cards on the bureau's surface, wondering if I should cut them to figure out what was going to happen. I had the power to divine the future. The voices that guided me through my readings, be they angels or just spirits, had not left me. I still felt their presence. Even as I thought of the tarot, I didn't need to prove that ability to myself. It would always be there inside of me. For now, I left the cards behind and left the apartment to clear my head.

I walked through the French Quarter, perusing the shops as if I were a tourist. The scent of jasmine lingered in the air as well as the coppery scent of rain as the clouds moved from light to dark. An oncoming storm, but I didn't mind the rain. The atmosphere contracted around me, making the air thick and dense. The storm would bring a welcomed relief from the humidity. It would cool off the area, driving tourists inside because they were afraid of getting soaked. For me, it was all a part of nature.

I came to the café where Veronica and I had first decided to sit and have tea. She had been so scared of what would happen between us that night. She so wanted not to come and meet me at the cathedral that day, but she faced her fears. I, on the other hand, had been so confident at how much I had charmed her when really it was she who had bespelled me. It had all been so different. It was only a few weeks ago, but a lifetime ago for me. I had been something else and had no idea what lurked around the corner of my destiny. I found my fate with her. I wondered if it would have been possible for me to continue on in the normalcy of my humanity, but I knew the answer to that question. I could never dream of going backwards. I loved what I had become. Everything was so wonderful; it made me pity mortals as they walked through life asleep. Not seeing and experiencing the things around them. I would have never known there were so many layers just in the scent of a rose. How first it was the subtle perfume of the morning dew that clung to it, the rusty clear smell of the minerals in the leaves, then the hint of acrid decay as the flower died ever so slightly each second, and finally, the burst of the rose's own perfume. All of these were things I smelled when just inhaling. But humans, no, they only smelled the beautiful perfume of the bloom. I owed everything to Veronica and was glad she had bumped into my mundane life.

"Ehh, Raven, long time no see. Where you been?"

I glanced up. Most people in New Orleans knew me by that name to keep my privacy. Either way, I felt an affinity for the dark bird, even after my changing. I looked over to the counter and saw Gerard. He had worked here for as long as I had been coming in, but he never seemed to age and always looked like he was going to the next frat party.

"Hey, what's up?" I said, glancing up at the menu.

"People've been looking for you. Figured you got holed up with some new fling and wanted the time away. You want the usual?"

I nodded, anticipating the taste of chai. The mixture of cinnamon, tea, and steamed milk as it slid down my throat like liquid silk. I took the tea and downed a sip, not bothering to let it cool. Gerard took in a breath through his teeth, marveling how I could drink it so hot, but I didn't notice the temperature. I savored the taste with my enhanced senses. The spiciness of it settled in my nose as the rest of it mixed on my tongue.

"Who's been asking about me?" I asked, licking my lips.

"Well, you know, the tourists referred by the hotels, and some of your regulars. There was this one though. A real looker came in demanding to know where you were. Had black hair, real nice figure too."

I nodded, assuming it was Devon. He would find us sooner or later. I assumed it would be later. I was surprised Gerard said he had made a scene. From my encounters with Devon he liked to keep things quiet, like everything was a game to him. Veronica and I were his pawns. But no more. Now it was time for us to checkmate. Veronica knew this. When he came this time, both of us would be ready.

"A real looker, huh? What did he look like?" I knew how fond Gerard was of good-looking men.

"Oh, this one wasn't a man, this was a woman. Real young. Once I told her you weren't here she calmed down a bit, and said…something—what was it? I can't remember, but I told her I didn't know when you'd be back."

I looked at him, my teeth lengthening. Why would a woman be looking for me?

It was unlike Gerard to notice women, even pretty ones. This one must have made an impression.

"Gerard." I lowered my voice a pitch so he would fall under my spell. "You remember what she said, now don't you? You can tell me."

His face went lax and he would have fallen if he hadn't been leaning up against the counter. He looked like a melting candle. I lowered my voice a little more and used less power, to give him back some of his self-control. I was still learning. After a moment, he regained his composure but still had a glazed look on his face.

"She said that she was staying in the cemetery, over across from Rampart. I thought she was a squatter, but she said for me to tell you she wanted to talk when you got back. It was important. She said something about a black rose."

He stopped when I withdrew my power. There was no other useful information stored in him. I felt that when I brushed against his mind with my thoughts.

"Thanks, Gerard, you've been a big help."

He blinked, wondering what the hell had happened, and then turned back to his work. I took another swig of my tea and threw it in the trash. I thought about it. A black rose. That meant nothing to me. Why the hell would a woman come looking—? Then it dawned on me. He wasn't talking about a flower. He was speaking about the club in Cambridge.

My back itched because my wings wanted to come out. My feet urged to be on the ground to know I was still connected to the earth. I rushed down the streets until I came to the edge of the French Quarter. The cemetery was across the street, surrounded by a ten-foot thick wall. New Orleans had a very high water table, so whenever it rained the buried bodies used to float back into town. Because of that they built above ground crypts. If you got a wall plot, you were baked by the sun until there was nothing left but dust. The remains were pushed down into a collecting bin and someone else took the resting spot. It was an economic deal.

A clap of thunder broke the sky as a torrential downpour unleashed itself onto the cemetery. The rain plastered the clothing to my skin, but I didn't mind much as it cooled me off and made me aware of my surroundings. Of course I was in a graveyard, but even though I was one of the dead, I was not going to be buried any time soon. I walked along the beaten paths between the ancient mausoleums. Many of them were nothing more than bricks, but a few of them were still in use. Wind came up from the storm and caught the plastic covering of those tombs undergoing restoration, flapping them wildly in the breeze, adding to the already creepy feel of the graveyard.

A few tourists squealed. They had been caught in the downpour, and since they were not used to New Orleans weather, they probably didn't think to carry an umbrella. I smirked as I caught the scent of their irritation. It made my mouth water as I thought of their blood exploding into my mouth, working its way into my stomach, warming me. No, I did not need to give into the urges I felt. I was not like the others and never would be.

Stopping in my tracks, I wondered where the other vampire would be. Obviously, she wouldn't let the other tourists see her. I closed my eyes and took in a breath, stopping my heart. I shut out the other noises, smells, anything that would interfere with me finding her. I cast out my mind, leaving the confines of my body and searching for this ancient vampire. Maybe she was as old as the one from the Black Rose. I assumed I'd find some trace of her energy in the cemetery, something of herself imprinted on stones or the environment. But with her being so old, she probably wouldn't make it easy for me to find her.

I scanned the whole cemetery. My mind moved in between the gravestones, and even the cracks of the mausoleums that housed ancient corpses. I did find one that was fresh, but I moved on. I weaved around the tourists, who were now venturing out of the cemetery because it had stopped raining. They were nothing, just ants, mere annoyances compared to me. Then I caught something toward the corner of the cemetery, hovering near one grave in particular. Before I decided to reunite my mind with my body, I took another quick scan of the property, including the walled crypts, wondering if maybe she had found some way to move into one of them and share the space with the baked corpses, but there was nothing.

I sighed and settled into my own body, restarting my heart to warm my skin. I came to the burial ground for nothing, knowing this was a wild goose chase. I figured I should get back to the apartment before Veronica woke so I could beg her not to leave me because

I needed her in my life. I began to walk toward the entrance and found myself drawn to the grave of the Voodoo Queen of New Orleans, Marie Laveau. Several offerings had been placed on her tomb, a full bottle of beer, stacks of three pennies, beads, and other paraphernalia that were representations of people's wishes. I wondered if the believers ever got their wishes granted by the dead Voodoo Queen.

I traced the carved letters of her name, questioning if this woman was aware of my kind even back in her day. If she had been, did she interact with us? Had she been a great psychic or just a fraud? I knew little of her, except the fact she was a living legend around the city. She had been a powerful sorceress in her day, but also knew the local gossip of the time, so she weaseled her way into the lives of many people, and it made her rich.

"I wonder how much you really knew," I said to the tombstone.

"She knew much about us, little one. She became one of my children, but sadly, she, like most when turned, didn't remember the creature she had been, and became something else. She lurks around here at times, visiting her gravesite, but remembering only pieces of the life she left behind. Most of her was consumed by the beast within us."

I spun around when I heard the soft, enticing voice behind me. I had not remembered the power of the ancient vampire, but maybe that was because I was trying so hard to protect myself from her I didn't have the capability to see her as I saw her now. She stood before me, her hair now shining purple-black as a raven's wing in the cloudy sky. She was dressed in a red silk dress, something from the forties. It fell to her knees and revealed pale, skinny legs. Her eyes were large and deep blue. Her lips were red, not from lipstick though, and she was shorter than I remembered. When I noticed her aura it was dark, cobalt blue, radiating light as a perverted beacon. I shivered as a whiff of her power swept over me.

"You're not a foolish one, child. I knew that the night we met. You tried to hide the fact you were human, pretending to be undead. You were powerful then. And now, you're one of the strongest vampires I've encountered, and I've met a lot of our kind. Unlike Marie and many others, you've retained all of your humanity, a rarity. You're very much like me, if you can believe that. I knew the night we met you assumed I was crazy, consumed by the beast. Isn't that right?"

I nodded, not really knowing what to say. I still couldn't believe she had gotten the drop on me. She was probably standing behind me, shadowing me the whole time I had been looking for her.

"Who are you?"

"I'm Aria, and I'm here to help you." She smiled, flashing a maw of uneven fangs.

CHAPTER TWENTY-SEVEN

My name is Veronica.

Someone traced the line of my jaw, urging me into consciousness. My first thought was of Brenna, that she had changed her mind and tried to seduce me into reality. It was a good concept after a restful sleep. I smiled as I savored the sensation of the tingling of my flesh underneath her nail as it moved along my cheek, down my neck, and digging into me enough to make me want more. Her thoughts brushed against mine. Without a second thought, I merged mine with hers. Her mental touch was gentle as her fingers were fingers on my clit, working me, making me hot and wet. I kept my eyes closed, not ready to open them, moaning loudly, beginning to come, and at the last moment, icy fingers moved inside me, making me jump. But oh, the ecstasy of the contrast of hot and cold. When I couldn't hold in my moans any longer, I yelled, giving myself over to the heaven that was Brenna's touch. All the while I knew everything had been mended between us and that was what made it all the more enjoyable.

Feeling the light touch of lips pressed against mine and the caress of her thoughts, I opened my eyes. At that moment, Brenna's mental caress became a leash that tightened around my mind. My hips still bucked against the fingers inside of me. My lips automatically returned the kiss even while I tried to get free from Devon. Then he was on top of me, ramming his cock into my depths. All because he wanted me to know that I was still at his mercy.

He grabbed onto my shoulders, his claws digging into my skin. I thrashed against him, but he was too strong as he began to transform.

"Don't think you can get away from me that easily, Ronnie. You're mine, always mine. And so is the little one you cherish so much. Oh yeah. I've missed thisssss," Devon hissed, his forked tongue dangling out of his mouth.

As much as I wanted not to enjoy it, I did. His actions and his mind reached down to Ronnie. I thought we had merged, but I realized how mistaken I was when she unraveled herself from our bond. I tried to fight her, but I wasn't strong enough. Ronnie rose to meet him, welcoming her Master. As the transformation overtook me, conscious thought and regret slid away. I became an animal rutting in heat, moving against another monster.

THE NEXT CONSCIOUS thought I had was waking again in Brenna's apartment, the scent of Devon all over me. Waves of joy and regret washed over me as I realized what had happened. I'd thought I'd been absorbed by the human part of me, but I guess that wasn't so.

I shivered and looked around the apartment, hoping that what happened earlier was just a bad dream, but I knew it wasn't. I caught a glimpse of the mirror and saw it had shattered. A piece of the glass still remained in the frame like a forgotten icicle waiting to fall with the spring thaw. I got out of bed, crunching on the remnants of the glass as they buried themselves in my feet. I leaned over and picked up one of the shards, staring at the reflection. I was in human form. My eyes were completely black, no longer lavender. Within the confines of my mind, Veronica turned over, ashamed she had given in to Devon. Now that the Master was back in my life, my human persona would not rule. I had been locked away for far too long. I was tired of her meat-lover morality and her late night visits to sick wards. My rage for Veronica grew. Now she was back in the shackles she had kept me in. I smiled at this. Never again would I give up my freedom. Our meshing had been a mistake. I could still feel parts of her meat-lover philosophy in the back of my brain and I wanted it gone. My Master would be pleased that I rose to meet his calling.

At the thought of the Master, I caught his lingering scent in the room as it led me out onto the balcony. It drifted on the breeze, waiting for me to follow it so I could finally be reunited with him. As I thought of our blissful reunion, a tear spilled over my eye.

I whipped it away, marveling at the new development in my tears. Never before had they been real blood. It meant I was more complete than I had realized. I began to shake at the realization. After so many years I could roam the streets and take what victims I wanted. I might even hunt down the dancer I had encountered earlier and take over her hunting ground. No, that could wait until later. My first obligation was to find my child. Oddly enough, I did care for her. Unlike Veronica, who craved to love and cherish her, I wanted to show Brenna that she must obey. She would be my gift to my Master.

"Brenna," I called out, wondering if she was there. I was afraid she had deserted me, and if she had, I would show her who the true Master was. No one disobeyed me. I listened and heard nothing, except the creaking of stairs and voices behind the door. One of them sounded like my child. "Brenna?"

The click of the lock sounded as the door opened. Brenna came in with another. My hackles rose, and my fangs grew as I caught the smell. The aroma of her companion was vaguely familiar, as if I should have known it, but I assumed it was something my defeated half had sensed so I threw it away and stepped out into the hallway, anger boiling over in my cooled body. My eyes bled red as the hunger came to the surface. I crouched low, waiting for them to come into view.

How dare she! She was mine, how could she seek to take another lover. Already she has thrown me aside, not showing respect. I'll get the bitch.

"I didn't know we could do that," I heard Brenna say to her companion.

"Of course, it's just another way of tapping into the powers of the mind. It's the same as being able to see spirits. When we change we are enhanced, but most of us don't retain the powers we had when we were human. Hell, I used to be one of the Oracles at Delphi, and then I saw too much one night."

"Really, what was it like?"

The door closed and Brenna came in along with the ancient vampire. She had thrown me aside like a piece of meat. I should have known it from the beginning. My instincts had been right when I thought she was just using me. I growled, letting my jaw change to contain all of my teeth. I took on a more animal shape, something in between a wolf and the hellhound form I normally took. Waves of power ran through me. The human in me was dead, but I had to reclaim my creation. She was mine utterly, just as I was Devon's, and when she was under my spell I would return to my Master and beg his forgiveness as I watched him pulverize my child.

The thought of her screams made me hot. I wanted to see her lingering humanity torn to shreds. Her scent became vile to me, something of the prey I fed on. She was not like the other vampires, some part of her was still human, an abomination. She had to be the beast, and I was sure my Master and I would to bring it out in her. I waited patiently for her to turn and see me.

"Veronica, what are you doing?"

Her words were muffled as her subtle heartbeat filled my ears. I growled. Not waiting any longer, I sprang, crossing the distance between us. The old one felt me coming and pushed Brenna out of the way. I collided with her, knocking both of us to the ground. My jaws snapped at her throat, but didn't dare bite. She was too powerful. Before I regained my balance and lunged again, she threw me off. I landed across the room, crashing through a window and out onto the balcony. My head collided with the wrought iron bars, knocking me into a daze. I opened my eyes to see Brenna coming at me.

Yes, let her come.

I waited, feigning injury as she bent over me, but the other stopped her, grabbing her arm and shaking her head. I opened my eyes after a few moments, staring up at my child, waiting for her to make the next move.

"Veronica, what's the matter? Don't you know it's me?" She came a step toward me, and then stopped, knowing something was terribly wrong.

"You chose another over me! I'm your Master. You human-loving bitch." I paused, loving the look of hurt on her face. Veronica stirred, but now that my Master had released me from my prison, I was not going to let the other side take over again.

Why are you doing this? she asked me, opening her mind.

She poured her emotions into my thoughts, allowing me to experience how much she cared for me. I took the advantage and pushed my mind into hers, claws and all, ripping around her thoughts as if they were paper. She screamed in pain, crumpling to the floor. I purred with triumph. Without the weakness she had just shown, I would not have been able to get into her brain; her mental abilities were stronger than mine. While inside of her mind, I noticed how much potential she had. She would be a great asset to help destroy others like her, once she was persuaded to join my Master and me. It would be difficult to get her to come over because there was nothing to entice her, but I was sure I could find a way.

"You think by showing me your love you can awaken Veronica. Did you think I'd fall on my knees and glorify in your return? The prodigal child. How little you know." I laughed and sniffed at the old one by Brenna's side. She could have the bitch for all I cared.

"Keep her for now, but once my Master comes to claim her, you'll be begging him to fuck you, begging him for mercy." I looked at them one last time and then leaped over the balcony, moving swiftly through the night, following the scent my Master left for me to follow.

I hungered for his touch. I ached, knowing soon he would have his hands around me and I would be dominated, bathed in my blood just as I had been on the day I had been born. That was the way it should have been, always.

28

CHAPTER TWENTY-EIGHT

My name is Brenna.

I sat clearing my head, trying to figure out what had happened to Veronica. Her mental attack had not done much damage to my psyche and whatever harm had been done would heal with time. Aria tried helping me up, and reluctantly I let myself be led to a chair and sat down, my head between my knees, still stunned.

"Why did she turn on me?"

"I surmise Devon got to her. It's the only explanation."

"I should have never left her alone. Why did I leave?" I clutched my head and screamed. Without thinking, I tore out two huge patches of hair and skin, revealing the bone. I hardly noticed the pain it left behind, just the itching as it started to regenerate.

"Don't."

Aria's hand restrained mine so I wouldn't hurt myself any more. I tried to move, but she held me.

"It's what he wants you to do. He knows you're a great psychic. Even I can sense that. It is strange for our kind to hold onto the gifts we had in humanity when we are turned, but he doesn't know you don't have another half."

Aria released my hands, removing the strands of hair and tissue. I didn't notice as blood trickled down the back of my neck and stuck to my dress.

"I know that, but how could Veronica suddenly change like that? She was fine last night. She accepted what she was, putting the two halves together."

"You said Veronica embraced the beast, and that's probably true, but the cement between the two personalities hadn't completely dried. Normally we accept the beast when we are first born into this life so the transition is seamless. It can't work the same way two hundred years later. That gave Devon a foothold. Now we have to get to her before she becomes his pet forever."

"Yes, but I don't even know where he's gone. I don't know how to track her if she's completely possessed. It's hopeless."

I got up from the chair and paced the room. I wondered how Aria had survived so long in a world of demons and monsters. In our few hours together she had revealed that we were not the only things that walked the earth. There were others: werewolves, fairies, other demons, and angels. So many things shared our reality it boggled my mind. I hadn't believed her at first until she pointed out the differences in the people we crossed paths with. Then I saw, with my own eyes, a real angel dressed in an Armani suit, rushing toward something. His aura, or halo, was brighter than the moon, and my skin tingled as his energy passed over me. It wasn't warm as I thought it would be, but cold as the grave. The quick glimpse I got of him made me catch my breath. He was beautiful. Pale as an opal with midnight hair and black piercing eyes that moved into my soul, reading what I was and acknowledging me. I laughed at the thought of an angel in a business suit. He nodded slightly, recognizing we were two other supernatural beings. Then he was gone.

I stopped laughing then.

Seeing him made me realize how little I knew. As a human I thought I knew everything, but it seemed I understood less now. It was interesting to watch, a human interacting with a fairy that looked like a white rapper, but to my eyes he had translucent blue wings, pointy ears, and was only three feet tall, but to the human, the fairy was six feet tall, wore at least seven gold chains, and a backwards baseball cap.

I had asked Aria how she had discovered all of this. She told me it came with age and experience. It took her about four hundred years before she detected all of the dimensions. I asked her why she had shown me all of this, and she replied I had the mental capacity to do it, and it would be for my benefit to know.

In the few short hours I'd known her, she had become a mentor, a good friend. She had shown me how to use a few telekinetic powers, such as working the mechanisms in the lock to my apartment and other small things. I could will a glass across the table, but nothing bigger. It didn't work that way. Just with little things, giving the door a small push to close, or even picking locks, but that was the extent of my ability. There were so many other things I wanted to ask her, and that was why I had decided to bring her back to talk with Veronica. Aria also said she knew a way to help us get rid of Devon.

Aria smiled. "I have an idea. We have to wait until midnight, but before that, you should find something to wear."

I gazed at Aria reluctantly. I did not feel like going out. All I wanted to do was go get Veronica and bring her back.

"Don't give me that look. Just do it. Besides, you're going to have to learn a few things before I can take you where we're going. So do as I say."

I smiled halfheartedly. "Yes, mother."

"Put on something revealing."

Great, I thought, wondering what I was getting myself into.

29

CHAPTER TWENTY-NINE

My name is Ronnie.

I knelt between Devon's legs. My lips worked his cock as my tongue slid up and down his shaft. It was cold and long in my mouth, but I shifted my shape to take it all in. Absently he patted my head as I worked him. The feeling of his fingertips on my skull was pleasure and payment enough for me to keep going until he shot into my mouth, releasing his salty cum into my throat.

I should have been with my Master all of the time I had been imprisoned, but Veronica had been stronger. She stirred a moment as I thought of her, but I ignored my other half. I was the one in control, and it would be like that forever. I grieved for all the lost nights with him, so many glorious evenings because of what I had become: a human-loving bitch. I purred inwardly, knowing this was what I had been missing.

To show my obedience, I swore he could have Brenna to do with as he pleased. It made him happy when I expressed my total and utter submission to him. He smiled and fucked me, hard and rough, until I bled from his claws and his dick. As I lay, drained from the exercise, I reveled in how much he loved me as he cleaned the blood from my wounds.

Yes, he was a kind and generous Master for allowing me to come crawling back to him, after so many years of disobedience. Soon we would have another to torture and play with. He had told me this as he cleaned my gashes, informing me of the plans he had for my offspring. He would break her until she was nothing more than a shadow and use her powers. I licked my lips, envisioning her beautiful, human demeanor ripped to shreds. When that happened, we would mold her into the perfect child. I smiled as Devon withdrew himself from me. The pure sweet pain of her torture enlightened my hunger. My forked tongue darted between my lips, taking in the last of him.

Master, may I? I asked.

Devon looked down at me, his mind searing through mine. I crouched lower, showing my obedience. He tapped my head, granting my request. I turned from him and set my gaze on the meat in the corner, a young mortal. Her fear called to my hunger the closer I got. When she saw me coming, she whimpered, but I didn't care about her pleas. She should have welcomed my ravaging. I was her God, just as my Master was mine. I smiled, showing her my maw of fangs. A terrified look still painted her face as I descended. I wrapped her in my wings so I would not splatter any blood on my Master.

30

CHAPTER THIRTY

My name is Brenna.

I screamed in frustration once again as I tried projecting the aura Aria wanted, a hardened shell, a bestial energy more like her kind. She wanted me to recreate the energy signature I had when I first met her. She and Veronica used similar projections to fool others of their kind to think they were not human-lovers. I understood now what Veronica meant about trying to blend in. Most of the mortal loving types were killed off swiftly if they showed signs of weakness, but a few fell through the cracks because they deceived the other bloodsuckers. The others were just monsters, masquerading as human.

It was a quarter to midnight, and Aria had wanted to leave by eleven thirty. She had me dress in a corset in which my breasts hung over the top. I slipped on a short, velvet skirt, but settled on my knee high Doc Martens. Dressing right was easy, but I couldn't reconstruct the aura she wanted. When I was human, I had pulled energy around me, focusing it outward so it was dark and pulsating, but as much as I tried, it was useless.

"Look, it's just not happening," I told her finally. "Why don't you go without me?"

Aria sighed. "I wish I could, but you're the one who has to do all the talking. I'm just going to get you in. Besides, you've never been among many other undead before. There were only eight of us at the Black Rose. That club's for both humans and our kind, but this place is exclusive. No humans allowed, unless they're food. If Malachai asks you why you're looking for Devon, tell him he's your Master and you wish to be reunited to show your loyalty. He'll eat it up."

"Why can't I say I'm your child? And why does it have to be me talking?"

"Brenna, you have to know how to play their games. Everything is about loyalty. You're the slave until you break free from your Master, or kill him. Very rarely will a Master let a vampire get strong enough to go out on its own. If that happens, then the Master trusts it or loves it in its own perverted way. How do you think I survived since my Oracle days? You show your allegiance to the owner. He's the head of the vampires in this area. He also used to be a sorcerer in his human days. He retained a power or two when he crossed over. He'd know where Devon is. You have to prove your devotion, just as you would to your Master. By me bringing you to him, it shows that even though I have free will, I'm showing acquiescence to him. But if Malachai doesn't believe you, well, he owes me a favor."

"Wait, you know this vampire? Did he make you?"

Aria laughed, her voice twittering like a flute doing scales. "Hell no, but we shared a few centuries together. He was fun, but we got into a fight over... Well, it doesn't matter. It's old news. I'm sure he won't remember. He was great in bed, though. But anyway. You have to ask him where Devon is. When you go in to see him, meet his eyes once, then keep your head bowed. Everything in your demeanor must be subservient."

"I don't bow," I grumbled.

"If you want to find Veronica, you'll play the game."

"Fine!"

I sighed, knowing I would do anything for her even if it meant acting like one of them.

Veronica must hate being under Devon's spell, locked away in her mind, unable to stop the torment her other half caused. She'd never want to live like that. I couldn't leave her the way she was, even if it meant destroying her. I realized that after she attacked me.

When I looked into her eyes it wasn't her. I would make Devon pay for the things he did to her.

As my hatred of him grew so did my hunger. My teeth lengthened, and something snaked around in my mind, crawling out of a long buried hole. The more I fed it with my anger of Devon, the more it matured into something. The more I was haunted by the notion of his hands on her pale, lithe body, the more I wanted to rip his ears and eyes out, tear his dick off and eat his liver.

"That's it! What did you do?" Aria asked.

I shrugged. I got pissed at Devon and something had opened in my mind. My wings itched to be released; my form wanted to reshape into something sinister. My hunger had flared up, but I didn't feel as if something were going to take me over. I was still in control. I thought about it, taking hold of my hunger, molding it, pushing that and my anger outward. I closed my eyes, hardening the energy, cementing it to me to look as if I were something akin to Veronica and Aria. It was the same process I had used when I had been human, though the energy frequency was different.

I understood now why I couldn't call up the energy I'd projected when I had been human. I had transcended death and become what I originally yearned for. Now I was something else, and I had to create another mask to make others believe I truly was like them. I laughed happily as I cracked the puzzle, understanding that even though I accepted what I was, I had to pretend to be something else. One always had to have a hidden face.

"Let's go."

"Do you think you can hold what you're projecting?"

"Of course." I smiled as my eyes inked red because I had found some semblance of the beast in me, and even though it was just an illusion, it was as real as I could make it.

We arrived in front of a house in the Bayou. It was a plantation house that had been there for a century or more. The paint on the columns was chipped; part of the roof sagged under the weight of a tree branch resting on the worn shingles. Shutters hung from rusted nails. The front steps were covered in swamp water. The buzz of bugs and the chirping of birds surrounded the house. In the distance, I heard the splashing of alligators rising and falling as they searched for food in the brackish water. In the swamps, the reptiles were the biggest predators. At least, that was what the humans thought.

We stepped onto the porch, and I let Aria knock on the door, which was surprisingly on its hinges and in good condition. She banged several times before the thing opened. When it did, I almost gasped at the sight, but I caught myself. A half putrefied human stepped aside and let us pass. She was naked from the waist up.

One breast sagged with the nipple all but gone. Her other hung from pieces of muscle that had begun to decay. Wisps of blonde hair fell out even as she moved, revealing the white of her skull underneath. She looked on us with one eye hanging out of her socket, the other gone altogether. I tried not to touch her as I passed.

The overwhelming scent of blood hit me as we stepped over the threshold. My mouth watered, the bones in my jaw creaked as more teeth pushed against my gums, but I fought the urge. On the ground floor I was astonished to see how well furnished the house was. The wallpaper was still intact, and pictures of old family members adorned the walls. The hardwood floors were neatly polished and not even warped from the moisture. Electricity sparked through the wires, illuminating a crystal chandelier. A wooden staircase ascended to the second and third floors, inviting weary travelers to find an empty room to sleep in. This would not be a place I would want to rest my head.

Aria caught my awe and disgust as we walked through the hallway into a furnished sitting room, and then into the kitchen. The house was empty except for us and the thing that opened the door.

"What was she...it...back there?"

"She's what happens when we don't get enough blood. She's the walking dead, literally. There's no consciousness. All she knows is the blood that animated her has bound her here, and she does whatever Malachai wants. He probably doesn't bother to feed her much. Usually they last longer. She seems pretty fresh. He had a few when we were together, but I hated them. They give me the creeps. They wait like hovering ghosts." Aria shivered as we got to the kitchen.

She rapped on what seemed to be the pantry door and waited. Her knocks echoed as she pounded on the wood, bouncing lower into a basement or dungeon, and then the door opened. I expected another one of the things that had greeted us before, but this time a mortal in his late twenties unlocked the door and let us pass. He was shorter than me and glared as I stared right back at him. I probed his mind, my power cutting through him like a knife. Memories of him being fucked and fed on entered my thoughts. He loved every minute that the vampires used him. It didn't matter if he died in a creature's embrace, he wanted to be used. His ultimate goal was to join the ranks of the undead, but just by piercing his mind I knew his vampiric master would never bring him over. He was too much of a weakling and loved the idea of grandeur too much. He would remain a slave.

As I released my mind from his, he came. I knew then how much of a junkie he really was, getting fixes off what other vampires did to him. I cringed in disgust at the thought of humans actually wanting to be turned.

Granted, when I was human I always thought they were monsters in long, dark capes, beings to be romanticized. I didn't know the whole truth. The more I learned of what my kindred truly were like, the more I despised them.

We descended a flight of stairs. The lackey led the way. The stairs led down into what used to be a basement or slave quarters. The scent of death lingered heavily in the air. Laughter echoed the further we descended. I heard the moaning and rattling of chains, of bodies slapping together in various stages of fucking. I tried to keep my eyes focused center, but there were so many distractions in the lavish rooms I couldn't help but peek.

In one room, a vampire in full transformation held a mortal by the throat, digging into her breast with its teeth, gnawing at the soft tissue. When it caught my scent its eyes panned my way, pieces of flesh hung out of its mouth, blood dribbling on the black fur. I averted my eyes and the thing went back to its feast. In another room, further down the hall, I listened to the moans of a man. I glimpsed in and saw a vampire mostly in human form. A woman had her claws shoved in the asshole of a man with her fangs submerged in his neck. Another female vampire behind worked the human's dick while suckling the other monster's neck. Waves of ecstasy radiated off the second female vampire. In another room there were no vampires, just a set of women, twins, chained to the wall. They wore nothing more than collars, but they were each mounted on a mechanical contraption. I sniffed and found them to be alive, the scent of old sex lingered in the room, and I caught the sound of some kind of generator. When I looked closer I saw five gyrating poles. Three metal phalluses were attached on the end of the unoccupied ones. I shivered as I thought of the poor souls being fucked to death, locked away with the monsters.

I glanced over at Aria as I saw her eyes lingering on some of the rooms.

"The good old days," I heard her mutter. She caught my eye and smiled.

"What?"

The junkie looked between the two of us and gathered I was new. "Those are the prep rooms. The Master likes his meat to be ready. Their orgasms give the blood a flavor he enjoys. You must be new. I've not seen you before."

"She's none of your concern. Now stop doddering and bring us to your Master. Or I'll tell him how naughty you've been and you'll get nothing. Now go!" Aria barked at him.

The junkie jumped, swearing under his breath and ran on ahead of us down to the end of the hall. He slipped past an oak door and closed it behind him. Mentally I checked my shields and found they still held, but to be sure I thought of Devon molesting

Veronica again, and how willingly humans like the junkie could give themselves to these creatures. I grew furious, reflecting the emotion outward.

"Careful. Don't let him think you're too powerful. Then he'll want you for his stable. Remember what I said. Don't look at him more than once."

I nodded, trying to relax. The door opened on well-oiled hinges. Aria stepped forward on the stone floor, and we were ushered into a large room. I kept my head bowed, casting quick glances to my left and right. Candles lined the walls and were scattered on a lush red rug. The color reminded me of dried blood; if there were any accidents there would be no way to know how much of a mess there would be. The whole room smelled like musk and frankincense. Sofas and chairs were scattered about the room, each housing vampires, and mortals in various stages of undress, some fucking, others just toying with the humans. From a quick mental scan of the victims, each of them was a willing participant. Or maybe they were now, but had been taken hostage once upon a time; now, every one of them was hooked on being dominated, sucked on like a straw.

"Master, they are here to see you," the junkie said, his voice quivering with fear or anticipation, perhaps both.

"I can see that, Joey. Now run along and tell every-one I am not to be disturbed. This will be the last of my audiences." His voice was smooth as oil and just as volatile.

The lackey ran out of the room, whooshing past us trying to get out of the path of his master's wrath. I smirked as he went past. I understood why he was on the bottom of the food chain. Even I could control the boy with just a word. One didn't even need a mental suggestion.

"Arriana, is that really you?" Malachai asked.

"Of course, love. It's been a long time."

"You haven't changed a bit. Just gotten a bit stronger, I take it. And who is this lovely specimen you have brought me. A gift?"

Malachai got off his throne and came to me. His hands cupped one of my exposed breasts as it sat atop my corset. It was the only one I owned that left my breasts bare and came to a point in the space between my tits. He tweaked the nipple, testing to see how hard it would get. He then slid a clawed finger under my black mini skirt and into me. The entry forced me to look up into his face. My eyes met his as I tried not to be shocked. I was not used to being a sex toy, and the world that I had entered was something new to me. I was the one normally making the decision as to whom I slept with. Being on the other side was not too pleasing.

His eyes were cloudy gray, his face white as a man-made pearl. He had brown hair that fell in waves to just below his chin, too short to put back. His mouth was full, almost like a woman's, and he had a cleft chin. I could have died in his eyes as he looked at me.

He moved his finger inside of me, pulling me closer to him, causing me to moan. He smiled at the sound, exposing two long teeth. "You liked that didn't you, little one?"

"Yes," I replied, and I remembered to look away after I answered him.

He moved his finger again, the sharpness cutting into me as if I had been impaled on a dagger, but I wanted more. After a moment, his hot breath exploded on my neck, as he was about to taste me. Then Aria's cool hand came around my shoulder, showing her claim on me. Malachai withdrew himself, but I didn't want him to. I desired him to use me as he would a piece of meat. I craved to be Malachai's, but with Aria's hand on my shoulder I snapped out of my daze and now understood why whatever human or vampire that came to him would stay with him forever. He was dangerous, enticing anyone with a hint of his power. I wondered how Aria had not succumbed to him, but I had a feeling she had had to fight to leave him.

"I did not bring her here for you to play with. I found this young one looking for her master, and as a courtesy I brought her to you, so you could reunite the two of them. She's practically lost without him, aren't you little one?"

"Yes," I answered obediently.

"So you didn't come here to make amends!" Malachai's voice grew cold and distant.

The back of my brain started to itch, the same feeling I got when I had been human. Something bad was about to happen. I wanted to tell Aria we should leave, but now would not be the time to break the charade. I just swallowed and held my tongue, hoping that whatever I felt was a mistake.

"Make amends? I have nothing to make amends for. What happened between us ended a century ago. I thought you would have let it pass. I came here hoping you could help this poor creature."

"Bullshit! You came here to get something out of me. This poor creature is not what she says, and if you don't know that then you're as stupid as the rest of the meat lovers you covet. No, this one is special. I can tell that about her even now," he paused and turned his dangerous attention to me.

"So what do you want from me? Tell me and maybe I'll help you," he cooed.

His mind pressed against mine like a warm blanket. He would caress me from the inside out and take away all of my fear and pain. I yearned to fall into his wonderful embrace, but there was a reason I had come here. I had to be strong.

I summoned my anger at the thought of Devon and then the thought of Malachai as he allowed the other vampires to ravage the mortals around him. I didn't understand how he could do that, or why they so wanted to be used by other vampires. Focusing this hatred, I was able to slice away his will from my thoughts.

"Brenna, don't listen to him."

The itching in the back of my head grew and even though I had cut his power from my mind, the problem hadn't been solved. Danger still lurked in the shadows.

I looked up from my feet and stared right at Malachai. A look of shock appeared on his face. He had not assumed I would stare at him, that I would have the will to do it. I didn't think I had the will to do it either, but I did. I cast off the aura I had been holding onto dearly, letting it shatter so he could see what I truly was, and what I truly wasn't. Aria took in a breath and waited, as all of the other vampires in the room stopped and stared. I took a step forward toward the throne he sat on, testing his strength more than my own. I knew how powerful I was.

"Aria brought me here so I could find one like you."

He was surprised I had challenged his power, but after a moment he recovered and tried again to bore his will into mine, to read my thoughts. However, he was not going to hold me this time. Malachai's mind pushed against my shields like a raging flood on a dam, but I was not budging. I knew with his power he had to be older than Aria by at least a thousand years. I stood my ground, not bending.

"You're a powerful creature, almost as strong as me, and certainly stronger than Arriana. You have a will of your own. You'd make a lovely addition to my stable. I could use one like you. Maybe someone to argue with. Soon you'd be begging me to ride you, to release you from your tortured mind. Wouldn't you like that?"

"I don't think so." I turned to Aria. "Let's go. He won't help us."

"No one ever turns their back on me!" Malachai screamed behind me.

Before I had time to face him, I'd already been thrown across the room, landing on my side, sliding across the rug. Bones cracked in my back as pain shot from my right side. It was hard to breathe as broken ribs punctured my lung. I turned to Malachai. He was still in human form but his claws extended, and his wings were drawn into his side. I took in a shallow breath, wiping the blood away with my tongue. He smiled at the sight, his forked tongue licking his lips. The itching had stopped in my brain. I was impulsive as ever and never listened to the advice I was given, even if it was otherworldly.

My own claws emerged as well as my wings. I was not afraid of him, or his kind. The other vampires in the room withdrew to the corners, knowing better than to get in the middle of the showdown. I got the sense of amusement from the master of the house. He thought he could bend me like a twig because to him I was a child. I smirked. I would show him what a child could do.

Gathering my strength, I ignored my wound and moved faster than he realized. I swiped with my claws, severing one of his wings. It fell to the floor, leaking blackened blood like a faucet. The thing looked like a piece of cardboard now that it had been disconnected. It flapped by itself and then stopped moving as Malachai shrieked from the pain.

He rushed at me fully transformed, his toe talons grating furrows in the red carpet. I saw him and ducked, taking advantage of the fact that he was off balance from the loss of his wing. He turned and charged again. This time I was not fast enough, and he scraped my arm to the bone, almost amputating it by the shoulder. It still rendered my left arm useless until I could heal it. I screamed in pain and was fueled by anger now more than anything.

I put my head down and tackled him with my good arm. Both of us collapsed on the ground. Before he recovered I got on top of him, planting my weight so he couldn't move. He struggled and tried to get free, but I held him fast between my legs. As he did I got an idea. I noticed one of the candles nearby and cast my mind out, calling it to me. It was only a small object so I could get it. It tottered across the carpet until it was within reach. I grabbed it and held it close to his face, close enough that several pieces of his fur caught on fire. He yelped in pain and fear. I smiled and brought it to his eye so he could feel the heat. It was already starting to sizzle as the hot wax dripped into his open socket. As this happened, he transformed back to human form under me. It was a good thing, too, because I was running out of strength, not used to fighting another vampire.

"Please, you've shown them who has won. I've been disgraced. No one has ever bested me. They're yours, take them. I'm sure that was why Arriana brought you here in the first place, to take over my brood."

I glanced at Aria and then back at him. I certainly didn't want the brood of subservient monsters he had under his roof. I just wanted Devon. "I don't give a fuck about what you've got going on here. I just want some information."

"Is that all you want? Then ask."

"I want to know where Devon is. That's it."

"If you would get off of me, I won't challenge you again. You have won."

Aria nodded. So I rolled off of him and moved to one of the chairs. My shoulder was beginning to throb, and I grew weary. I needed to feed. The thought of warm blood in my body gave me something to look forward to and gave me an extra boost to stay focused, but it wasn't going to last long. Maybe he was going to be loyal to his word, but somehow I doubted that.

"I'm looking for Devon. He's your height, has short dark hair, skinny, long fingers, big hands. He may have had a woman with him, his slave. I need to know where they're staying."

He closed his eyes, relieved I had moved the candle from his face. He took a moment to compose himself, and then faced me. "There was one you spoke of. He was here about a week ago. He didn't have a woman, but he brought me a delectable meal. He said if he could do anything just to contact him, but sadly I do not know where he is staying. I didn't need to ask. He has always been welcome to move about my territory."

I searched his face. He couldn't lie now that I had taken his honor from him. Everything he had worked for had been taken away in a matter of moments. It was degrading for him just to be talking with me. He would rather I had killed him. I sighed, all my hopes of finding Veronica melting away. There was nothing I could do, but wait and hope that somehow, some way, she would come back to me. I wanted to leave the lush dungeon he had set up. I scanned the room, surveying the other vampires that waited expectantly for me to make a move, to bid them to do or say something. They had lost a Master but gained me as a Mistress, though I wanted nothing to do with the foul smelling beasts that lingered in this plush basement.

A piece of me wanted to stay and rule the brood, just as it had wanted to be dominated by Malachai, but this was one of the remaining things that connected me to the race of vampires. Even though part of me wanted to be conquered, it would never happen because I would always remember what I was and overcome that small flame in me. No, I would go one step further and free the humans he had captive. Yes, that seemed like a good move.

"Release the mortals," I instructed Malachai.

He looked at me in shock. "You've got to be kidding!"

"Brenna, what are you doing?"

"You said I had won. Release them all."

Before he could answer a loud howl split the noise of the room. I glanced around the room and saw the other vampires were salivating, and they got the sense that I wasn't going to instruct them. Hunger bled into their eyes as they anticipated something and then the door burst open. A large man-wolf came barging into the room, driven by the scent of blood. I caught a whiff of its animal scent and knew it wasn't a vampire. I wondered if this was a werewolf.

Malachai looked at me and smiled. "I don't think I'm going anywhere. Nor are you."

"But you said I won—"

"Child, you bested me, yes, but you are nothing more than a meat-lover. And I would never relinquish my brood to one like you."

I took a few steps backward as I watched his brood take a few steps toward me. Malachai was a monster, just like the others I had encountered. Only Aria had proven to be different than all of the rest of the cretins. Aria grabbed me, but his brood turned away from me and then back to their Master. Malachai's look of triumph faded and was replaced by fear. The skin on a few beasts' faces rippled and contorted as the undead pushed forward.

"She's a meat-lover. I have not lost my place among you," he screamed to his children. Aria pulled me toward the door as I watched his children descend. The werewolf howled again and jumped on one of the unsuspecting humans. Claws shredded flesh, sending a torrent of blood across the room. The monster sank its muzzle into the human. High-pitched wails erupted from the prey as they were broken from their spells. I tried to help the mortals, but Aria grabbed my arm and pulled me with her.

"You can't help them. Come on. It's them or us. I don't know about you, but I'm not ready to meet my Maker." We made it through the door as Malachai's pet feasted on what was left of the human. We slammed the door behind us and then made a run for it.

We passed the two gyrating twins and I noticed the gaping holes in their chests where their hearts had been eaten. The obscene orgy had evolved with a new twist. Two of the female vampires had transformed their faces and had their wings out, while the rest of them remained human. They had their victims sandwiched between them in mid-air, while they fucked and sucked them. The third female I had seen was now lying on the bed, spread eagled, letting drops of blood cover her naked body, so the others could lick it off her. I cringed at the sight. I went to enter into the room to try and free them, but Aria tugged on my arm.

"Come on," she yelled.

"We have to help them." I stood my ground when I heard a loud banging behind us. Screams of humans and vampires alike still sounded from behind the large oak door, but when I looked back the door was splintering. The large shape of something had already become embedded into it.

"Shit." That was not one of the vampires. It was Malachai's pet.

"Come on," Aria screamed.

I stayed one more second, wishing to help the poor mortals when I knew I couldn't. It was either them or us.

We made the stairs just as the door broke and something else happened. The stairs went soft as clay. My foot got stuck in the top one. I stumbled, tried to pull it free from the boards, but it was like putty, and when I looked up, I stared into the red, beady eyes of Malachai's pet. Blood dripped from its long, brown fur. Its sharp teeth grinned at me as a pink tongue laid waiting in between them. I screamed. The muscles in its haunches bunched as it was about to pounce. Aria grabbed hold of my arms and pulled me into the kitchen just as the wolf landed. Its claws raked my leg to the bone. Aria half dragged me out the door as the werewolf struggled to hang onto the doorframe with his enormous claws. Like everything else the whole house was beginning to bleed together like a wet painting. Nothing was substantial as Aria made it through the back door and into the swamp just as the house dissolved into the mists and waters of the bayou, taking everything, including the wolf, with it.

"What the hell was that?" I asked.

"I told you Malachai used to be a magician before he was made into a vampire. He could create illusions, but when he crossed over that power became more substantial. Not that it matters. He's dead." Aria helped me. I was soaked with bog water. My hunger burned within my veins, as my body used the blood I had taken earlier to heal itself. I needed more if I was going to be completely recovered by dawn, or whenever I awoke from my slumber.

"What was that?" Aria asked. Her talons extended as she searched the remains of the swamp.

"I didn't hear anything. Can we just go?"

"No wait. It's coming from over there." She pointed to a tree.

I tried to hone my senses to the area she indicated, but everything was fuzzy from the blood loss. I just shrugged my good shoulder as she went up to the tree and came back with a writhing bundle.

"Look, what we have here," she purred.

"M-m-master," the boy whimpered.

I groaned. It was Joey the junkie. Aria offered him to me, but I turned my nose up at him. There was no way I was going to take anything from one of Malachai's brood, especially this one, who got off on just the thought of being bitten.

"Suit yourself. It's a shame to waste a good meal." She smiled.

Before I could protest, Aria's claws cut through Joey's neck. His cranium flew like a Frisbee across the swamp and plopped somewhere in the water. A second later, I heard the swishing of alligators going after the morsel. His body stood erect, blood erupting from a geyser in his throat. Aria opened her mouth wide to catch the blood, and then let the deadweight drop, his body folding like a lawn chair on the ground. Aria licked her fingers clean and smiled at me.

"What?" she asked as if nothing had happened.

I shook my head, disgusted over the display. I really wasn't like her in any way.

"What was the quarrel between you and Malachai anyway?" I willed my wings out so we could venture back to the city.

"It was over nothing, really. We had this game. Whoever could lure in the most humans in a century won. Well, I won by one mortal. He lost. He never let it go. He was such a sore loser, going on about how his honor was hurt and how I was a woman and all that bullshit. Finally I had enough so I left."

Both of us flapped into the night, our wings making slight swishing sounds against the breeze.

"I'll never understand what makes you guys tick. When this is over with I want nothing more to do with any other vampires."

I yearned for Veronica to be back in my arms, but I was no closer to having that. Malachai didn't help. The only real lesson I learned coming to this place was how perverted other vampires were. I just wanted everything back to normal.

Aria laughed. "You can say that now, but one of these days you might be knee deep in a brood yourself. Don't discount the future. Things have a way of coming back to you. Just you wait and see."

"Is that a prophecy from the Delphic Oracle or are you just saying that?"

"Oh, I'm not telling. You're the psychic, you figure it out."

I groaned, not even acknowledging her, and moved even more swiftly into the night, to a soft bed where I would lay down my head and fall into a dreamless sleep.

31

CHAPTER THIRTY-ONE

My name is Ronnie.

"Ronnie," Devon called my name.

His voice was smooth and strong. I melted inside as the syllables of my name twisted around on his tongue. I gazed up at him and then bowed my head, rubbing up against his knee. He ran his fingers along my spine and I shivered. The sensation made me want him then and there, but I waited expectantly.

"Your child is coming for you. Do you know this?"

"Yes, Master. I've sensed her in my dreams." I paused, my voice nothing more than a whisper so it wouldn't hurt my Master's ears. I knew my child was coming for me. In my dreams I had seen her fighting with an Ancient. Devon knew she was searching because she wanted me back, but he did not have the daymare visions I had. He was not blood-bound to her. He hadn't given her a new life. I had wondered if he had dreams of me, being able to track me over the years, but somehow I knew he hadn't.

When I woke that night to the glorious rays of the moon, my child had been on my mind. In the vision I had, I felt fear for her. That was strange and I surmised Veronica had somehow unshackled herself and was running rampant in my mind. I hadn't wanted Brenna to get hurt. Something in me desired to comfort her, and even as I woke to greet the night, I had troubling emotions. I should have gone to my Master, but he wouldn't understand. He would think that I was turning into my human counterpart, that I was turning into a meat-lover, too.

"What is it, Ronnie? You have something on your mind. I can read it in your thoughts. Tell me; I won't be angry."

I sighed, looking up at my Master briefly to get a read of his face, but it was as blank as uncarved marble. Veronica turned as I mulled over the decision of whether or not to tell Devon how I felt. I decided against it. I didn't think it would be the best. I didn't want to fall out of favor.

"It's nothing, Master. I only fear for you if she comes. I wish nothing to happen," I lied, lowering my head, hoping he had not been monitoring my thoughts as I said this. I felt ashamed. For the first time I lied to the one who had brought me into this glorious life, where I was a god to the mortals we fed on. I simply did not know how to tell him the truth. I did not want to appear weak, but the more I thought of my child, the more I craved to be reunited with her. In my visions, I experienced feelings for her. This was not related to my human side. I truly felt something for the girl. I wanted to nurture her, and as much as I loved my Master, I felt something was wrong.

His hand ran down my spine again. I responded, but for the first time his touch elicited no true thrill. The more I thought of this, the more I realized he didn't care for me. I worshipped him, showed him kindness, was an obedient servant; but now that he had me back, he was bored. It seemed our rutting was only to relieve his tension. Inside I cried out in frustration.

See what have I been trying to show you for years, Veronica whispered in my thoughts.

I whimpered, trying to ignore her, but her words echoed in my thoughts. I leaned against his leg, but it was only to regain my composure. My Master thought it was to get more attention. He patted me again, his claws digging into the vertebrae of my back. He traced the curve of my muscles and went to my ass, swiftly inserting his talon into my asshole. I drew in a breath and backed into his talon as he impaled me. I heard him sigh as if doing me were a job. Within a second he had withdrawn his talon and mounted me, sticking his cold, hard dick into my cunt. He reared up against me and I participated as expected, but this time I took no enjoyment from his touch. For the first time, I distrusted my Master. I closed my eyes, wondering if my human side was actually right.

My Master withdrew from me, but it was an automatic response. He slapped my ass and mumbled something, dismissing me. It was all I could do to keep from hissing at him. I held my forked tongue and crawled away, back to the corner in which I slept. I sat, closing my eyes, trying to figure some way to warn my child before she came here, before she was broken and turned into something like myself. I did not want to see her get hurt.

I curled my lips at this thought. No, my Master would not turn her into a slave. She would outsmart him. I knew this. As the sun rose over the horizon, signaling my sleep, my only thought was of her.

32

CHAPTER THIRTY-TWO

My name is Brenna.

My nostrils flared at the scent of crackling bacon. The smell of it turned my stomach. I yawned, wondering what day it was. The last thing I remembered was my shoulder aching after my confrontation with Malachai.

Then I had fed, drinking from a victim who crossed my path. My attack had been vicious, but like my first victim, I could not kill him. Even then, with the wounds I had sustained, I took another, drinking until I was sated, leaving my prey alive. Aria laughed at me, as I had been so vicious with Malachai. I paused, looking up at her, blood dripping on my naked breasts, and growled. Aria made the comment that I wasn't as different from her kind as I thought. I projected a mental slap into her mind and she quieted down after that. I finished my meal, sating my hunger. Blood surged through my system, renewing some of my strength. It cleared my brain, moving away the cobwebs so I could focus. It warmed me, making my heart speed up as the blood settled in my system.

I licked my lips again as I thought of the thick, salty fluid. My stomach growled, but then the smell of eggs wafted to my nose and the contents of my stomach threatened to come up. The thought of what Aria was doing in my kitchen made me get out of bed.

I stretched, noticing the stiffness of the muscles in my arm and my leg where the werewolf had clawed me and Malachai had almost severed my arm. When I examined the wounds, only faint pink marks remained.

"Humph!" I was impressed with my body's ability to heal. I slipped on a robe.

"Hi," Aria called, chipper as the morning sun trickled in through the shutters.

I winced at the light, letting my eyes adjust to the brightness. "What the hell are you cooking?"

Aria smiled as she moved breakfast onto two plates and offered one to me. I picked up a piece of bacon, sniffing it. The hardness cut into the ridges of my fingers. The scent of it impaled my nose, causing me to sneeze. Never before had I smelled something so hideous. The burnt pork, which I used to eat on occasion, held no appeal to me and reminded me of burned rubber. I dropped the piece of blackened meat, marveling that it didn't break when it hit the porcelain plate.

"You should have some. You've been asleep for two days, so I thought you might be hungry. I hope you don't mind."

I shrugged, listening to her chomp on the bacon, grinding it between her teeth like broken glass, pounding it to dust. I cringed at the creaking her jaw made as she swallowed the meat. I didn't understand how she ate the stuff when all we needed was blood to survive.

"How can you eat that?" I finally asked.

"Just because our bodies don't need this stuff to survive, it doesn't mean we can't take in human food. Most of us lose the taste for it, but it helps when you're eating in public. Then there are no questions. Besides, I find that what humans eat is delectable. You still drink things, so why not eat? Besides, don't you wonder what chocolate tastes like now that you've changed? Trust me; mortals don't know what they're missing. It really is better than sex. Well, human sex anyway. So why not have some?"

I scanned my plate one more time and knew I couldn't eat the bacon, but the eggs looked edible. I grabbed the fork and popped a few of them into my mouth and chewed. Their rubberiness was nothing new to me, and their taste was the same, still disgusting, but I swallowed them anyway. I took another bite of breakfast and saw Aria smile. I didn't want to hurt her feelings. It seemed this time they were easier to eat, probably because I didn't need their energy to keep me going. It made me wonder what other foods tasted like. It was awkward to have the food lingering in my stomach, weighing me down as though someone had lined my belly with stones.

"Silly." Aria laughed at me. She had been monitoring my thoughts as I examined the effect the food had on my body.

"What?"

"You have to think about digesting the food. It doesn't happen automatically anymore. Just tell your stomach to start. It'll get the juices going. If not, you're going to have it sitting in there for as long as you want. I have to warn you though, it'll be quick. Our bodies normally expel anything that is unwanted."

I eyed her, willing my body to focus on the food in my stomach. Nothing happened at first, then my body responded to the foreign substances. She was right. It was quick. My stomach lurched forward, like I was going to puke, and then I heard it gurgling, sputtering, like a motor turning over, and my digestive juices started, working on the food.

"How do we get rid of it, after it's digested?"

"What do you think the toilet is for?"

"Oh!"

A few minutes later I found myself in the bathroom, getting rid of the food. Aria had also said it a was up to me to think about digesting and then it would be gone, so theoretically I could wait a year before I had to dispel the food, but I didn't think that was a good idea.

Back in the kitchen, Aria gave me a devilish grin. "I told you."

I started to respond when images flashed in my head. At first I ignored them, thinking them to be memories of the other night, but this was different. The pictures raced in my head like neon signs. They were pieces, only fragments. They filled my head with heat and pain as I tried to make them out a second time. Soon they came too fast, and all I could do to stay conscious was to let them flood over me.

I saw images of someone's feet. There were white walls, a black rug. There was a painting on the wall of spattered colors, but when the image came again, I realized it was the splattering of blood. There was a taloned hand, pointing at a window. I couldn't see what it was. When I tried to focus on the object outside the window, all I saw was a box, brown and gray in the distance. It was too bright to see. The sunlight streaming in the window blinded me when I knew it shouldn't have.

There were feelings mixed in with the flashes: hatred, pain, anguish, love, and determination. I tried to understand where it all came from, but I ended up with a black wall. My eyes rolled up in the back of my head. I thought I smelled the scent of burning hair, and when I looked down at my skin it had blackened and crisped. I shrieked and fell, landing hard on the floor. I pulled my hand into the darkness out of the light, huddling in the corner. While this happened I wasn't exactly me, I was someone else, someone who sent me these visions. The pain was so overwhelming I didn't know where I was. I screamed again, and then felt someone shaking me. I looked up, seeing the shadow of a man, but it was only an outline in my blurred vision, and then Aria was there, holding me. The man backhanded me, sending me across the room. I hit the wall hard, bending the sheetrock behind the paint. I tried to look up to please my Master, but when I gazed up it was only Aria, looking down at me and calling my name.

"Brenna, are you all right?" Her hand was shaking me. I cowered in her arms as she held me, afraid that he would beat me again. I had woken him and this was my punishment, but maybe I had accomplished something. I didn't know.

Suddenly a sharp sting across my face brought me back to reality. I opened my eyes, growling at my assailant. Instinctively my fangs descended. I raised my hand to slash at my attacker but found it held fast.

When my eyes focused, Aria held my wrist. Her fingers were clawed as well. Her eyes had begun to bleed red, her beast awakening, ready to defend her if she had to.

"Brenna." Her voice was thick as she yanked at my hand, cutting into my flesh as her talon pierced my skin. I was intrigued by the blood moving down my arm. It trailed like oil down my flesh, which I expected to be burned, but it wasn't. I touched my arm, ignoring the stickiness, and felt the cool, perfect flesh underneath. It had all felt so real. I touched my cheek, smearing red liquid on my face. No bones were broken. There was nothing wrong with me. I stared into Aria's face, her eyes were now totally red, and as she breathed I saw her forked tongue protruding between her lips.

The scent of my blood permeated my nose, as I know it filled hers. I watched her tongue darting out, caressing her lips as her grip on me tightened. I stared into her eyes and offered my healing wrist to her, the blood seeping as the wound had began to close. She hesitated. Her hand trembled, the only movement she displayed, and then after a moment she brought my wrist to her waiting lips. She inhaled the scent of my blood as if testing the nose of a fine wine. Her tongue wrapped around my flesh, taking in the last bits of blood. I moaned, pressing my wrist against her lips, begging her to suck harder, and she complied.

My hand found her breast and rubbed the nipple as it rose against my touch. I grabbed her hand and moved it to my sex. I was hot and freezing at the same time as she drank out my life. Her fingers found my nub, her other hand pulling loose the tie of my robe. She sucked my blood and worked me for a few moments. I closed my eyes, enjoying the sensations. My free hand sought her moist depths, so I could make her come, but she clamped her knees shut as my hand reached her. She pulled away from me, letting my wrist drop and backed away. I whined my sorrow.

I waited there, letting out a few ragged breaths. When I had calmed down I addressed her, resting my head against the cool tile floor.

"Why did you stop?"

"It's not right. You didn't know what you were doing. If you truly wanted me, it wouldn't have been like that."

I laughed. I was getting lectured by a vampire who was turning me down because I wasn't in the right frame of mind. I wondered when the last time had been for Aria. Maybe it would explain why she was so cold. She thought she was high and mighty just because she was over a thousand years old. Here I was giving myself to her, doing her a favor, and she didn't want me.

I growled, exposing my fangs. She knew I was angry, but it didn't seem to matter.

I laughed, more hissing than anything.

"Brenna, snap the fuck out of it. Damn it, girl. Stop tripping on the superiority complex already and tell me what the hell happened!"

It had all come on me so fast, I didn't know. It wasn't like me to treat Aria so. She had helped me. Pangs of guilt rose, burning me, but I dismissed them as I looked at my hand again, marveling over how it had not been burned. The images didn't make sense, but the man in them did. I knew him as Master, but I knew him in other ways, too. He was connected to me through blood. We had been one. I had looked up into his face when I had been dying. For kicks he had given me a trace amount of his elixir, lining my lips with it, just enough to taste, to keep me in my body as I waited for either death to take me or for Veronica to make up her mind and let me become one of the undead.

Then it all clicked. Veronica sent me the images. The burn wasn't on me. Why did she burn in the sunlight? Her tolerance was high. Then I remembered what she had told me, of how bestial vampires had no tolerance in the sun. The way she attacked me the other night made me realize that her other half was more in control than her mortal self.

She was loyal to Devon. Something must have caused that to change. I felt the anger and humiliation in the images. Something transpired in her brain to make her realize what an asshole he really was. That gave me a bit of hope. Maybe she wasn't totally lost to me. I dreaded the thought of killing the one who made me. She would not want her bestial half in control. If that happened, I would take her head, sending her soul to heaven where it belonged. Maybe then she would be reunited with her sister and the family that was taken from her. This was an improvement over what had happened the last time I encountered her. My Master—my love—was still alive, and it seemed the demon in her wanted freedom as well. If that were the case, then I would gladly give it to both of them. Cold tears seeped out of my eyes before I realized what was going on. Veronica had done her best and in her own way contacted me. I knew there was hope and that made my spirits soar. I gazed up into Aria's eyes, which had gone slightly back to normal.

"I'm sorry. I didn't know what happened. I thought you were someone else."

"I figured that, the way you acted. What happened to you? I heard you scream. Are you all right?"

I nodded slowly, realizing how I must look. I got up, helping Aria at the same time. I gave her a quick hug and led her into my living room. I marveled at the sun as it shined onto my skin and didn't burn me. Veronica's feelings still lingered in my mind. I pushed them aside and thought of things that were in the images. Obviously she wanted to show me something out the window. That was why she was looking out it. Also, there was a large box thing. It looked like a warehouse. I sighed. That was mostly the whole section. There had to be something else.

"So what happened?"

"Veronica contacted me. I don't know how she did it, but she did. She wants me to come and get her. I just know it."

"It could be a trap. Devon could have told her to contact you." Aria reclined on my couch, out of the direct light of the sun.

"There was so much anger and hatred toward him. It couldn't have been a trap."

"So then you know where she is?"

I sighed. That was the only problem. "Isn't there any way I can sense her? Trace her through my blood?"

Aria shook her head. "The only way you can trace someone is through a mental connection. You would think since we are bound by blood it'd be easy, but it isn't. Nothing is simple. If Veronica reached out to you and found you mentally, you should've been able to follow the connection back and find her on the other side. But—"

"I tried, but there was only a wall. I think Devon was close so her shields were up," I jumped in.

"If that's the case, the only way you can find her is when she's asleep, and from what we saw of her the other day, she was consumed by the beast, so you're going to have to track her. Maybe in a few hours when she's asleep, I can help you. It's dangerous. If Devon suspects anything, he can attack you psychically through her. If that happens, you're toast. You won't be able to throw your shields up quick enough."

"I have to take that chance. I have to find her."

"Then it's settled." Aria glanced at the clock. It was only eight-thirty in the morning. "We need to wait two hours or so, just to make sure she and Devon are both in a deep sleep. Think you can wait that long?"

"I don't have a choice, do I?"

"No, but in the meantime, do you want any more eggs?"

I glared at her and she laughed. I collapsed on the sofa, basking in the light of the sun, hoping in some way it would impart some of its strength so that I could find Devon and free Veronica before it set. I was only dreaming, and the sun was something to warm my skin and light my way.

33

CHAPTER THIRTY-THREE

My name is Ronnie.

I cupped my burned hand close to my chest, hoping it would heal. I smiled over what I had accomplished.

When the sun rose that morning, I had pretended to go to sleep, waiting for my Master to fall into his dreams. When I was sure he was settled in bed, I searched my mind for some connection to my child. I had to call to her, to let her know where I was. With all of my searching I found nothing. I had almost given up when I felt my humanity stir deep within my mind. It held back and then came forward, assuming it could help me. It was the part of me Brenna had more kin-ship with. Even though it was our blood that ran in the child's veins, it was the mortality of my personality she was connected to.

Veronica came forth as if coming onto a stage. We stood side by side on the same platform, evaluating one another. For the first time, there was no animosity between us. I had finally realized she was right about Devon. Our merging into one being earlier had been the right thing to do. There were still some things we had to work out though. Veronica showed me her love for our child and that it was because of Brenna that we could now be truly whole. We sized each other up, circling the stage, wondering what the other would do. We needed Brenna to survive to keep us together be-cause we both loved her so much. It wasn't just me who would find her. It would have to be a combined effort. At that moment, she wanted to come back and take control, but it wasn't a good idea. The Master must not know. If he did, then he would rip us to shreds. Just the thought of his claws touching my skin made me shiver with disgust. I didn't want him fon-dling me anymore, let alone fucking me. I wanted to feel the soft hands of my child. I pulled the memories from Veronica of when our body had been engaged in the act of love with her. That was what I wanted. I desired to drink her in, making her feel what it was like to be really and truly loved by another of her kind. Or someone like her kind. It was true we were different because she had no beast. The Master did not know this, and I was not about to tell him.

As he slept, I merged briefly with Veronica and let her find the bond we shared with Brenna. She found it quickly. I closed my eyes and stared at the wall. I thought of Brenna, and suddenly I was in the child's head as she thought of Veronica. As she thought of me. I had to get used to the name as it echoed inside of my head. I was so used to being called Ronnie, for it was what my Master called me on the night of my birth, but I could learn to hate it.

My humanity cheered as we made contact with Brenna. It suggested we go to the window and let Brenna know where we were. I agreed, but the sun would hurt. I hesitated, and then drew back the shades, looking out briefly and being blinded by the sun as I put my hand up to shield my eyes. My skin caught on fire. I shrieked loudly, breaking a glass coffee table my Master had in the other room from the pitch of the wail. It woke him, and he came running.

My mortality retreated so he would not suspect anything. He saw me looking out the window and pushed me aside, back handing me so that I flew against the wall, crunching the material it was made of. He stood over me, his row of fangs ready to burst from his mouth. I cowered in front of him.

"Never do that again. Don't you know sunlight will kill us? Kill me?"

He threw me into a closet and locked the door. "Stupid bitch. I knew I should've disposed of her when I had the chance," Devon muttered to himself.

Once darkness enveloped me, I smiled. My humanity surfaced and said it would be all right. Brenna would find me. I believed that, and that was what I thought of as I drifted off to sleep, with my humanity settling back into my personality. I knew there would be some adjustment, but I didn't think that we had to be at war anymore. Our differences could be worked out, if not for the good of our existence, then for the good of our child, who was braver and stronger than both of us. She had faced what was inside of her and knew what it was like not to fear the light of day.

34

CHAPTER THIRTY-FOUR

My name is Brenna.

I paced anxiously, waiting for the sun to climb in the sky. Aria finished the eggs and sat down to read a book. I tried to remain calm and keep myself busy. I screened my answering machine, listening to the desperate clients who needed my help. I took a paper and pen and began to record their numbers, categorizing which ones were more important and how old the messages were. I made it through most of them without thinking of Veronica. The last few, the most recent ones, were all whining about lost loves. In frustration, I yanked the answering machine from the socket and threw it against the wall. Aria gazed up at me and laughed.

"That's a great way to conduct your business. Don't you ever wonder why they want to know what the future will bring them? I mean, when people came to me as I sat in the temple, I often wondered why they bothered. We all have free will, but no, humans are too stupid to accept that. They all wanted me to solve their problems. Did you ever find that to be true when you did readings?"

I wondered if Aria retained her psychic powers after she had been turned. When I shifted my gaze, focusing on her aura, I noticed it wasn't as bright as mine, as those of people who were psychic. Normally, those who did psychic work had brighter energy fields due to the fact they were conduits of energy from another realm of reality, another dimension. My aura had not changed much. It had grown brighter. I had thought about going back to doing psychic readings. It would be easier now that I was a vampire. Some form of higher consciousness gave me the ability to continue my life as well as help those who crossed my path, and it had let me keep my abilities.

"There were times, as a mortal, they got on my nerves, but I always helped them in some way. It didn't matter if the information was wrong. It was important that the clients walked out with a lighter heart. Many times this happened and I felt complete just in that knowledge. Humans might be my prey, but that doesn't mean that I have to con them, or pry into their minds. All it means is that I have more responsibility. Didn't you ever feel that way about the ones you helped? I mean, you must have had kings and queens coming to you for advice, considering you were supposed to be the direct connection to the Divine."

"At first it was great and then it got boring. I'd go into a trance and things came out of my mouth, but I had no connection to the words. I liked the status. Do you know how many men and women begged for me, just to touch them, to spend the night? Of course, I was supposed to be a virgin, like any of the priestesses were. That's a laugh. At night there were so many orgies. So many things happened to me that I didn't know where one thing began and the other stopped. After a while I thought I was indestructible, a goddess. Now look at me. Perfect body, great skin, and all I can eat without gaining a pound."

"Don't you miss it though, the connection to the other side, to the cosmos?"

"We are the other side, honey."

"Yes, but—"

"But nothing," Aria glanced at the clock. "Come on. Veronica and Devon should be wrapped in dreams."

I sighed, hating how she changed the subject, but it gave me the answer. She truly did miss the feeling of being plugged in. It wasn't the all-powerful feeling she talked about, that was just an ego trip. No, the plugged in feeling was the ability to know things, to understand the universe on a basic level without having to think about it. At those moments, it didn't matter how old you were, or what race, or where you were on the planet. You were part of everything, part of the universal consciousness that kept the world intact. You had an awareness of yourself that let you float along with the atoms of dust on the wind, be part of a cat basking in the sun, or just be the energy between two lovers as they kissed for the first time. It was an experience that really couldn't be put into words, but it was what made the job worth it.

"Come on. Stop thinking of your future, past, present, whatever. I need you to focus in on Veronica."

I nodded, knowing she was right. There would be many times I could contemplate the mysteries of the universe and how they now fitted into my life. It was not the time to compare and contrast the differences in my psychic channels. This was the time to find the one I loved.

I sat down next to her on the couch as she pulled the curtains across the window, putting the room into semi-darkness. I sighed as the temperature dropped. Still, it was a welcome relief. Up until then I had not realized how hot I had been. I closed my eyes and let myself relax. Focusing on my aura, I felt the magnetism it put off as it interacted with everything else in the environment. I grounded myself, pushing my energy down within the earth so I wouldn't have to call upon my own energy to defend myself. If need be, I could pull energy from the elements around me. In my mind, I cleared my thoughts, waiting for Aria to help me.

Her hand lingered on my temples. I shivered as I felt her aura contracting against mine. She massaged my forehead, urging me to relax more. I tried to comply, but I was too keyed up on trying to find Veronica.

"Quiet your mind. Pull one thing from your memory that is the strongest connection you have to her. It can be an emotion, a picture. Find that and hold on to it."

Images of her flashed in my mind, but I cleared them away, as they would do me no good. I needed to find an emotion because that was how my psychic abilities worked. I got feelings about things. Of course there were images, but emotions were stronger than all of them, and the emotion I had for her was love. I grasped onto that, and held it close to my heart, bringing it into my brain.

Aria's mind brushed against mine. I had no shields up against her. I trusted her and didn't need to close my thoughts.

"Now, cast out your mind, holding on to that emotion. Send it out like you would when you read a person. Move like the wind latching to the one you love and push past her shields. Invade her mind and let her know who you are."

Aria's words faded as I concentrated on Veronica. I had to find her in the myriads of people in New Orleans. I had not used my psychic powers since I had been turned, so it was like using them for the first time and not knowing what I was doing. As I held to the love for Veronica, I knew I was getting closer. Her aura vibrated like a beacon in a midnight cloud-filled sea. It was bright and I was drawn right to it. I moved faster than I ever imagined, until I was there and the light blinded me. When I thought it couldn't get any brighter, I opened my eyes and saw that I was standing in a room. A king sized bed took up most of the space. I moved closer, noting the hardwood floors, and saw a familiar figure sleeping on it. Devon. He wasn't why I came. Veronica was nearby. I scanned the room for any sign of her and heard breathing inside the closet.

I grasped the knob, but my flesh passed through the metal. I tried again, but the same thing happened. Even though I was with Veronica, I was nothing more than a ghost. If Devon suspected me, I wouldn't be able get back to my body soon enough to raise my shields to protect myself. I was too inexperienced to understand how to do damage on this level. He could do more than enough mental damage to my psyche if I were unprotected. I didn't want to chance that.

Not being able to open the door, I stepped through it. Passing through the wood was interesting. Each tiny sliver impaled me, tickling my insides. Inside I crouched down, watching Veronica lost in a soundless sleep.

My heart thumped loudly as the innocence of her was so wonderful. This was the woman I had fallen in love with, the one who would take care of me over the next few centuries. Absently, I tried to move a piece of hair out of her face.

My aura connected with hers and her eyes snapped open, staring into space, knowing someone was there, but not being able to see me. The piece of hair I touched actually moved a few millimeters.

When her eyes opened, I knew the beast was awake in her. Her eyes were partially red from hunger. I glanced down at her arms to see one bore the burn I thought I had on mine. It was true; I really had been there. Unconsciously, I moved my hand over the area, feeling the energy. There was a hole. My aura moved into hers, filling the gap as I concentrated. A golden light encompassed my arm and moved over her hand and into the break in her aura. The flesh underneath began to mend, the burned skin turning white and then pink, until there was nothing left of the wound. The golden light lingered a bit longer and then died down. The heat that entered my body left me, and then I was lightheaded.

"Who's there?" Veronica whispered.

Brenna, I thought to her.

"It can't be."

I didn't know what to say to her.

Brenna, you must come back, Aria shouted across the distance. Her voice echoed in my mind, calling me back.

I only had a few more moments with Veronica. Closing my eyes, I focused the energy in my hand, brushing my palm against her cheek, sending her my love at the same time. She felt the depression of my hand on her flesh. She looked into the empty space, knowing I was truly there.

"Is it really you?"

Yes.

Her eyes grew wet as she heard me. Something was tugging deep inside me, trying to get my attention. Aria tried to pull me back.

Come with me.

Veronica shook her head no. She didn't have that much courage, and the height of the sun would kill her because of her demonic personality. I had to try anyway. I needed her, wanted her to be with me.

Then how can I find you?

"The same way you found me now. All it takes is one time to establish the link."

Then why didn't you do this before?

"How could I when my Master needed me? Now...it doesn't matter. You shouldn't come here.

He'll kill you. Don't come looking for me again. Please go! I—"

The door opened. Devon snarled at Veronica and pulled her out of the closet. I stayed where I was, afraid to move in case he sensed me.

"Who the hell were you talking to? Don't you know I'm fucking trying to sleep? This is the second time this morning. Are you trying to drive me mad?"

"No Master! I'm sorry. I was dreaming, talking in my sleep. Please, forgive me."

My heart went out as I saw the strong woman I loved broken in front of the demonic bastard who had made her. Devon's cruelty had made her dependent on him. She tried to be complacent, but he just wasn't listening. He was too much of a dumb ass to want to believe her.

Instead of leaving her alone, he threw her across the room so she landed on the bed. He lunged at her, talons poised over her heart.

"Is this want you wanted?" he screamed.

"No, Master. Please, I'm sorry," she whined.

Devon paused, horrified at what she had said. "Did you say no to me? You fucking whore. Just for that I'll show you what it's like to deny your Master."

Veronica covered her face as he swiped at her, trying to defend herself as Devon shredded her tits. Blood and tissues flew around the room as if an automatic shredder had gone crazy. I screamed in frustration, but he didn't hear me. He kept attacking her, slicing away muscle and chips of bone. If I didn't stop him, then she might lose one of her arms, or worse, he could graze her heart and kill her. I noticed one of Devon's slippers by the foot of his bed. Without thinking I made a grab for it, and to my amazement it came with me. Not taking the time to wonder what made me able to hold it, I lobbed it. It landed squarely on the back of Devon's head. He stopped in mid-slash and turned around, looking to see who had thrown the slipper. He couldn't see me. I thought I was safe, and his nostrils flared as he caught my scent. He smiled a wicked grin. The muscles relaxed around his mouth, and his arm fell to his side. I didn't know what he was doing, but I knew it was time to leave.

I thought of Aria and returning to my flesh. I tugged on the connection I had stretched so very thin, and like a rubber band rebounding, I snapped across the distance and was thrown into my body. The scene at Devon's house retreated, as I was pulled backward through a long black tunnel. Devon's feral presence descended upon me. I slammed back into my body, opening my eyes. I drew on energy from the earth, picturing a thick, circular, clear wall around me, before Devon arrived in the apartment. He snarled as he tried toppling my barriers, but he couldn't. I had gotten back just in time.

Don't think you can have her back. She's mine. Just like you'll soon be.

"You'll never have me. And I'll get her back. Just you wait. Now get out of here."

I felt Devon smile. His grin seemed to spread throughout the room, pressing on me at all sides.

If you do come for her, maybe there won't be anything left.

"I'll kill you."

I'd like to see you try, little one. How about this: you come and I'll let her go. We'll trade fair and square. You see, I really want you.

"Brenna, don't. It's a trap."

"I know Aria, but what am I going to do?" I paused. The only way Veronica would be set free would be by playing by his rules. She would not be able to survive with him much longer, and even if he did get me, there was no way I was going to bend to his will. He had me and he knew it. "Fine. Where do I meet you?"

Devon's energy grew silent as he contemplated his plan. This was all a game, and I had to play if I wanted to get back the one I loved. I would win, no matter what.

Meet me tomorrow night at St. Louis Cemetery #1. I'm sure you know where it is.

And then he was gone.

"You can't go. He'll kill you."

I got up from the floor and stretched, relaxing for the first time, realizing how tense I was. I had to save

Veronica. "There's no argument. You and I both know that. Besides, Veronica would do the same for me. You would do the same for your child."

Aria remained silent behind me, knowing I was right. I opened the shutter and wondered how I would overcome Devon. He was stronger than I, but I was faster and more tolerant in the sun. He wanted to meet me after sunset. I would be ready, no matter what it took.

PART FIVE
DEATH

35

CHAPTER THIRTY-FIVE

My name is Brenna.

At nightfall, the hazy sunset hung over the city like a curtain being lowered, and I waited to make my curtain call. I stood outside my apartment, ready to go. I pulled a cloak of energy around me, shielding myself from people passing by. Aria wanted to come, but I told her no. I had to take on Devon alone. Besides, if he sensed her then he might go back on his word and hurt Veronica. I couldn't chance that. What was the point? I didn't know what to expect and if he won it was either my life or my sanity at stake. I didn't know which was worse. I wasn't afraid of dying. I had already done that. I was more frightened of ending up his obedient servant. I doubted that would happen. He thought I was like all the other vampires; he didn't know I wasn't torn asunder by a bestial personality. He thought I was some human-loving bitch trying to take his child away from him. By challenging his authority, I pissed him off, just as I had done with Malachai.

Well, I had played the subservient pet once, but I was not about to do it again.

I would never bow my head to another. I was as independent as a bird. I would not play the vampiric game. It was time the game had a new set of rules. I smiled at this. Their society was going to change. I would be the catalyst. It didn't mean I would go out killing others of their kind, but I would defend myself if I had to. Never would I recruit mortals and make them in my image.

A slight breeze kicked up a few of the fallen leaves, and I knew it was time for me to make my voyage. Pulling the energy skin closer, I began my journey to the outskirts of the French Quarter, where the cemetery lay. By the time it had grown fully dark, I got to Rampart Street. I glanced at the projects on the left of the cemetery, hearing the inhabitants talking inside. Some lingered on the porch, watching the passing traffic, while small children played in the parking lot. I took a quick mental scan of the cemetery, detecting no living things in there. There could have been a hundred or so ghosts lingering in the place, but I didn't care. There were no detectable heartbeats, human or otherwise. That meant nothing. Devon was probably keeping himself and Veronica cloaked.

I crossed to the other side and leaped over the wall of the cemetery, clearing it and landing on top of one of the raised crypts inside. I left my wings in, so I would not use the energy of pulling them out. The more I kept myself cloaked the better chance I had of taking them by surprise.

I surveyed the tops of the graves and didn't see anything. I took a breath and hopped down, landing silently. I moved through the cemetery and found myself in front of Mary Laveau's tomb. The cool surface helped to steady me. I moved in between a few of the rows, cautiously wondering when Devon would jump out and try to take me. I found nothing until I came to a crypt with a small bench in front of it. Someone lounged on the stone bench, hands clasped. I noticed the long, girl-like fingers and swore to myself, hoping that it would have been Veronica, but why would Devon keep his bargaining chip out in the open? No, he had hidden her somewhere.

"You won't find her," he crooned. "Do you think I'm stupid enough to bring her here?"

"You promised an exchange. Her for me."

I stood a few feet from him. He sat calmly picking the dirt from underneath his fingernails. Irritation welled up in me, but that was just what he desired. He wanted me to give in to my anger so he could catch me off guard, but that wouldn't happen. I took a deep breath and quieted my distraught emotions.

"I never said anything. I just said to meet me here." He paused and grinned. His eyes shifted to a nearby tomb. "Isn't that right?"

"Yes, Master." Aria's distinct treble echoed in the night as she stepped out from behind a crypt.

I turned, shocked to see the ancient vampire standing there. She grinned, revealing a mouthful of sharpened teeth.

Fuck! How could I have been so stupid? I let her into my home, into my mind? I kicked up a cloud of dust from the gravel path.

"You were my friend. I trusted you."

"Oh, poor Brenna. Did you really think I was just going to show up out of nowhere and help you? I've always done my Master's bidding. He knew you would need some guidance. Why not send me?"

"Everything you said was a lie."

She knew where I was vulnerable, what things were precious to me. I didn't think. Devon had given her the perfect assignment. Infiltrate the enemy and get them to trust you.

"Not everything. I really was a Delphic Oracle, and you did wonderfully by killing Malachai. Before I lost my powers I told Master about the birth of a new kind a vampire, one that would be stronger and could survive in the sun. With it he could rule our kind. Moreover, it would be in his bloodline. He just had to control it. And then you came along. Just like I predicted."

"Yes. Aria was wonderful in her day. And you have so much potential, Brenna. All you have to do is accept me as your Master. Veronica is a weak link in our world. Come with me, and I'll make you greater than anything you have ever dreamed."

I swallowed and took a quick assessment. I was outnumbered. I wouldn't be able to take on two vampires all by myself. I gulped. My heartbeat picked up. Tension grew in the air. There was no way I was going to be Devon's slave or become the prodigal child he wanted me to be. Without thinking, I bolted. I wove in and out of the gravestones, trying to make it to the back wall. If I could do that, then I would be all right. I rushed past worn down tombs and saw the back wall in sight, the part of the cemetery dedicated only to Protestant parishioners. Ten feet from the wall, I leaped, my wings bursting out of my back. My hand found the top of the wall when hands grasped my waist, throwing me off balance. Claws raked deep within my shoulders, stopping my wings in mid shift, as the pain of the wound overtook me. I cried out as I hit the ground, and Aria's claws hooked me like a side of beef, dragging me through the cemetery over the worn paths with gravel digging into my ass. I struggled against her grip, but her claws only tore into me more, so after a while I stopped.

Aria brought me back and stood me up. Devon smiled, exposing twin fangs. His eyes bled red as he anticipated having a meal. A long, curved talon caressed my cheek, drawing blood. His tongue connected with my skin, lapping at the seeping wound. I pulled back as much as I could, but Aria held fast so I had to stand and endure him enjoying himself. He laughed deep in his throat when I tried to pull away, savoring the look of disgust on my face.

"You're as good as I remember you. The first time I saw you on the street, I knew all about you. I peeked into your mind, discovering all your desires. Why do you think you took me home that night? I was what you were looking for, something to replace the meal you lost earlier. You are the most fun I've had in ages, and it got better when I fucked you. You didn't even know I tasted you. Now that you've crossed over you're even better. Aria has told me all about you like I instructed her to. You don't have the beast. Intriguing. You're unique like she said you would be, and now I own you. Hmm. Yes, you'll be a wonderful one to break. I have to thank you for getting rid of Malachai, by the way. He's been a nuisance ever since he created me. He thought he could control me. Forcing me to stay out of New Orleans, exiling me to Boston. I don't know how one deals with the snow, but now I have reign over New Orleans and Boston. Hmm. What am I going to do? So much power, so little time. But you wouldn't know that, now would you, little one? Or should I call you Raven? Yes, that name suits you better than Brenna. Raven it shall be. You'll be my bird of prophecy. Be able to spy on others around me just like a modern day Marie Laveau. Arriana tried to turn her because she thought Marie was the one she had seen in her vision. Now Marie's only an insane creature with too much bestiality. I couldn't control her. But you. You'll do wonderfully."

I laughed.

Devon stared at me. Anger rose in his eyes.

"You think I'll become your poppet. No one rules me. I call no one Master, not even my own creator. You're dreaming, Devon. You know, you got me. Sending Aria in so I would trust her. That was brilliant. Honestly, though, I don't know what it was I saw in you when I was human. I mean, your dick is small. Now I can really see how minuscule it is."

He slapped me. The force of it could have broken my neck, but Devon hadn't hit me at the right angle. I opened my eyes once the stars had cleared and worked my jaw as the pain dissipated. My power stirred inside of me, coming out of its hole, but I held it back. There were still too many things I had to take into consideration before I let loose my powers.

"You have no idea what you're talking about, Raven. It's no use fighting me. Aria did at first and then saw the error of her ways, didn't you Arriana?"

"Yes, Master." She bowed her head.

"I don't know what the hell you see in him, Aria. He's nothing but a murdering monster."

"Enough," Aria yelled.

She plunged her talons deeper into my back. Something ruptured.

"There's nothing you can say to change her mind. She's completely under my control. She has been since the beginning. When she was the Delphic Oracle, she saw her own future. When she first saw me she gouged her eyes out, hoping what she had seen had been a false vision, but when I brought her over, her lovely eyes grew back, and she was my slave. Now Veronica. She was a chore. I knew she would be trouble when I first bit into her. She's nothing more than a meat-loving bitch. But you, you could be so much more. You could rule beside me."

A feeling of dread washed over me as he said that. He wasn't lying. Something about his words hit the psychic chord in me. I understood why Aria must have gouged out her own eyes when she saw the future, being in service to a thing like him for the rest of her days. I wondered what type of human she had been as the Delphic Oracle. Whatever psychic powers she'd had had been used up ages ago. Devon must have sucked her dry, taking away all of her individuality, which severed her cord from the universe. I shivered at the thought. He was not going to do that to me.

"So you say she predicted all of this? What was the outcome? Didn't she ever tell you that the future isn't written in stone? It can be changed, you know."

Devon smiled, growing all of his teeth into points. The beginnings of horn buds poked through his forehead. His face bubbled and twisted as hair sprouted and bones rearranged themselves. He laughed, the sound becoming garbled like grating stone in his throat as his vocal chords reformed. His shoulders grew broader and his talons became their full length. I didn't cringe as his foul-smelling breath swept over my face. I stared up at him as he looked down upon me. His curved talon snuck underneath my shirt, ripping it and my bra as his claw moved against my skin. He pulled my shirt off, throwing in it somewhere into the cemetery. His cold, hard talon moved along the curve of my breast, embracing the nipple as to not hurt me. The gesture was almost tender. His other hand came around and pulled me closer to him, caressing my ass. He growled something to Aria, who let me go. He moved one claw under my chin, forcing me to look into his eyes. They were cobalt red, no irises, just red, as if his eyes were a liquid storm swirling around. I felt pulled into them.

The coarse hairs of his fur poked into me, burying themselves like wooden splinters into my skin. The more I struggled, the more embedded they became. His claw forced me to fall deeper into the storm. His mind pushed against mine. I resisted the best I could, but he knocked down my barriers as fast as I erected them. My eyes closed. His forked tongue snaked into my mouth. I didn't want to respond to him, but my body didn't know anything else. It wanted the ecstasy of his touch. His other hand pulled me against him. His dick throbbed against my thigh. I moaned, grinding my hips, wanting him to fuck me. All I wanted was him. I would do anything for him as his will took over my thoughts.

His cold talon moved inside of my jeans, finding the crack of my ass. I pressed in closer to him, not minding the small hooks of his fur, not caring that wherever it touched me bled; my body yearned for his dominance. "Tell me what you want, child. All it takes is one word and you can have it forever. What is it? Tell your Master, Raven, and I'll be kind. I promise."

The sound of my name on his lips was music to my ears. I was his Raven. His bird. I would use my powers to give him whatever answers I could. Anything. All I had to do was tell him what I wanted. And oh, how much I yearned for him. How much I wanted him to fuck me, ripping me apart with his cold, hard cock, working me with his fingers until I was raw. But...Master?

He had my jeans down around my ankles and backed me up against one of the cold crypts. His claws ran furrows in my flesh as he sought to get a good grip on my hips to lift me up and enter me. The smell of my blood perfumed the air. I heard footsteps on the gravel path coming this way, probably Aria coming to see if the master needed her help, or possibly other predators coming, being drawn by my blood. I didn't care. They could all have a piece of me as long as I could have the ecstasy of having him ravage me over and over again, until the end of forever.

"Come child, tell me what you want?"

What did I want? Devon's will pushed harder, wearing me down, but something deep inside wouldn't give in to him, even though everything wanted to. That was an insignificant part that didn't matter. It was nothing, something lingering from a past I hardly remembered. Something I had lost to my master's hands. I opened my eyes and peered into my master's face.

"I want you, Master. Take me; I'm yours. Forever and always. I'll do whatever you want." I grinned, exposing a mouth full of my own jagged fangs.

"Good girl," he groaned as he pushed himself into my waiting cunt.

I moaned loudly with his entrance, reveling in the fact he had chosen me to be with him. As he pounded into me, my head whacked against the cold marble of the crypts. With each move he made, his hold loosened, and my own will came back. I worked against him, moving at will, letting him do whatever he wanted to me, and as we both came he bit into my neck, ripping out a piece of flesh with it. The pain was exquisite, and I didn't care. I wanted more. I wanted all of it.

As he sucked me dry, still releasing himself inside of me, his control diminished, and I snapped. My eyes bled red. My hunger overtook me. There was a roar from deep inside of me, breaking my soul, but it was not a beast to speak of. It was remnants of the demon race that still lingered in me. Only now did I understand my true nature. I was not like the others. I was a separate kind of being. I was neither human, nor demonic vampire. I was the seed of a new race. That was why I couldn't kill mortals. My hatred for this man emerged and ran rampant through me, exposing what was truly inside of me. I saw a beast that looked similar to Devon, but instead of leather, its wings were made of black feathers, it had no horns, and most of its features were human. The energy surrounding it was golden, something connecting it to the other side. If I was part angel I didn't know, but I was not some evil being. Acceptance filled me and took over my body.

Bones cracked, realigning as I became what I had seen inside my mind. My teeth returned to normal, and I was left only with a double set of elongated fangs in the front. I had talons, black as a raven's claw, but no fur. My wings burst forth and pushed out against the stone, causing Devon to lose his grip and fall backwards, letting me go. I got up in a hurry, not waiting to see what he would do.

I heard a crack behind me and saw Aria standing there in full transformation. I grinned at the thought of taking both of them on. Aria took a step forward, but I saw a shape lunge from the shadows and take her down. It appeared to be a large wolf of some kind, a hellhound. I smiled, knowing who it was. I turned from Veronica and let her deal with Aria. My beef was with my Master.

"Please, Master, why are you hiding? Are you afraid of me?"

A few rocks fell, and I turned to see Devon perched on the outside wall. He looked down at me and grinned. He thought he was going to get away, but I knew better. He jumped into the air, gaining some altitude before I took flight. I willed my wings to beat and went after him. We flew over the city before he landed in Jackson Square. Then he was off running, pushing through the crowds of people. He crossed the street, not bothering to cloak himself. Mortals screamed at the nightmare that ran them down. He went up the steps and ran across the bridge to the River Walk, heading toward the Mississippi River. He landed on the concrete walkway adjacent the river and stopped, waiting for me to catch up with him. I licked my lips, spitting out any last taste of him. My will was clear. No more would he try to control me.

I landed only a few feet from him. We stood in the ultimate showdown. Boats passed us in the background on the Mississippi, their passengers unaware of what was happening on the shore. I opened my mind, pulling in the energy around me until my shields were up. In that second I took stock of my body and its wounds. I was bleeding badly, outwardly as well as in. Aria had probably hit a few major organs. Holding this form was taxing. I wouldn't have the strength much longer to keep it up.

As I pulled in energy, Devon took me off guard. He charged me like an overgrown football player. I flew about ten feet across the concrete, landing hard on my back. I got up and saw him behind me. I ran at him, claws outstretched, and before he dodged I raked my talons through his arm, severing it right above the elbow. He howled in pain. I smiled. He came at me, this time taking to the air. I tried to get under him, but every time I swiped at him he moved a little further out of my reach. He toyed with me like a cat playing with a ball of string. So I waited, gathering strength and then sprang, propelling myself into the air. I grabbed onto his leg and let gravity pull us down.

His remaining claw began ripping out the feathers of my wings as we both fell to the ground. I got on top of him and sat there. He struggled and then quieted down. I stared into his red eyes, knowing mine were shining with my own hunger. He was still hard underneath me. His dick was slick and partially fur covered as I sat on top of it. It moved on its own, seeking entrance into my depths, but that would never happen again. I licked my lips as I hovered inches from his face, smelling his putrid breath.

"You could surrender. It would be so much easier, don't you think?"

Devon smiled at me, revealing his rows of teeth. "Child, why are you trying to hurt your Master?"

His eyes swam red again, tried to pull me in, but I wasn't going for it. "You're not my Master, asshole."

And with that, I slashed my talons through his neck, severing vertebra and flesh. His head spun around, rolling a few feet, teetering on the edge of the concrete. It stayed and then landed with a plunk in the river. Blood poured out from the stump of his neck. I got up, watching as his body transformed back to human. I picked up the carcass, not wanting to leave it where humans would find it, and hoisted it over my shoulder.

I took to the air, using a little energy to shield myself from prying eyes. I made my way back to the cemetery and landed near the front wall. I dropped the body, propping it up against the wall. I looked up at the tombs in the wall and pulled against the marble slab, but the bolts held tight. I focused my mind around the screw. I willed it to come undone. At first the bolt creaked on the rusted screw, but then it spun around faster until it dropped to the ground. I focused on the second bolt and it did the same. I pulled the marble slab back and then threw in Devon's body. I also walked over and grabbed Aria, stuffing her in as well.

I smirked as I put in the remains. The keeper, in a year or so, would wonder why there were three mummified corpses. I didn't care. I just knew that the sun would bake the shit out of what was left. That was the beauty of the eight-foot thick wall. It acted as an oven.

I put on the slab and screwed in the bolts. With my task finished I wound my way through the cemetery to Veronica. She was curled into a ball against Marie Laveau's tomb, weeping. I sat down next to her and just waited. After a moment, she looked up at me through bloodstained tears. I knew by looking into her face something had happened, something that she could never fix.

"You killed him."

"I had to, love. For both of us. He'd have destroyed you and me. You didn't want to live with him the way he was. He used us. You know that. That was why you tried to keep me from him. Remember?"

"I know, but he was still my Master. He gave me life. How could you?"

She took a halfhearted swipe at me, but I just took her in my arms, understanding how she felt. Devon had tried to control her for so many years and for a brief moment she had a taste of freedom, but he lured her back in, just as he had me. I found the strength to overcome him. Maybe it was because I wasn't bound by his blood, or because I was a different type of creature than the rest. I didn't know, but in the end it didn't matter. He was dead, and would no longer haunt us. All I knew was Veronica and I were together and with the moon overhead, we would continue to see eternity.

EPILOGUE

My name is Brenna.

"Good morning, Boston Tearoom." I tried to sound as polite as I could on the phone, but sometimes people got to me. The woman on the other end asked me for directions and what kind of readings we offered. I answered and then she hung up.

I clicked the phone off and put it back into its cradle. Someone else could get it the next time it rang. Voices in the background alerted me that customers were coming in, but I made a dash for the back room and asked Peter to take care of the clients. I grabbed a seat on the couch and looked at the collage of photographs on the wall. Many of them were of Edmund, my former boss and friend.

Little did I know at the time, but after he died, he left the Tearoom to me. I was shocked when I found out, but it made sense. Six months after his death I was still getting used to the fact that this place was mine.

"Raven, telephone," Peter's voice called from the front, a hint of his German accent surfacing.

I sighed, retrieving the phone. "Hello."

"Hey, how's it going?" Veronica's voice moved through the phone like a welcome relief, caressing my insides and making me quiver.

"It's going?" I didn't dare ask how she was. After Devon's death we'd tried to be together, but there were a lot of things she had to work out. She chose to stay in New Orleans, and I decided to go back to Boston to make the Tearoom take off. I was living in her house for now, but it was up for sale. Both of us wanted to get rid of it.

I thought of the past six months. The woman I loved had changed in so many ways. She considered herself a meat-lover, as her kind called vampires who loved humans, and she wasn't ashamed of it. Neither did she try to hide it. She and her beast had come to an understanding and had meshed somewhat into one personality, but Veronica was still volatile. As much as she cared for me, both of us knew we needed time apart to discover what we were, what we had become.

I was reading everything I could get my hands on to try and discover my origins, but there was nothing.

I only knew I had some connection to the Divine in me, and I was part demon and part angel. I was still able to see angels walking around everywhere. At least Aria had shown me one useful thing. I hadn't gotten up the courage to actually stop and talk to one. When I did see them, they acknowledged me, and that was it. Other than that, life was normal. I continued to do readings, waiting for Veronica to give me some signal she would be coming home.

"It sounds like you're busy. I'll let you go"

"No, not really. It's just the normal crowd. It's great to talk to you. The energy in here is dead today. Besides, the weather is starting to warm up. It gets awful hot in New Orleans this time of year. Maybe you might think about coming up North to cool off for a bit?"

There was a silence on the phone. Longer than what I wanted. "I had noticed the weather getting kind of sticky and had that same thought. I didn't know if I would have anyone to come back to."

I smiled. "There's always someone waiting. All you have to do is get your ass up here."

Veronica chuckled. "Soon, love, soon."

"Good." I clicked the phone off, knowing the conversation was over, but things between us were just beginning.

ABOUT THE AUTHOR

Crymsyn Hart is a bestselling author of Erotic Romance. Her worlds are filled with luscious vampires, gorgeous gods, quirky witches, and everything else that goes bump in the night. Crymsyn worked as a psychic for many years in Boston while attending Emerson College. She graduated with a BFA in Writing, Literature, & Publishing. When she gets bored, she sneaks away to local cemeteries and coffee shops to find peace and quiet. Crymsyn shares her life with a small zoo, two playful puppies and her hubby Mark. If you come after dark, you're more than likely to find her snuggled up with a gory horror movie, or a bloody vampire movie. Crymsyn has a collection of Living Dead Dolls and five bookshelves overflowing with books. Of course there's always room for more.

Visit her on the web at:

www.RavynHart.com

Also available from Crymsyn at Purple Sword:

Tarnished Choices
Tarnished Souls
Tarnished Wings
Remember Me?
Role Reversal
Murmurs
Violet and Silver
Bitten By Love

PURPLE SWORD PUBLICATIONS

Romantic Speculative Fiction

www.purplesword.com